A Husband's Vow

Anya's rage was like her sensuality. Raw and tangible, it flared to life. She looked around for something breakable to throw, her eyes landing on the nearest table and the vase of flowers that sat there.

"Don't," Julian whispered.

She turned slightly and reached for the vase. Julian had no choice. He reached out and grabbed her, yanking her away from the doomed vase and into his embrace, pinning her arms down with his, holding her tightly against him.

His body's response was immediate and perfectly natural. She was, after all, more naked than not. And she was, he had to admit, quite lovely. Unconventional, but lovely. And soft. So very, very soft and sweetly scented.

Anya looked up at him, her anger magically gone. An almost sweet smile crossed her face. "Now you will ravish me?" she whispered.

His body was so close to hers, she no doubt felt his response. "No," he answered softly.

"You are determined to keep to your vow of chastity?" she asked, moving the length of her body ever so slightly against his, undulating gently, moving in a way so subtle that those who stood behind him surely could not see what she was doing to him. "I think it is a vow doomed to be broken."

LINDA JONES

De Buty & The Beast

LOVE SPELL BOOKS  NEW YORK CITY

A LOVE SPELL BOOK®

April 2002

Published by

Dorchester Publishing Co., Inc.
276 Fifth Avenue
New York, NY 10001

ISBN 0-505-52476-7

The name "Love Spell" and its logo are trademarks of Dorchester Publishing Co., Inc.

Printed in the United States of America.

Visit us on the web at www.dorchesterpub.com.

Chapter One

Julian stood, his back ramrod straight and his feet firmly planted, in the center of the Sedley mansion south parlor. His demeanor was purposely nonchalant, his face a mask of propriety. He gave no outward sign that his heart was about to burst through his chest, or that he had never in his twenty-six years seen such opulence.

He'd never expected to see the interior of Rose Hill, or any home like it. The Sedleys were a well-respected and filthy-rich family that had made its fortune in shipping and trade since the days of the American Revolution. They were known not only for their fortune, but for their place in North Carolina society.

Elizabeth Sedley, matriarch of the Sedley clan, paced before a cold fireplace, wringing her hands in an uncharacteristic display of nervousness. She was attractive, still, for an older woman. Her hair was stark white, her face only lightly wrinkled. She stood barely five feet tall, and while she was far from thin, she was not what one would call heavy, either. Healthy, Julian thought as he watched her. She looked extraordinarily healthy.

"You are aware of my situation," she said, keeping her voice low.

"Yes," Julian said simply. Who was not aware? The reappearance six months ago of Mrs. Sedley's granddaughter, who had long been assumed dead, had stirred up much excitement. The girl had been thought lost at sea, along with her parents, nearly twelve years ago. Her mother and father had perished when their ship went down in a storm, but the girl had drifted to the Caribbean island of Puerta Sirena. Mermaid's Gate. The idyllic island was inhabited by a ragtag group of people. A few of the original Hispanic natives coexisted with pirates from around the world who, for the past one hundred and fifty years or so, had made the island their home. Apparently they had made a retired English pirate their king.

"I've tried everything," Mrs. Sedley said in a lowered voice that spoke of desperation and confidence. "In the past six months we have lost eight tutors, three governesses, and five companions. Most do not last a full day. It's not entirely Anya's fault," she said a mite defensively. "On the island where she has lived the past twelve years of her life, she was called a goddess. She was treated like a queen. She

2

is understandably having difficulty adjusting to this new lifestyle."

"Understandably." Julian's nose twitched. He had heard the stories of the heiress's behavior since her homecoming. In muted whispers, the gossips were calling Anya Sedley the Beast of Rose Hill.

"My granddaughter can be difficult." Mrs. Sedley glanced his way, her eyes pleading. "But she is also bright and lovely, and she needs a guiding hand. That's all she needs," the old woman said optimistically. "A firm, guiding hand."

Julian's heart sank a little. He now knew why he had been summoned. He was not a tutor, he was not a companion. And even if he were, he had no desire to take on the Beast of Rose Hill.

"Why, she reads constantly," Mrs. Sedley said, a note of pride in her voice. "And speaks not only English, but quite a bit of French, Spanish, Portuguese, Italian and . . . some island nonsense. Sometimes all in one sentence, and from the tone of her voice I suspect that much of what she says is inappropriate for a lady, but still . . . such knowledge is an accomplishment, don't you agree? Why, she's already read everything in my library, and is rereading her favorites. If only she had the proper guiding hand."

"Mrs. Sedley . . ." Julian began, anxious to cut the elderly lady off before this conversation went any further. The longer he stood there, the more desperately she pleaded, the more difficult it would be to say no.

Apparently she knew his weakness quite well. She did not give him an opportunity to continue. "A tu-

3

tor is not enough," Mrs. Sedley said quickly. "Anya needs someone to take her well in hand. Someone of high moral character who will dedicate himself twenty-four hours a day to her reformation. Someone who—"

"Mrs. Sedley . . ." Julian tried again.

"A husband who will take this wild creature and transform her into the lady she should be," the old woman finished, undaunted by the interruption.

"A husband? Mrs. Sedley, surely you don't expect—"

"Your grandfather was a good friend of mine," she interrupted.

"I know."

"He shared your interests," she said, walking unerringly toward him, the gleam in her eyes strong and intelligent. Elizabeth Sedley would soon be sixty-eight years old. Her face might be wrinkled, her hair snow white, but there was youth and vigor in her eyes. "A study of cultures not our own, a dedication to academics."

She played on his weakness. A physician by training, Julian had no tolerance for sick people. He was awkward around his patients and much preferred research. Like his grandfather, he was fascinated by tribal cultures. Their similarities the world round. Their differences. Unfortunately, such study would take years. A lifetime. And it would also take lots of money—money he did not have, thanks to his father's love for and bad luck with games of chance.

Mrs. Sedley faced him bravely, tilting her head to look him in the eye. "Marry my granddaughter," she

4

said succinctly. "Turn her into a young woman worthy of her station by her twenty-first birthday, and you shall have your own ship from the Sedley line, a worthy crew, supplies, and whatever funds you need to get your studies underway."

Julian's heart thudded. He was not so sure he would be able to hide his excitement. "When is her twenty-first birthday?"

"September 15. You will have just over four months to complete the task."

From what he had heard, four months would not be nearly enough time to tame the beast. Still, the rewards were high. "And what does Anya think of this plan?"

Mrs. Sedley's lips thinned. "She knows only that I have set about finding her a husband."

"And what does she think of that?"

The old woman's eyes flitted away nervously. "She seems quite willing to take that step."

"Why will another, more dedicated tutor not do as well as a husband?"

Mrs. Sedley sighed. "Anya responds better to men than to women, I have found. The companions we hired almost always left here in tears. And for her training to be effective, her tutor needs to be here twenty-four hours a day. There can be no rest, no respite from this task." She laid her eyes on Julian. "And I need no more scandal. If you live under this roof, you must marry her."

"I see your reasoning," he began, "but marriage seems a bit extreme."

"Anya's portion of the Sedley fortune will be hers

Linda Jones

when she turns twenty-one." Mrs. Sedley's voice was all business, now. "She will be prey for every fortune hunter on the east coast, and she is so impulsive I fear . . . I fear she will choose the wrong man, if she's given the opportunity to choose for herself. Even when you are away on your travels, you will be her husband, and so you will protect her from the vultures."

"I see."

"Julian," she said, her voice changing to a more maternal tone. "I have made up my mind. What Anya needs is a husband. I called upon you for this task for many reasons. I admired your grandfather greatly, and you are a man of high moral character, as he was. I read your latest pamphlet on the degenerating moral character of our nation, and I must say, it played a great role in my decision."

Julian looked humbly to the floor. "I appreciate your confidence." And yet . . .

"That said," Mrs. Sedley continued, "I feel I must tell you everything."

Good heavens, there was *more.*

"I mentioned that Anya was called a goddess."

"Yes," Julian said suspiciously.

Mrs. Sedley set about wringing her hands again. "Apparently she was a . . . ummm . . ." She lowered her voice to a whisper. "A love goddess."

"A love goddess."

"And I told you she was treated like a queen?" Mrs. Sedley continued.

Julian's heart dropped. "Yes."

6

"Well, actually she was the king's paramour, his . . . his concubine."

The same heart that had dropped a moment earlier rose into his throat. "I see. This would be the English pirate, Terrence Whetherly?"

"His son, Sebastian."

The offspring of the pirate and an island woman, no doubt.

"Naturally, we don't want the world to know of these transgressions, but I did think you should have all the pertinent details."

"Very kind of you to be so honest."

"Anya tells me she cannot have children, but since this will be an arranged marriage, and you will be leaving in a few months time, I don't see how that detail would affect your decision."

Julian tried to decline, but the "no" caught in his throat. Was he actually considering this preposterous proposition? A love goddess? The mistress of a self-proclaimed king? Four months of his life to see his dream come true.

"Perhaps you should meet Anya before we go any further."

Mrs. Sedley turned slowly, took two steps, and lifted a silver bell from the end table by a burgundy velvet padded chair. Almost immediately, the butler appeared.

"Show Miss Anya in, Peter."

With a barely disguised sigh, the servant nodded and briskly left to do as he'd been instructed.

"I should warn you," Mrs. Sedley said in a lowered voice. "We have tried to reform her, but Anya continues with her unconventional ways. Some I am learning to accept. Others are more difficult to withstand. You should be prepared."

"For what?"

"For anything." She sighed.

Julian heard the butler's clipped step and harried voice moving closer to the parlor where he and Mrs. Sedley waited. "But Miss Anya . . ."

"Silence," a crisp, feminine voice ordered. "I have asked you not to speak to me unless you are bearing a message of some importance. Your opinion is of *no* importance."

"But Miss Anya . . ."

"I should have my grandmother whip you for your insolence. Did I not tell you to be silent?"

Julian turned to face the doorway as the voices came nearer. Peter was not deterred by Anya's threat. "But your grandmother gave specific instructions . . ."

The butler stopped speaking when Anya reached the open doorway and stopped there, laying her eyes on Julian in a bold, almost fearless way. She had long, unbound red hair that fell well past her waist. Lush lips that would never be proper, no matter what training she received. Wide eyes blue . . . no, green . . . perhaps both . . . that latched on to his as she stepped into the room.

She wore an array of jewels. Dangling pearls at her earlobes barely peeked out from her wealth of red hair. Around her neck she wore several necklaces. More pearls, a ruby pendant, an onyx teardrop, and a worked gold piece of delicate leaves. Her wrists, both of them, were similarly adorned, as was one ankle.

And she was naked, but for a brightly colored scarf that had been strategically placed around her waist, knotted there, and left to hang so that it covered the apex of her thighs and half of one shapely limb. Her unbound hair covered her breasts to some degree, but an abundance of bare flesh was most shockingly revealed.

"Anya!" Mrs. Sedley whispered hoarsely. "What did I tell you. . . ."

"I am not naked," Anya said as she placed herself before Julian and lifted her eyes to his face.

"You promised you would wear shoes this afternoon," Mrs. Sedley continued, reprimand in her voice.

Anya was not affected by the rebuke. "They pinch my toes." She began to circle around Julian, her movements like that of a cat, slow and graceful and . . . deadly. Her eyes raked up and down his body. Julian remained still, not circling to follow her, but allowing her to study him as she wished.

Peter, the harried butler, sighed once again and made his escape.

"You were right, Grandmother," Anya said softly. "He is a beauty."

"I never said—" Mrs. Sedley began.

"Julian the beauty," Anya interrupted. "That is what you called him."

"No, no," the older woman said patiently. "Julian DeButy. Dr. Julian DeButy. That is his name, the way

9

your name is Anya Sedley. DeButy sounds similar to 'the beauty,' I suppose."

Anya completed her circle and stood before him once more. Julian fixed his eyes on the ruby at her throat. To look at anything more would be improper. To study her body the way she studied his would be beneath him. He should pay no attention to the way her very red hair fell across the swell of her bare breasts. He definitely should not allow his eyes to dwell on those lush lips, or the sprinkling of freckles across her nose, or, dear God, the valley between her breasts and her bare midriff, with skin so smooth and flawless it surely felt like silk.

His eyes should most certainly not drop to the portion of exposed hip, shapely thigh, the length of that one completely exposed limb that almost brushed against his trousers. No, he stared at the ruby at her throat and thought of . . . of ships. Long, wooden ships that sailed across the seas, tossed by the tremendous waves so that it pitched up and down, up and down, in a rhythm deep and certain. He could feel it even now, roiling in the pit of his stomach as the ship carried him—Oh, this was not helping at all. So he thought of . . . of last night's meal.

That was a safe enough topic for his beleaguered brain, surely. He'd dined with his aunt before taking the train to Wilmington. She'd served a succulent roast hen that had been quite tasty. The way it had lain on his tongue, tender and luscious, had been quite lovely. Just thinking about it made his mouth water. Yes, there was nothing so satisfying as a well-prepared meal: chicken and potatoes and greens, followed by delicious caramel cake. Oh, that cake had been marvelous. Sticky and sweet and decadent. Sinful, surely, it was so rich and just the memory made his stomach tighten and his heart skip a beat. Smooth and silky and warm . . .

Good heavens, what had this woman done to him?

Neither ships nor food calmed him, so he thought of the money Anya's grandmother offered, the opportunity to circle the world and write books about his travels. To discover tribes that still lived as their people had lived hundreds of years ago, each with their own society. Their own rules and mores.

It did not matter that Anya had been a queen and a goddess, or that she could not have children. The only dignified reason for a man and woman to lie together was to conceive a child. The civilized man was above his baser instincts, though at times those instincts were easier to ignore than at others.

Julian usually had no problem ignoring his own animal instincts. He rigorously avoided temptation, keeping to his books and avoiding situations that might prove . . . uneasy. This situation was most definitely uneasy. Any man who was confronted with a naked woman might feel aroused.

He turned his mind to business. Since Anya could not conceive, and he would not stay long at Rose Hill, there was no need for their marriage to include the marital embrace. They would have separate beds. Separate *rooms*. He would be a mentor, a teacher. Not a lover.

"You wish to marry me?" Anya asked, her words clipped and precise, with just a hint of a foreign accent. Not Spanish, not French, but something exotic and . . . no, *not* arousing.

He was being ridiculous. This was just a woman, no different from any other. He would give her four months of his life, he would train her, mold her into the lady she should be. Those tutors who had come before had simply not been strict enough.

"Yes," he said crisply. "I do believe we'd make a suitable couple."

"You have not asked me if I wish to marry you," she said, a hint of censure in her voice. "My grand-mother tells me I must have a husband, and to be honest I am tired of sleeping in a large bed all alone."

Julian's eyebrows went up, just slightly. Before they were wed he would have to make things clear to her. He would make her understand that they would not share a bed, and that she should not count on him to stay indefinitely. He could surely explain to her the benefits of a marriage of convenience.

"But why should I choose you?"

"Anya, dear," Mrs. Sedley said, "I have told you all about Julian. He is a fine, upstanding physician, he comes from a wonderful old Southern family, and he has all the qualities any woman might want in a husband."

"Does he?" Without warning, Anya reached out and laid her hand on his crotch. He tried to back away, but she grabbed onto the fabric and what lay beneath and would not let go. Her grandmother, standing at his back, could surely not see this indig-nity. Just as well, as it was a truly mortifying moment.

12

In spite of Julian's resolve to think of other things, he twitched and grew in her hand. Anya responded with a wicked smile.

"He will do," she said softly.

Satisfied, Anya let her hand fall away. "When is the wedding?"

"There are a few things we need to discuss before we go any further," her intended said. He was so very stiff . . . in more ways than one.

But he was also very beautiful. He could easily have been called Julian the Beauty, and no one would question the fitting name. His hair was thick and dark brown, and worn longer than Cousin Seymour wore his. The strands curled over his ears and down the back of his neck. He was slender, but not thin, standing tall and straight and nicely built in his form-fitting black suit and white shirt.

His face was truly beautiful. Eyes so dark a brown they were almost black; a nose so straight and finely shaped it was a wonder; a mouth firm and wide, but not too wide. Already she detected a hint of an afternoon stubble on his chin. His skin was a little pale, perhaps, but not a sickly pale like that of her boring, insipid cousins, Seymour and Valerie. Yes, if she must take a husband, Julian DeButy would most definitely do.

"What do we need to discuss?"

He glanced over his shoulder to look at her grandmother. "I don't believe in starting something as important as a marriage with falsehoods. Mrs. Sedley, would you leave us for a moment?"

Anya smiled. He wanted to be alone with her. Oh, she was so very ready to take a husband. Someone who would hold her close and listen to her. Someone to share this new life with. She was tired of being lonely, and she had never been as lonely as she had been since coming to Rose Hill.

Grandmother left the room, but it was quite clear that she didn't want to go. She kept turning her head, pausing in her usually steady step. Anya gave the woman a fleeting, reassuring smile as she left the room.

Anya turned slowly. "I will close the door." She did not get far before her intended stopped her with a hand on her shoulder.

"That won't be necessary."

She spun around and glanced up at Julian. "You do not wish for privacy? I thought you wanted to make sure I would please you before we married." Why else would he ask Grandmother to leave? Anya reached out to touch him once again. This time he was faster than she. He jumped back quickly.

"No." He ran a nervous hand through his hair, ruffling the dark strands. "Please sit down." He indicated a chair, which she dutifully took, sitting, pulling her feet off the floor and crossing her legs so that her knees brushed against the padded arms. The jewels on her ankle jingled prettily, catching the light from the afternoon sun that streamed through the window behind her.

Julian took the chair facing her, glanced in her direction, then quickly jumped back up again. His face flushed pink and he averted his eyes. "I'll just

14

stand over here," he mumbled, moving to a station at her side.

Standing beside her, he placed his hands behind his back and fixed his gaze on Grandmother's walnut desk. "Mrs. Sedley tells me you cannot have children."

Her heart fell. Her curse, her most dreaded failure, and already he knew. Surely he did not want to marry her now. "No. If that defect displeases you I will find another husband," she snapped, refusing to allow him to see the hurt.

He looked down at her. Oh, he really was beautiful. As he studied her, she saw something beyond the startling physical beauty. A kindness, perhaps. A good heart. "No, that does not displease me," he said gently. "And I would not call the inability to have children a defect. I don't really care for children, to be honest."

She lifted her chin. "Neither do I." It was a lie, but a well-delivered one. She did not want this man, or anyone, to be honest, to see the pain her failing brought her.

Julian fidgeted, just a little. His spine stiffened, his nose twitched. "But in truth, the only moral reason for a man and woman to lie together is to create a child."

"What about pleasure?" she asked before he could go further.

Again, his cheeks flushed pink. "We are not animals, Anya," he said sternly.

"But we are."

He lifted a silencing hand. "This is not a discussion we should have at the present time. I only mean to make it clear that you and I will not share a bed."

"Not until we are married."

"Not at all."

She took a moment to study his profile. "You do not find me pleasing?" No, she knew he was attracted to her; she had felt his response, seen it in his eyes, and felt it fill her hand.

"You're a very attractive young woman," he said primly. "Even if you are most inappropriately attired."

"You will not sleep with me because I cannot give you a child, and yet you wish to marry me?"

"I have taken a vow of celibacy," he said, his words clipped.

"You are a holy man?"

"No. I have taken the vow because we as civilized human beings should be above our baser instincts. We should be able to control our desires and put the energy within us to work in better, higher ways." He did not look at her as he delivered his ridiculous speech. His eyes were fixed on the wall ahead.

"That is bloody stupid," Anya said with a grin. "Who told you such a thing?"

"It's a widely accepted fact—"

"It is very stupid."

"You need a husband. I need a wife." Still, he did not look at her. "In a few months' time I will begin my travels. I am a scholar, you see, and I wish to study and write about primitive cultures. This venture will require me to spend most of my time in the coming years away from home."

"Then I do not see why we need to marry at all," she said succinctly. "You do not wish to bed me, and you do not wish to live here. Why do you need a wife, Dr. DeButy?"

He glanced down at her, his dark eyes penetrating and yet still kind. "Your grandmother has offered to finance my travels. In exchange, I will do my best to take up where your tutors have failed."

Julian DeButy intended to be yet another teacher. He wanted to change everything about her, just as her family did. Anya's heart fell. She would never be good enough to suit the people around her. "What makes you think you will succeed where they have failed?"

"I am a very persistent man, Anya. I do not take on any task even considering the possibility of failure."

She smiled up at him. "They call me the Beast of Rose Hill."

"So I have heard."

"And I do not see why I need to be more like my insipid, boring, fat cousin Valerie."

"Insipid and boring mean basically the same thing," he said calmly, "and it's rude to refer to your more robust kin as fat."

"Even if she is?"

"Even if she is."

Anya unfolded her legs and slowly rose. She should throw something breakable across the room and tell Julian DeButy to go to hell. If she did that, he would leave. Somehow she already knew he was not a man to beg.

17

Linda Jones

But if Julian left, Grandmother would only bring in another man. Perhaps someone who was not so handsome or tall or honest. Perhaps a man who did not have a good heart, as she sensed this man did. She had met so few good-hearted people since coming here, she did not think she could bear to send this one away.

Julian was so sure they would not share a bed as man and wife. She did not agree, but now was not the time to oppose him. She would seduce her husband when the time was right, and that seduction would not be difficult. He already wanted her. He looked at her and responded. In truth, enticing Julian DeButy into her bed would be no challenge at all. Had she not been trained since the age of fifteen in the art of seduction?

He was so sure he would not stay here at Rose Hill . . . but, again she did not agree. She would be a good wife and she would please him, and Julian DeButy would stay. Anya accepted his proposal, conditions and all, with a solemn nod. She was decided.

Chapter Two

Someone had suggested the main ballroom for the ceremony, but Mrs. Sedley had declared the rarely used room too cavernous for such an intimate gathering. She had chosen this room, the formal north parlor, for her granddaughter's wedding.

Julian faced the door in breathless anticipation, awaiting the appearance of his bride. He heard her approach, and in spite of his determination to remain calm, his heart kicked in a restless manner. And then she was there, framed by the doorway and smiling like no other.

Like many brides, Anya wore white. Unlike any bride Julian had ever heard of, that white garment was a well-placed scarf much like the one she'd worn the day before, when he'd first met her. She moved toward him, her hips swaying with each step. Her unbound hair danced, and she sparkled and jangled, as she had apparently donned every piece of jewelry in the house for the occasion. One piece had been pinned atop her head, and sat upon brilliant red strands like a pearl-encrusted tiara.

The flowers she carried were a traditional bouquet, apparently provided by her grandmother. Fashioned of roses in yellow, white, and pink, each bloom perfect, the roses were complimented with a simple white satin bow. Magnificent as they were, the color and beauty of the flowers paled in comparison to the woman who carried them.

The preacher, who had apparently been warned to expect anything, stared at the floor and muttered a prayer. Seymour Sedley gaped at the bride, wide-eyed, his jaw practically hitting the floor. His sister, Valerie, sniffled and turned up her nose in disdain.

Elizabeth Sedley smiled and whispered, "Isn't she beautiful?"

Outrageous, lewd, uncivilized . . . and definitely beautiful.

As she walked toward Julian, Anya smiled. It wasn't a demure smile, of course. The grin was wide and invigorating and full of decadent promises. Promises he would not allow her to keep.

Marriage to Anya was a test, he told himself as she came near with swaying hips and loosened hair that danced with each step. She was a challenge to be met and mastered. His beliefs were stronger than his libido.

The wedding ceremony was brief, the preacher's words spoken quickly and in a low voice, with his gaze steadfastly pinned on the floor at his feet. Their party was small: the bride and groom; the shy preacher; the two cousins; Elizabeth Sedley; the butler Peter and the two live-in maids, Betsy, who was in charge of the kitchen, and Hilary, who seemed to spend most of her time upstairs. Only Anya and her grandmother smiled.

What on earth had he done?

The preacher pronounced them man and wife, and mumbled that Julian could now kiss his bride. A chaste peck on the cheek, he decided as Anya turned to face him. There would be no passion, no hint that when he looked at her she stirred something savage within him.

He leaned slightly down and forward. His bride awaited him with a wide smile on her face and a wicked gleam in her eyes. Before he had an opportunity to lay his lips against Anya's cheek, she threw the bouquet aside, spun around, and ran.

Cousin Valerie squealed as the bouquet pelted her in the face. It bobbled there, and she caught it instinctively. Anya laughed and glanced over her shoulder as she ran away from Julian, heading straight for the double doors that opened onto the massive Sedley gardens.

Julian took a single step after her, placing his hands on his hips as Anya laid her hands on the cut-glass doorknobs, preparing to toss the doors wide open.

"What on earth do you think you're doing?" he asked succinctly.

The doors still closed, her hands resting on the

knobs there, Anya's smile faded. "You are supposed to chase me. It is the custom."

"It is not *our* custom."

Anger flashed in her eyes as she turned and took a few steps in his direction. "You are to chase me into the jungle and ravish me."

"Good heavens," Valerie muttered.

Anya looked at him as if he had lost his mind. "Do you know nothing? It is the way a husband claims his bride, making her his in the way of man since the beginning of time."

"There is no jungle here," Julian said sensibly.

"But there is a bloody garden," Anya argued. "It will do."

He tried to preserve his calm. No one had ever maintained that this chore would be easy. Anya should be reprimanded for her language, but that could wait. There were more important matters to address.

"Our customs here are different, Anya. We will celebrate the wedding with your family, sharing cake and lemonade in the dining room."

Her lush lips hardened, and his bride muttered something in a tongue-twisting language, something hard and biting that could only be a curse. "I would prefer to be ravished than to eat too much cake and get fat like—"

"Anya," he interrupted. "It's the way things are done here."

She passed by a table near the sofa, picked up a figurine of an old woman, and threw it. Not at him, but soundly against the nearest wall. The piece shattered into a thousand pieces. One of the house maids sighed loudly.

"I do not like the way things are done here," Anya snapped, reaching out as she stalked toward him to lift yet another breakable piece of porcelain from yet another small table. "If you wish me to be your wife, you will chase me into the garden and . . ." Her hand reared back.

Julian took two quick steps forward and deftly snatched the figurine from Anya's hand. "Would you stop this?" he asked in a lowered voice that only she could hear. "You know quite well that I am not going to ravish you in the garden."

"But I want . . ."

"It doesn't matter what you want, Anya. I am your husband, and you will do as I say."

The anger in Anya's eyes was so deep and real he almost flinched. "I always get what I want," she whispered.

"No more," he countered.

"I am a goddess."

"You are my wife," he insisted. "From now on you will do exactly as I instruct you. Right now, we will go into the dining room with your family, have cake and lemonade, and be civil. You will be polite, you will compliment the cook who made the cake, and you will thank your grandmother for this fine wedding."

"I am not your slave."

"You are not a goddess, either."

Her blue-green eyes flashed in anger. "I could have your head for this."

23

"Not in North Carolina."

Her rage was like her sensuality. Raw and tangible, it flared to life. She looked around for something breakable to throw, her eyes landing on the nearest table and the vase of flowers that sat there.

"Don't," he whispered.

Anya turned slightly and reached for the vase. Julian had no choice. He reached out and grabbed her, yanking her away from the doomed vase and into his arms, pinning her arms down with his, holding her tightly against him.

His body's response was immediate and perfectly natural. She was, after all, more naked than not. And she was, he had to admit, quite lovely. Unconventional, but lovely. And soft. So very, very soft and sweetly scented.

Anya looked up at him, her anger magically gone. An almost sweet smile crossed her face. "Now you will ravish me?" she whispered.

His body was so close to hers, she no doubt felt his response. "No," he answered softly.

"Why not?"

"You know why not."

"You are determined to keep to your vow of chastity?"

"Yes."

She moved the length of her body ever so slightly against his, undulating gently, moving in a way so subtle that those who stood behind him could surely not see what she was doing to him.

"I think it is a vow doomed to be broken, *marido.*"

"Marido?" he repeated.

"Husband," she whispered.

Julian purposely set his wife away from him. He was steadfast, but a man could only take so much temptation! "I insist that you come with me to the dining room so that we may properly celebrate our marriage with your family. Please."

"Of course," Anya said sweetly. "You needed only to ask."

"Anya," Julian said, his voice nothing if not patient. "Why don't you sit here and have a piece of this wonderful cake?"

He spoke to her as if she were a child, but she knew quite well that her husband did not think of her that way. In spite of his morals, his vow, his insistence that he was not an animal, her husband wanted her. There had been nothing to interest her since arriving at Rose Hill, nothing but the books in her grandmother's library. But this . . . this would be interesting.

The dining room was large and well furnished and somehow cold, even now as the spring weather turned warm. The long polished table was made of walnut, dark and gleaming, and the buffet against one wall matched it perfectly. There were always fresh flowers on the table, but today, in celebration of her marriage, the arrangement was more elaborate than usual, and a smaller, matching arrangement had been placed on the buffet, next to a layer cake decorated with white frosting and sugared violets. There were two large gilt-framed mirrors in the long dining room, as well as a small oil painting of

a dreary landscape. Of hills and a lake, it was a painting Anya found lifeless and boring. The drapes were
heavy and a dark, jungle green, and they shut out
much of the light, even now in the afternoon, when
they had been pulled back to allow some sunlight to
break through. She longed to be in the sun. In the
garden. Being properly ravished by her husband.

"You will sit beside me?" she asked sweetly as she
looked up at her husband.

"If you'd like," he answered. He appeared calm
enough, but his throat worked slightly and his
cheeks turned just a little pink.

Anya feared her new challenge would be no challenge at all.

She took the chair Julian offered, sitting properly
as her grandmother had taught her. Knees together,
feet on the floor. Her husband took the chair beside
her, and one of the kitchen maids placed a piece of
cake in front of each of them. The other girl was in
the main parlor, sweeping up what was left of that
awful, ugly figurine of an old woman. Surely no one
would miss that dreadful piece. And it had felt so
good to throw the figurine and watch it shatter.

Julian kept his eyes on the cake. "It looks delicious, doesn't it?"

"Yes, it does," Anya said sweetly. She waited for
Julian to glance her way, as she knew he eventually
would, and then she ran her finger through a thick
glob of white frosting, carried it upward slowly, and
brought her finger to her mouth. Wrapping her lips
around that finger she sucked gently, closed her
eyes, and moaned. "Delicious," she said as she slowly

removed her finger from her mouth and scooped up another glob of icing.

Poor Julian, he went quite red in the face. "You have a . . . a fork, Anya. Use it."

She glanced around the room. Cousin Valerie was lustily eating her own cake. Seymour ogled the maid who was filling fine glasses with lemonade, and Grandmother was trying to convince the preacher to stay for a piece of cake. None of them were watching the bride and groom, at the moment.

"It tastes better this way, see?" She lifted her finger to his lips, dabbing at his mouth with the white frosting. He grabbed her wrist but it was too late. Her finger was there, the frosting was there, and when he parted his lips, no doubt to tell her to desist, she slipped her finger into his mouth. He had no choice but to close his lips around her finger and suck off the frosting. Her heart beat a little harder as he sucked so briefly against her finger. She felt the tug of his mouth and the warmth of his tongue . . . everywhere.

"See?" she said as he pulled her hand away. "That is so much tastier than the same frosting taken to your mouth on a cold, silver fork."

"Will you behave?" Julian whispered as he released her and licked a small amount of frosting from his lips.

"No." She laid her recently freed hand on his knee and he twitched.

The preacher took his leave, and Grandmother took her usual place at the head of the table. She smiled so sweetly, Anya was forced to smile back.

Linda Jones

"How is the cake?"

"Very tasty," Anya said. "But a poor substitute for—"

"Anya," Julian interrupted.

She smiled and said nothing more, but her hand climbed a little higher up her husband's thigh. Oh, it was a nice, firm thigh, she noticed as she gave it a little squeeze. Beneath the table, he took her hand, lifted it, and placed it firmly on her own knee . . . where it did not stay long. This time she placed her hand even higher on his leg, and he jumped. His knee banged against the underside of the table.

The table shimmied, just a little, the glasses of lemonade quaked, and all eyes turned to Julian.

"Pardon me," he muttered.

Anya's hand slid up his thigh. Her fingers slipped beneath the hem of his jacket.

With a surge of energy, Julian pushed his chair back and stood. "You look chilly," he said through clenched teeth. "Here, let me give you my jacket." He began to unbutton the garment, but stopped short of removing it.

"I am not at all chilly," Anya said calmly.

"Humor me." Julian deftly turned so that his back was presented to all those at the table. He slipped off the jacket, stood behind her chair, and slipped it over her shoulders. She even leaned forward to accommodate him.

When he returned to his chair, moving quickly, she could not help but see the bulge in his trousers, the evidence of his desire that he tried so deftly to hide.

28

"It scratches, a little," she complained, lifting her shoulders to shrug out of the garment.

As she tried to push the jacket off, Julian reached over, grabbed the lapels and pulled them together so that they covered her breasts and caught her hair. "Please," he asked.

Anya was demanding, she did not deny it. She was accustomed to getting what she wanted, *whatever* she wanted, without question. But she was also a woman, and she knew when she had gone far enough.

"If you wish," she answered softly, lifting one arm to snake it through a sleeve, then lifting the other to repeat the process. Once that was done, her husband released his hold on the garment and sighed in relief.

"Julian?" she said, leaning slightly forward. "Would you assist me?"

He shot a suspicious glance her way. "Assist you in what way?"

She lifted her arms. Her hands were hidden beneath the long sleeves of his jacket. "Would you roll up the cuffs so I can eat more of this delicious cake without getting frosting on your wedding clothes? I will, of course, use a fork."

He efficiently and quickly turned the sleeves up until they were well clear of her wrists.

"Thank you, *caro*," she said, her soft words for his ears alone.

Julian moaned lowly and leaned over his wedding cake.

Anya smiled. This was going to be much too easy.

*   *   *

29

Julian paced across the Persian rug in the opulent bedroom that was to be his for the next four months. The coverlet and draperies were in shades of deep blue, the fine furniture crafted of mahogany. The lamps would be filled each day, so that he would never have to worry about conserving oil.

He was in such pain, he barely noticed the unaccustomed luxury. His physical arousal had decreased hours ago, but inside—deep inside—something still churned.

A test, he reminded himself once again. Anya was a test, sent to try his courage and his principles and his moral fiber. But who had sent her? God or the devil himself? At the moment, Julian suspected a demonic hand in this particular trial.

The door that connected his chamber with the sitting room opened, and the demon herself walked in. Tonight she had not even bothered with a scarf around her waist. Everything had been taken off. She was all fair skin, red hair, and the gleam of one small gold wedding band.

"Must we sleep in separate rooms?" she asked, pouting prettily.

"Yes," he insisted. Her own bedchamber was on the other side of the sitting room. Too close, he thought as he averted his eyes. Much too close.

Undeterred, she walked to the bed and lifted his nightshirt. "Do you sleep in this?"

"Yes."

"Why?"

He sighed and closed his eyes. "I don't want to get chilled in the night."

"It is very warm here. You will not get chilled," she sounded very reasonable, and so he was on guard. "I think you are much too concerned about getting chilled, *cher*. This afternoon in the dining room, tonight in your own bedroom." She sighed. "When a man and wife need *never* be chilled," she added, lowering her voice to a slightly deeper pitch.

He ignored the way his gut clenched, opened his eyes, and looked at her. He would have to learn to deal with the sight of Anya, no matter how unnerving she might be. "It isn't proper to sleep unclothed."

"But it is much more comfortable. My grandmother bought me several nightgowns." Anya wrinkled her nose. "They all scratch. I tried to wear them, I swear I did. But I always woke in the middle of the night and tore them off. I felt like they were choking me, binding me down. Do you never feel that way when you wear your nightgown?"

"Night*shirt*," he corrected testily.

Anya gave him a wide smile and lifted the garment to hold before her bare body. "If you insist." She lowered her head and sniffed lightly at one sleeve. "Your nightgown—night*shirt*—is much softer than mine."

"It's old and worn," he confessed.

Anya hugged the garment to her body. "I rather like it."

"You may have it," he said, hoping she would take the nightshirt and go. She made no move to leave the room. "In fact, why don't you try it on right

31

now." Yes, clothing would be good, if she insisted on remaining here.

She lifted the garment and her arms, revealing more than he wanted to see . . . and he could not make himself look away as she pulled the nightshirt over her head. The linen hung on her, loose and misshapen. So why was she still beautiful, in an impossibly endearing sort of way?

"It is not so scratchy," she admitted, raking her hand over the linen. Her fingers danced over her full breasts and down across her flat belly, the motion making the linen cling to her flesh for an all-too-brief moment. "Not like the nightgowns my grandmother gave me. But if I take your nightshirt, what will you wear to bed to keep from getting a chill?"

"I have another," he said sharply.

Anya very slightly puckered her full lips. "Too bad."

He simply could not bear four months of this. They'd been married a few hours, and already Anya was beating down his defenses. Beating them down, slipping past, sneaking inside . . .

"Anya," he said sternly, "have a seat. We need to talk."

She ignored the chair he indicated and sat on the side of the bed. She crossed her legs as she had the day before, but fortunately tonight the length of his own nightshirt concealed the forbidden view he had been afforded at that time.

He gathered his courage and faced her. Hands behind his back, he glanced down at her. "I will not allow you to seduce me. We have not married for your amusement."

"Then why have we married?" she asked, wide-eyed and deceptively innocent.

"We have married so that I might make you into a proper young lady. So that you might take your place in society and make your grandmother proud."

"I would rather make you proud," she said, her voice low and slightly husky. "I would rather make you . . ."

He ignored her. "It looks as if I will have to set some rules for you to follow."

"Rules?" she smiled. "*Marido,* I make rules, I do not follow them."

"You must behave like a proper lady," he continued. "There will be no more episodes where you . . . touch me beneath the dining room table."

"When can I touch you?"

"Never," he answered quickly.

"Never?"

"It would be best if we maintained a platonic relationship."

"What does that mean?"

"It means we will be friends, and that is all." He nodded with a note of finality.

"You do not want me to touch you?" she asked, her voice low. He had expected she might be angry, as she had been that afternoon, but she took the new edict very well.

"That is correct."

She left the bed, moving with a cat's grace. "If you wish, *querido,*" she said agreeably.

The hairs on the back of Julian's neck stood. "I appreciate your agreement on this issue."

She headed for the door to the sitting room, turning just before she reached it. "You will find that I can be a very agreeable person. Thank you for the nightshirt," she said, running her hand over the soft linen, letting the palm of her hand hug the curves of one breast, her side, one hip. "I like it very much. It smells of you."

His traitorous body reacted as she had no doubt known it would. Who was he kidding? She didn't have to touch his body to tempt him. She could be two rooms away, whisper a word, and he would respond.

"*Marido,*" she said, her voice softly accented and so low his ears strained to hear each syllable. "You are here to teach me, I know, but I have a feeling I will become the teacher before many days have passed."

"Anya . . ."

"You think I am the beast, but be warned. There is a beast waiting within you. It sleeps deep and quiet, but it is there. I see it. It has fangs and claws and it is hungry."

"I do not have—"

"I am going to awaken the beast, *cher.* And then I am going to tame it and make it mine. And then I am going to feed it well." With that, she turned and left the room, tossing back a cheerful, "Sweet dreams."

The devil, Julian thought as he collapsed onto the bed. Anya had most definitely been sent by the devil.

Chapter Three

"I refuse to wear that," Anya said, pointing at the monstrosity that lay across the foot of her bed. Constructed of wires and strings and bones, it was an instrument of torture her grandmother had enticed her into once. That was a mistake she would not make again, no matter how ardently her husband insisted.

Julian walked to the edge of the bed, bent forward to study the corset through narrowed eyes, and finally reached out to pluck the thing between two fingers and lift it as if the ghastly garment might decide to bite. "Your grandmother insists that you learn to dress properly, and the corset is apparently a part of the required ensemble."

Anya planted her bare feet and lifted her chin. "If you want me to wear that hideous thing, you will

35

have to hold me down and place it on my unwilling body. I will fight you."

Julian barely canted his head in her direction, laying his eyes on her fully for the first time this morning. "In truth, I have no liking for the corset myself. It isn't at all healthy."

Anya smiled.

"We will save the corset for special occasions," he finished.

"No matter how special the occasion, I will not willingly don that . . . that . . ."

"You will fight me."

"I will."

Julian lifted his eyebrows and moved his attentions to the other garments on the bed; a pale blue dress, a lacy chemise, petticoats, drawers, hose, garters . . . shoes. "What a lovely dress."

"Ha! There is nothing wrong with what I am wearing."

Her husband sighed. "You're wearing a scarf and half of your grandmother's jewelry. That's hardly proper attire for a lady of your standing. For any lady at all, to be honest. You're more naked than not."

"You should try being more naked than not," she shot back. He wore layers and layers of *proper* clothing. Shoes, trousers, a starched shirt, a tie, a jacket, things beneath it all, she had no doubt. And it was such a lovely, warm day! She longed to feel the sun on her skin, the warmth of a spring breeze. At times she felt like she was suffocating in this fine house.

Julian lifted the chemise. "We will begin with this."

"We will not."

Her husband assumed a superior air. "Must I assist you as if you were a child?"

Anya smiled. "Yes, you must." She rather liked the idea of Julian the Beauty dressing her. He had asked her not to touch him and she was doing her best to comply, but he had said nothing about him touching her.

Julian, however, obviously realized that it was not in his best interest to follow through with his threat. He sighed, dropped the chemise onto the bed, and raked his fingers through his hair, as he often did when he was distracted. She found his discomfiture unexpectedly charming.

"Surely you understand the concept of compromise," he said lowly.

"Of course."

He paced beside the bed, his eyes falling now and then to the feminine garments that had been placed across the yellow bedcover. He was clearly uncomfortable being in her private chamber, among her private things. She wondered if as he paced he pictured her sleeping in that bed, wearing only his nightshirt.

If his thoughts took that turn, he did not allow the weakness to show. "Perhaps in these early days, as you accustom yourself to your new surroundings and customs, you could wear this appropriate clothing during the early hours of the day. Your grandmother will be pleased, your cousins will be relieved, and Peter will not have to divert visitors from your path. In the evening, when you and I are alone in our quarters . . ." He sighed again and pushed his fingers through his hair, mussing the dark strands. "You can wear whatever you want."

Anya glanced at the clothing on the bed, and then up at her harried husband. "No."

"What do you mean, no?" he snapped. "It's a perfectly generous and reasonable offer."

"I like things better as they are, when I wear what I want all day long."

"But it isn't . . ."

"Proper?" she finished. "I do not care for being proper."

"So I have noticed," he mumbled.

"I gain nothing with this so-called compromise," she said brightly. "Why should I agree? It is true that you are stronger than I am, and I have no doubt that you could force me to the bed." His eyes flickered up and met hers. She licked her lips. "And you could very easily hold me down while you place that detestable clothing onto my body." He swallowed hard, and she lifted her arms and offered her crossed wrists. "You could hold me down, press me to the bed with your body against mine—"

"Anya!" he interrupted.

She dropped her hands and shook her hair back so that the thick strands no longer covered both breasts. One was revealed, and her husband's eyes fell there and stayed. "You could force me to do as you wish, but as soon as you let me go I would remove the clothes and rip them into shreds. Still, if you would like to try . . ."

He turned his back to her and took a deep breath. And another, and another. Anya smiled at that broad back. Those wide shoulders. His long legs.

"All right," he said tersely, turning around to face her again, pinning his unerring gaze on her face. "You want something from me."

"Yes, I do."

"I understand you like to read."

Anya's eyebrows arched. It was not the offer she had expected. "Read?"

"Your grandmother says you've gone through every book in her library."

"Yes." It had been her only peace in this household, closing herself in the library and reading all those marvelous stories.

"My own things will be arriving soon, including a collection of books. If you cooperate, I might be willing to share."

No, it was not the offer she had expected, but she found the prospect of more reading material . . . intriguing. "What kinds of books do you have?" She tried, very hard, not to reveal her interest.

"Shakespeare."

"I have already read *Hamlet*," she said, sniffing as if she did not care. "It was quite good."

"There is more to Shakespeare than *Hamlet*. Much more. Have you read *Romeo and Juliet? The Taming of the Shrew?*"

"No. *The Taming of the Shrew* sounds intriguing."

"Of course it does," he said, his lips twitching just slightly.

"What else do you have that I might like?"

He quit fighting the twist in his lips and smiled at

her. Oh, he did have such a lovely smile. "Tales of men who have traveled the world."

Her heart nearly skipped a beat. "What about women who have traveled the world?"

"Sorry."

"What else?"

"Medical books," he said with a wave of his hand. "You would likely not be interested in those. I also have a few volumes of poetry, and a couple of novels I have never found the time to read."

The medical books sounded quite fascinating. Poetry was boring. Novels . . . she did enjoy novels. "And you will be a generous husband and share your library with your wife?"

"If she agrees to be cooperative and dress like a lady when she is among others."

She walked to the bed and lifted the linen drawers. "But at night, when we are alone, I can wear whatever I desire? Even if what I desire to wear is . . . nothing at all?"

Julian swallowed hard. His easy smile faded. "I am willing to compromise."

She took the step that brought her to him, so close her nose was almost touching his chest. So close she could feel the heat radiating off his body. "I understand," she whispered. "You wish to save my nakedness for you and you alone."

"No, that's not at all . . ."

"You wish to keep that part of me to yourself."

"Anya," he said in a warning voice.

"You are jealous," she whispered.

"Fine," he said, slinking past her and stalking to

40

the door. "I am jealous. Just put on the damned clothes."

She lifted the chemise and held it over her breasts. "Yes, dear."

Her husband groaned as he left the room.

Anya was lovely, and he told her so. In answer, she kicked at the hallway railing and complained that her shoes pinched her toes.

"When someone compliments you, the correct response is, 'thank you,' " he said as he took her arm and escorted her down the stairs.

She made a noise of pure disgust.

In truth, she was more than lovely. She was devastatingly beautiful. No matter how proper the clothing, Anya still looked untamed and lusciously seductive. Perhaps it was because she continued to wear her hair loose and flowing, an impropriety he would remedy after breakfast. Then again, perhaps it was her luscious lips, the way she smiled, the sparkle in her eyes. There was nothing tame about her face, and he had a feeling that could not be changed. Her spirit was wild, and that wildness could not be disguised with a plain day dress and a pair of shoes.

One step at a time, he reminded himself as he and his wife entered the dining room.

Anya's grandmother and her cousins were already seated at the table. They all perked up and took notice when a suitably attired Anya made her appearance.

"Anya," Mrs. Sedley exclaimed, "you look"—her

41

Linda Jones

expression softened—"so much like your mother."

Anya allowed Julian to pull out her chair, and she sat demurely. "I do not remember her," she said, a trace of coldness in her voice.

Julian sat beside his bride, wishing the change of clothing had subdued her sensuality. Perhaps if it had, he'd be able to steer his mind in a safer direction than the one it had chosen to take—the sight of Anya tossing her hair and baring her body, wondering what tactics she would use on him tonight, when they were again alone. Wondering how he would continue to resist her.

And he would. He had no choice.

The maid who hurried into the dining room was as surprised as the others had been. Her eyes widened, and she halted in the doorway between the dining room and the kitchen.

"I am hungry," Anya said, without so much as lifting her eyes to look at the maid. "And I have a yearning for roasted boar this morning."

The poor girl went pale. "Madam, we have no . . ."

Anya raised her head slowly and pinned her eyes on the trembling servant. "I have a yearning for roasted boar," she repeated, each word precise. "See to it."

The maid looked pleadingly to Mrs. Sedley. The poor girl was terrified.

"Ham," Julian said gently. "Ham will be just fine. Do you have ham?"

The maid nodded vigorously. "Yes, sir."

Anya laid her eyes on him. "I did not ask for ham, I asked for roasted boar."

42

"Don't be unreasonable," he said in a low voice.

Her hand shot out and she grabbed the vase of flowers that sat, most foolishly, within her reach. With her eyes pinned to his, she reared her arm back, readying a throw. Seymour ducked. Valerie covered her eyes.

Julian reached out and snagged her arm. "Return the vase to the table," he said calmly.

"I will n—"

He tightened his grip and forced her arm down, very softly repeating his order. This time Anya complied, setting the vase down with such force that water splashed onto the tablecloth.

"We do not throw things when we do not get our way," he said.

"Yes, we do," Anya snapped.

"And I do think you owe Betsy an apology."

Anya's face went blank. "Who?"

"Betsy." Julian lifted his hand to indicate the maid in the doorway. "You treated her quite badly."

A hush fell over the room, as everyone awaited Anya's response. She just shook her head in wonder. "She is a servant, here to do as I ask. I need not apologize when she is the one who is inadequate."

"You know quite well there is no roasted boar in the kitchen," he said. "You asked so you would have an excuse to raise a ruckus at the table. Offer an apology."

"Why should I?"

He smiled at her. "Because if you do not, the medical books that will be delivered with the rest of my things will be declared off limits."

Her lips thinned and her eyes sparkled. "And what makes you think I care at all for your silly medical books?"

He leaned toward her and lowered his voice to a whisper. "Because when I mentioned them upstairs your eyes positively lit up."

"They did not," she protested.

"They did." He leaned a little closer. "Apologize."

Anya lifted her chin, faced the servant in the doorway, and took a deep breath. "Forgive me . . ." She glanced at Julian and he whispered,

"Betsy."

"Betsy," she repeated curtly. "Ham will be just fine." Her nostrils flared, and Betsy made her escape.

"See there?" Julian said with a smile. "That wasn't so difficult now, was it?"

"I cannot believe you made me apologize to a mere servant."

"She is more than a servant, Anya, she is a person. A person with feelings just like yours."

Anya snorted.

"Don't make that noise," he commanded. "It's very unladylike."

"We have been married less than one day," she said beneath her breath, "and already you annoy me."

Thank God. Perhaps if she decided to find him annoying she would quit trying to tempt him so shamelessly when they were alone. "I'm sorry to hear that."

Betsy arrived with ham, eggs, coffee, and sweet

bread. Anya behaved herself as the maid placed the hearty meal before them. But when Betsy had left and the others had returned to the chore of consuming their own meals, Anya leaned close to him and whispered, "Do not worry, *cher*. Just because I find you annoying, that does not mean I do not want you. You are my husband, and you *will* come to my bed."

Anya sat on the stool to which Julian gestured, plopping down too hard in protest. "I do not like pins in my hair," she insisted. He had directed her to the south parlor for this exercise, away from the family and away from their beds. Perhaps he found this room . . . safer.

"You must wear your hair up, Anya," Julian said in that sensible voice of his. "It's—"

"Proper," she interrupted.

"Yes," he agreed. "Hilary, who often assists your cousin Valerie in fashioning her hairstyle, will be happy to . . ."

"No," Anya said, lifting her head defiantly. "Only you."

"What?"

"If I must wear my hair up, only you will touch it." She turned her head and looked up, giving her husband a smile. Hilary, a docile girl who rarely said a word, stood meekly behind him. "If anyone else but you so much as touches a strand of my hair, I will cut off their fingers, one at a time, and feed them to the wild dogs that howl at night."

"Anya!" Julian snapped.

45

But his protest came too late. Hilary was gone. Anya turned her head forward again, glancing out the window to the lovely, warm day beyond the panes of glass.

"Your manners are atrocious," Julian accused.

"It is your job to teach me, is it not?"

He groaned, and slipped his hands beneath the long locks. His fingers brushed against her back, and the hairs on her neck stood. She closed her eyes as he lifted and twisted the strands. Oh, such strong hands he had. The top of her head positively tingled as his fingers moved clumsily through the motions of arrangement.

"This is going to look ghastly," he mumbled.

"If I must learn new things, you must also learn," she said softly. "I will be patient while you master your new skills, as I hope you will be patient with me."

His fingers worked through her hair. Some strands were piled heavily atop her head, others fell around her shoulders. Julian tried to hold it all in place while he reached for the pins on the table at her side. "I cannot believe you threatened that poor girl with physical violence," he said as he stabbed at her hair with a pin. "You actually threatened to cut off her fingers!"

"She left, did she not?" Anya said, unconcerned. "Just as I desired. And you are learning to style my hair as you wish me to wear it. We should both be pleased."

Her grandmother had complained that she had a difficult time keeping help, as of late. Besides Peter,

46

only Hilary and Betsy remained as live-in servants, though there were a number who came in and worked odd hours or odd days. They all avoided Anya like the plague, just as she wished. She knew quite well what Betsy's name was, and that Hilary was easily frightened.

Again Julian stabbed at her hair, lifting some of the strands that had fallen. His hands were gentle, strong, and capable, but tender. He would make a wonderful lover, when he finally capitulated. And he would capitulate. When he did, he would be hers to command. Her willing slave, a submissive husband. He would belong to her, in every possible way.

"Hilary should have known better than to run," he said evenly. "Even if you had been serious with your ridiculous threat, there are no sharp objects within reach for you to . . ."

Moving quickly, Anya lifted her skirt and unsheathed the knife she wore at her right thigh. The leather strap rested over the linen of her drawers, today, instead of against her bare thigh, but she had no trouble slipping the dagger from its sheath and lifting her hand high to display the weapon for Julian.

His hands stilled. "Where did that come from?" he asked softly.

She lifted her white-stockinged leg and slowly drew back the pale blue skirt of her blasted dress so that he could see the leather strap and sheath.

"What on earth made you decide that you needed to leave your bedroom armed this morning?" He tried to sound calm, but did not quite manage.

47

Linda Jones

"Caro," she said softly, "I never leave my room un-armed."

"Yesterday . . ."

"Of course."

"Last night at dinner . . ."

"Naturally."

He poked at the twisted hair atop her head with more pins, remaining silent for a long moment. "This is your home, Anya. There is no need for you to carry a weapon. When you do leave the house you will be escorted, so at that time there will be no need. Do you . . . do you think someone here will try to harm you?" His voice was so gentle, so thoughtful, she felt something shift inside her. She had been right when she looked into his eyes that first day and determined that he had a good heart.

"As long as I have the dagger, I have no need to fear anyone."

His fingers worked at stray, misbehaving strands, touching her scalp, brushing against her neck. She felt his warmth and presence behind her, and savored it. Yes, he was a good man. And he was hers.

"Anya," he finally said. "Have you ever . . . have you ever used that knife?"

"Of course."

"On a human being?"

She sniffed and hesitated before answering. "No. The threat has always been enough."

He placed the final pin in the hair, circled around her, then dropped to his haunches so that his face was close to hers. He looked her in the eye, deep. So deep. "You are home," he said softly. "Among

48

family and friends. No one will ever hurt you here."

She wanted to believe him, she did. But she had been too long alone, she had been too long an outcast. No matter how she wished otherwise, she knew she could count on no one else. Not for protection. Not for security. Not for anything. If she were successful and Julian came to her—*when* she was successful, she amended—she would buy his devotion with her body. It was the only way. Nothing was free. Not loyalty, not affection.

He laid a hand on her cheek. "You are not so fearless after all, are you?"

Unwilling to let her husband see too much, Anya grinned and shook her head gently. Her hair came tumbling down.

Julian's eyebrows lifted slightly, in obvious dismay. "Well, we'll get it right eventually, I suppose."

She thought, for a moment, that they were finished, but Julian simply stood over her and crossed his arms. "Our first lesson will concern your language."

"I speak many," she said innocently.

"A lady carefully considers every word that leaves her mouth. People will judge you by your manner of speaking."

"I do not speak well?"

He narrowed his eyes, like a hawk. "You know perfectly well what I'm talking about. Ladies do not curse."

"Never?"

Julian shook his head.

"How bloody boring that must be."

49

Her husband ignored her deliberate jab, staring at her as his eyes went dark.

"Well, what does a lady say when she is upset or frustrated?"

"A simple *mercy*, if you must. Or perhaps, *goodness gracious.*"

Anya smiled, stood, and patted her husband lightly on the cheek. "Thank you for trying to teach me, *marido,* but I prefer to continue to speak as I always have."

"Anya . . ."

"Are there any other lessons for this morning?" She placed her foot on the sofa, lifted her skirt, and returned the dagger to its sheath. When she glanced up and over at Julian, she found that his gaze was pinned to her leg. It was an opportunity she would not waste. She took her time making sure the dagger was secure in its leather housing, and then she picked at a nonexistent wrinkle in her drawers, raking her palm over her thigh. That done, she moved her hand lower to smooth out the stockings.

Julian said nothing, so she asked again. "Lessons? Manners? Speech? Corsets?" She smiled and raked her hand down her side, where there was no corset.

"Not right now," he said hoarsely. And then he turned his back on her and stalked from the room.

Anya's smile faded. Her husband might want her, but she was beginning to realize that he was also very stubborn.

Chapter Four

The next day, Julian stiffened his spine as he and Anya walked into the sitting room that connected their bedchambers. Afternoon sun streamed into the fine, spacious room. He had never in his life lived in such a place. His last, inadequate apartment had not been as large as this one sitting room. But what a price he was paying for this fine place.

Reason, he needed reason. He was a professional, a scientist, and his wife was a fascinating subject. She was a project; walking, talking evidence of the effects of a pagan society on a woman of good stock. She was a fascinating medical and sociological subject. There was no other sane way to approach the situation.

Now that a fairly pleasant lunch with the family was over, Anya was to take a nap and he would make notes on the travels he would undertake after his

Linda Jones

chore was done. Unfortunately, Anya did not look at all like she wanted or needed a nap.

He watched, fascinated, as she walked to the window and lifted her face to catch the rays of sun that streamed through the panes. With Valerie's help, they had managed to restrain his wife's abundance of red hair atop her head. Only a few strands had gone astray, wispy curls of red dancing around her cheeks and neck.

For the first eight years of her life, Anya Sedley had lived a fairly normal existence. As normal as possible, for a child living through a barbarous civil war. She had been as protected as possible, by her family and her family's wealth. She had been schooled, sheltered, and taught the ways of a well-bred young lady. The war had ended, and perhaps for a couple of years Anya had been a part of the ideal family: a mother and father, a loving grandmother, cousins to play and learn with. And then her father had tired of Reconstruction and packed up his wife and child to leave it all behind, to join a colony of disenchanted Southerners in Brazil.

Sole survivor of the shipwreck that had taken her parents' lives, Anya had lived the next twelve years as a pagan; and had taken quite well to her new lifestyle.

Anya was beautiful, that was true. But she was also an utterly primitive female. Sometimes he was quite sure his wife was more animal than human. Her self-control was non-existent. She said whatever came to her mind, no matter how inappropriate it might be. Her natural sensuality rose to the surface on occa-

52

sion, and she was not ashamed. She was never ashamed.

In a very small, very reluctant way, he envied her that freedom. To say what she thought without reserve. To truly dismiss the cares and expectations of the civilized world. She was fascinating. Seductive. Free. She was everything Dr. Julian DeButy was not.

There had been times, terrible moments, when he'd looked at her and wondered if there had been other men in her life, men besides the king of Puerta Sirena. She had been the king's concubine, not his wife. Had there been other men before the king? Did the king's concubine entertain other men? When his thoughts turned in that direction, the wondering made him a little crazy, so he never wondered for long.

She turned from the window and began to unbutton the bodice of her gown.

"What are you doing?"

"You said when we were alone I could dress as I like." She sent her hated shoes sailing, with a hearty flailing of one leg after the other.

He had said that, hadn't he? "Yes, but it's an awful lot of trouble to remove . . . all that, and then have to dress again for dinner."

Her eyes met his. Challenge and defiance sparked there. "Grandmother will expect me to wear something hideously adorned for dinner. Lace that scratches my throat, bows so large that when I try to sit they get in my way; little, tiny roses made of satin." She scoffed. "In the past I have thrown the awful dresses she leaves on my bed out the window, or cut

them up with my knife in protest. But if I must wear
clothes . . ." She seemed to pout, in a way so naturally female, it must come easily to every girl-child
and woman on the planet, no matter what their age,
no matter what their education.

"You must."

"Then I will be comfortable in my own room." She
continued unbuttoning. "And I am not going to take
a nap," she said, sounding thoroughly disgusted at
the idea. "I do not know why Grandmother always
insists that I sleep in the afternoon, when I sleep very
well at night."

"Many young ladies find that an afternoon nap
refreshes them."

Anya again snorted in disgust.

"You must stop making that noise," Julian said.

"Why?" Anya peeled off her dress and stepped out
of it, kicking it aside with a vengeance before beginning with her chemise and petticoat.

"It's not . . ." Something rose up in Julian's throat
to choke him. "Not . . ."

"Ladylike," Anya supplied with a smile.

"Exactly."

He had to admit, grudgingly, that her smile was
enchanting. It was so real. So honest and unfettered.
Anya had surely never stood in front of a mirror
and practiced that grin, or worried that such a smile
would give her wrinkles in her later years. She
simply . . . smiled.

In a matter of moments she had shed her clothing. Entirely. Here in the privacy of their sitting
room, she apparently felt safe enough to remove the

knife and sheath from her thigh and set it aside.

After looking her over once, Julian turned his gaze to the floor. And he had thought restraining all that unruly hair was such a fine idea. But with those red tresses atop her head, there was nothing to cover her breasts, no soft curtain of hair to conceal at least a portion of her body.

"I imagine you will want to put on your scarf and let down your hair," he said, walking to the window and lifting his head to look to the East. One could almost see the ocean.

"No. I am perfectly comfortable as I am."

Out of the corner of his eye, he saw Anya stretch this way and that. She lifted her arms and twisted slowly, moving like a cat. He had never seen so much flesh. He had never studied a woman's curves and softness and . . . freckles. In desperation, he tried to appeal to her feminine side. "That very colorful scarf, the one you wore on the day we met, it was quite lovely. Very beautiful, in fact. I was rather hoping you would wear it again."

She stilled. "You liked it?"

"Very much."

Anya slipped through the door and into her room, and appeared moments later with the large scarf positioned so that it covered one thigh and the apex of her legs. Her hair was still up, though, her breasts still bare.

"You wouldn't have . . . another scarf, would you? Perhaps something in blue or red to match the one you're wearing."

"Grandmother gave me many scarves when she

discovered that I was willing to wear them," Anya
said, her voice low and suspicious.

"I have an idea," Julian said, shooing her into her
bedchamber and following.

Without being asked, Anya opened a long drawer
filled with scarves. Fancy and plain, they were
stacked high. Julian plucked a bright blue one off
the top and closed the drawer. "Here," he said,
handing it to Anya without looking directly at her.
"Wouldn't it be lovely if you wore this over your . . .
if you used it to cover . . ."

"You want me to cover my bosom?"

"Yes." The scarf slipped from his fingers as she
took it from him. Slowly.

"Why?"

Ah, there was no easy answer to that one. He had
a feeling Anya would be delighted to discover that
her nakedness disturbed him. Hell, she probably already knew. She had a way of seeing things. Of knowing what would rattle him. And she seemed
determined to rattle him.

"A man is always more interested in what he cannot see than in what he can," he said, trying to sound
reasonable.

"You want to be interested in my bosom?" she
asked, holding the scarf before her.

"Of course not." He hoped the blush he felt did
not show. He feared he hoped in vain. Glancing at
Anya out of the corner of his eye, he caught her
smile.

"I will wear it," she agreed, "if you will help me
put it on."

"I really have no idea how to affix such a thing."
To such a place.

"Neither do I."

Julian took a deep breath and snatched the blue
scarf from Anya. Placing his hands on her shoulders,
he turned her about and discovered that her well-
shaped back was almost as fascinating as her front.
Perfectly formed, feminine, soft . . . and somehow
strong as well.

He folded the scarf, his hands shaking just slightly
as he accomplished the task. To soothe himself, he
thought of the places he would travel when his task
was done. Islands of the Indian Ocean, Africa, the
wilds of Australia. So many places he had not yet
begun to think of them all.

He instructed Anya to lift her arms, and she complied. Taking a deep breath, he wrapped his arms
and the scarf around her. When he had difficulty
getting the scarf correctly positioned, Anya was no
help at all. She simply stood there, stock still, while
he was forced to straighten the silky material over
her right breast. His fingers brushed her warm skin.
The fullness beneath his hand gave in a most won-
drous way.

He removed his hand, closed his eyes, and
counted to ten.

"What is taking so long?" Anya asked patiently.
Her arms stayed raised, she swayed slightly, and her
backside almost brushed against him.

"I've never done this before."

"So I see," she whispered.

He quickly completed the chore, tying the scarf

snugly at her spine, and stepped back. Anya turned so Julian could admire his handiwork. Her breasts were covered, in a way, but there was still so much skin exposed, so much . . . temptation.

"Very good. I will make you my own personal maid," she said. "No one else seems to want me."

"Perhaps you have trouble keeping a personal maid because you break things and threaten those around you with physical violence."

"No," she said matter-of-factly. "They do not like me because I am different."

"You know," Julian said, seizing the opportunity that presented itself. "If you would dress properly and take to heart all the manners and ways I teach you, you will soon not be so different."

Anya's easy smile faded. "I could make myself look like my cousin and my grandmother and all the other women who live in this part of the world, but inside . . ." She raised a fist to her chest. "Inside I will always be different."

He was almost certain he saw the gleam of a tear in her eye before she spun around and stalked into the sitting room.

Her husband did like her. He might not admit to such a fault, but he did like her. She had known it from the moment she had first laid eyes on him. From the moment he had first laid eyes on her.

She needed to be with someone who liked her. Even if it was in this way, where she sat in a chair by the window trying to read a boring novel she had already read twice, and he sat at the desk across the room and furiously scribbled notes on a sheet of paper.

Julian must not leave when the time came. He must not leave her in this house where she was called beast and whore and barbarian. Sometimes she was called these names to her face, but usually they were whispered behind her back by the servants. She heard, though. She always heard.

She had to convince Julian to stay, and she knew of only one way to tie him to her. Only one way to persuade him that he could not live without her.

She dropped her reading and began to take the pins from her hair.

At the sound of the book hitting the floor, Julian lifted his head and laid his eyes on her.

One strand at a time, her hair came spilling down. "These pins are giving me a headache. No wonder Valerie is always in such a foul mood."

"I can imagine," Julian said softly. He still had not returned his attention to his work.

"Are all women in this country so . . . so . . ." She ruffled the loosened strands and let them fall around her body. "Disagreeable?"

"Of course not," Julian answered. "Most women are perfectly agreeable. I'm sure Valerie is a lovely person, in the right circumstances."

"You have known many women," she said, knowing in her heart of hearts that it was not so. "You have taken many beautiful women to your bed."

Julian returned his eyes to the paper before him and scribbled something new. "Not really," he said, his voice low.

59

"But you are handsome and strong," she protested. "Surely many women have offered themselves to you."

Julian took a deep breath, as he often did when he was disturbed. "It is important for you to realize that proper women do not offer themselves to anyone. To do so would be undignified and morally wrong."

"Even if the man a woman offers herself to is her husband?"

He swallowed hard. "We have had this discussion before, Anya."

"But I still do not understand."

"When my books arrive later this week, I will give you some pamphlets to read. They explain everything."

"I want *you* to explain—" Anya stood and walked toward her husband. He tensed with every step she took—"why here it is not proper for a man and woman to come together as they have from the beginning of time, as they do around the world? With power and pleasure and a divine unity."

He blushed. "We are better men."

"Or simply foolish men," she countered. "What do you gain by your chastity?"

"The energy expended in marital relations can be better used in thought," he said calmly. "In truth, the only reason for a husband and wife to submit to their sexual powers is for reproduction. In denying their sexual selves they can discover the joys of a true, pure friendship." A small muscle in his jaw twitched. He was not able to meet her eye. "This is best for everyone, as misuse of and overindulgence in man's sexual energies can lead to sickness, even death."

"Who told you such nonsense?" Anya stopped before her husband, placing her hands on her hips and staring down at him.

"It's a widely held fact that—"

"Nonsense," she interrupted.

"Anya, you have no idea what you're talking about."

She knelt before him and placed her hands on his knees. "But I do, *marido*. Since I have come here, everything has changed. I am no longer a goddess. I always say and do the wrong thing. I feel like I am living in a nightmare."

He laid a comforting hand in her hair.

"I am wrong; more often than not, but I am not wrong about this. No man ever lost his ability to think or died because he took pleasure in his wife's body."

"As I said, marital relations are best reserved for procreation. For . . . for creating life."

Her heart fell. "And I cannot have children." It was her greatest heartache. "That means I am imperfect in your eyes."

For the first time since Julian had initially spurned her, she believed him. He did not want her. It had nothing to do with his ridiculous excuses, though. She could not give him a son, and so he did not want her. It was that simple.

"No . . ." he began.

Anya did not sit at his feet to listen to his vile

excuses. She jumped up and returned to her chair.

"I will not make a fool of myself by asking you again to bed me," she said, her eyes on the window and the bright sun beyond. "I would not ask you to sink so low as to sleep with a flawed woman."

"Anya, you are not flawed. But this is . . . this is . . ."

She sat in her chair and scooped her boring book from the floor. "You are the teacher and I am the student."

"Exactly." He seemed relieved.

"You will teach me to behave in the way my family expects, and then you will leave and never come back."

"Yes. This is a business arrangement, Anya. Nothing more. A man and a woman can expect more from marriage than a physical relationship that might very well do them both harm. There is companionship to be had in marriage, as well as a dedication to higher and better morality. We are not savages, Anya. We are civilized men and women who have risen above the physical."

She had been so certain, when she had looked at him, touched him, smelled him, that he wanted her. How could she have been so wrong?

She had not been wrong. Julian did desire her, but he did not want a wife who could not give him a son.

Like Sebastian. Poor Sebastian. He had terrible bad luck, for a king. His first concubine, Emelda, was also barren. As was Anya. As was the woman he had taken to his bed when Anya had proved unable

to give him a child. Three women, all of them un-
fruitful. A king needed a son, yet each of the three
women Sebastian had taken as a lover proved to be
unable to give him a child. Poor Sebastian, he had
surely been cursed.

Julian smiled at her. "One day you will know I am
right about this."

She threw the book at his head.

"My darling, you look marvelous!" Mrs. Sedley
crossed the parlor with quick, delicate steps, her radiant smile for her granddaughter and no one else.
Valerie and Seymour exchanged a look and then left
the room together.

Mrs. Sedley took Anya's hands, clasped them between her own, and looked the girl up and down.
The gown Anya wore was a colorful rose, with a neckline lower than Julian approved of. It was rather de
cadent, and Anya filled it out rather nicely.

"Just marvelous," the older woman continued.
"Why, you'll be a proper lady in no time."

Julian rubbed the small bump on his aching head,
a reflexive action Anya surely saw.

"It is too tight," she said tersely. "And the lace
makes my bosom itch." To make her point, Anya
delicately scratched at the rising flesh above the low
neckline.

Mrs. Sedley's smile faded, just a little.

"And must I wear this large bow on my arse?" Anya
turned to display the satin bow in question.

"Anya," Julian scolded in a low voice. "That's not
a proper word."

She looked at him as if he were daft. "Bow?"

"You know perfectly well what I mean."

"Arse? That is the forbidden word. There is a better word?"

"Of course there is, but it's always best not to speak of such things at all."

"What things?"

Mrs. Sedley muttered, "Oh, dear," and excused herself to check on supper.

"Parts of the body," Julian continued as Mrs. Sedley left the room.

"We should not speak of them at all?" Anya stepped toward him and lifted her hand. He almost flinched when she placed the tip of her finger there. "Nose," she said, running her finger downward. "Mouth. Chin. Neck." Her hand drifted steadily down. "Chest. Belly."

Julian grabbed her wrist and stopped her inspection. "It's best you stop right there."

"I see," she said, not at all surprised that he had stopped her when he did. "You are telling me that it is perfectly acceptable to discuss some body parts, but if those parts are below the waist . . ."

"Anya . . ."

She leaned closer. "Perhaps I should whisper."

"Perhaps you should behave."

"Julian DeButy," she said, her eyes glued fearlessly to his. "You are a prig."

He didn't deny it, though he didn't care for the word at all. No more than he cared for *prude* or *puritan*. He'd been called all that and worse, in the past two years. "I am a moral man."

Her eyes softened, became dreamy and inviting. "You are afraid of the animal that lurks inside you."

"There is no . . ."

"You are afraid."

He didn't deny it.

"In the moments we have before dinner, perhaps we can discuss the way you walk."

Anya smiled. "You like the way I walk?"

Julian took a deep breath. "Well . . ."

Before he could form the words, Anya turned and walked toward the doorway, her hips swaying in their own rhythm, her every step a seduction. At the doorway, she turned and began to walk toward him, her satisfied smile adding to the seduction.

"Your manner of walking is . . . lovely, in its own way," he said staidly. "And while such a manner of walking might be perfectly acceptable on Puerta Sirena, it's not quite demure enough to be acceptable here."

Her smile faded. "You want me to change the way I walk?"

"You should watch Valerie and your grandmother. They both—"

"They walk like they are in pain," Anya protested. "They move like something inside them is broken."

"You needn't alter your way entirely," Julian said, as he noted the displeasure on his wife's face. "But if you could subdue the, uh, sway of your hips."

Her displeasure faded. "I do not know if I am capable of changing the way I walk. My hips simply sway." She turned her back on him and took a luxurious step. "See?" she said as she took another languid stride.

Julian crept up behind her and laid his hands on her hips. He had to make her stop. She did, and he stood there with his hands on her hips and her back to his chest. "All right," he said softly. "Take a step."

She did, and he stilled the natural sway of her hips as she moved forward. Her flesh moved beneath his hands undulated gently beneath pink satin. But it wasn't satin he felt. It was his wife. The swell of her hips. Her warmth. Her softness.

"Is that better?" she asked softly.

"Much," he choked.

She took another step, and his hands remained where they were as he tried to contain the swing of her hips. His step was in time with hers, they moved in symmetry, as if they danced.

Julian lowered his nose to her hair and closed his eyes. Heaven above, this woman smelled so good. What made her hair smell so enticing? Perfume. Maybe the lingering aroma of a scented shampoo. They took another step, and his body pressed more insistently against her back.

"Marido," Anya whispered softly, "if this is what our lessons will be like, I believe I will enjoy having you as a tutor."

Julian dropped his hands and took a step back, as he realized how close they were, how intimate. Good Lord, Anya had done nothing blatant, and still he had allowed his thoughts to take a dangerous path.

"Just . . . observe your cousin Valerie. She walks quite properly."

Anya turned and smiled up at him. "I rather like the way you assist me, *marido*."

A test, he reminded himself. The test of a lifetime.

Chapter Five

She had never been afraid of storms. The cottage she had lived in on Puerta Sirena had been much less substantial than this house, and yet she had never quaked at the sound of thunder.

Tonight Anya quaked. She quaked so hard her bones rattled.

Without making a sound, she crept through the sitting room and into Julian's bedroom. She eased the door open and closed again, tiptoed to his bedside and stood there, looking down at the indistinct lump in the darkness. Somehow knowing he was close made her shake a little less.

For more than two weeks he had attempted to reform her. He taught her how to speak, how to walk, how to dress. And she indulged him because it suited her to do so. She had not thrown anything in days.

She did not know why she liked Julian DeButy so much. He would not allow her to seduce him, even though it was clear to her that he did desire her. Like everyone else, he wanted to make her into something she was not. A lady.

And yet there were times when she knew he preferred her just as she was. Those moments were rare, but she had begun to treasure them.

Lightning flashed, the room was bathed in bright light for an instant, and in that moment she saw Julian staring up at her from the bed, where he lay wide awake and suspicious.

"What are you doing here?"

Thunder shook the house, too soon after the lightning, and she jumped out of her skin. When she had recovered, she answered confidently. "I thought you might be frightened by the storm."

"No," he said calmly. "I'm fine, thank you."

Well, she was not fine—and if her husband was any kind of man at all he would see that! "That is good," she said softly, turning to go.

"Anya," Julian called as she laid her hand on the doorknob and prepared herself to weather the storm alone in her own room. "What's wrong?"

"Nothing."

She heard the rasp of a match behind her, the rattle of Julian's bedside lamp. A moment later a warm glow filled the room, and she breathed deep in relief. Yes, that was much better. Still, she did not turn around.

Julian left the bed. "You're shaking," he said, his voice low.

"I am . . ." Another flash of lightning interrupted her, and she braced herself for the thunder that would follow. Something she did not like at all welled up inside her. "Not," she finished when the rumble faded.

Julian laid his hand on her shoulder. "Is it the storm? Are you afraid?"

Ashamed, wanting to deny the fear, Anya forced herself to nod and whisper, "Yes."

"There's nothing to be frightened of." His voice was calm, soothing, reasonable, and kind.

Anya turned to face her husband, tilting her head so she could look him in the eye. "I do not know why I am afraid. Until I came here I was never afraid of storms, but now . . . each one is worse than the last. It seems they always come at night." Her heart hitched.

"Does the storm make you remember when your ship went down?"

Anya shook her head fiercely. "No. I remember nothing before Puerta Sirena. Nothing at all." But lately she did remember. Pictures in her mind, mostly. Small remembrances. Sitting on the steps with Valerie, the two of them playing with their dolls. Eating gingerbread in the kitchen. Seymour, as mean then as he was now, pulling her pigtails. And sometimes, for brief flashes of time, she remembered her mother. A tall, slender redheaded woman with a warm smile and . . . and . . . she didn't want to remember. Remembering hurt her heart.

"Come and sit on the bed," Julian said, taking her

arm and leading her there. "We'll wait out the storm together."

Together. It was such a nice word. She sat on the edge of the bed, but Julian did not. He stood before her, his head cocked to one side so he could study her face. And she could not help but smile, just a little.

His nightshirt was the silliest thing she had ever seen. It hung to his knees, and beneath the hem he had very nice, strong legs, dusted with dark hair. Fine man's legs that should not be constantly hidden. Usually his clothing fit him snugly, showing off his frame, but this nightshirt was misshapen, horribly baggy.

She wore his other nightshirt, as it was more comfortable than the gowns her grandmother had provided. The garment she had taken from her husband was soft, and worn, and it smelled of him, just a little. She had put it on before coming to Julian's room, knowing that if he woke and found her there naked he would surely throw her out.

Her smile disappeared when the lightning came again, and again. Her heart thundered and she could not breathe. Most of all, she wanted to scream. She did not.

"It's all right." Julian was obviously concerned. He paced before her, stopping only to study her face on occasion.

The storm grew fiercer, and her body shook. She hugged herself tightly, but no matter how she tried she could not make the quaking stop. Julian finally sat on the edge of the bed and placed his arm

71

Linda Jones

around her. She turned her face into his shoulder and buried it there. Yes, that was better.

She took a few deep breaths, but when the thunder came again she lurched. Julian tightened the arms that encircled her.

"I should awaken your grandmother," he said, starting to move away. "Perhaps she'll know what to do."

"No!" Anya clutched at his nightshirt and held on. "Do not go. I . . . if I can only stay here until the storm ends." Not just here in this room, but right here with Julian's arms around her and her face buried against his shoulder.

"All right," he agreed softly.

The storm did not let up, and Julian did not release her. It was very nice, the way he held her so close. He mumbled a lot, and she could rarely tell what he was saying. Sometimes he seemed angry. Other times he did not seem angry at all. But he did not let her go. Not once.

Julian was a good man. A good husband, even if he would not lie with her.

The storm lasted longer than any of the others she remembered. A couple of times she started to doze off sitting up, but she never quite went to sleep. Julian quit mumbling. Her heart stopped pounding like it was about to burst through her chest, and settled into an even, steady rhythm.

Anya was not sure how she and Julian ended up lying on his bed, but it was very nice. She rested her head on his shoulder, and he kept his long, strong arms around her. He breathed deep and even, and when she hid her face against his shoulder she was not so afraid. Still, just before she drifted into a deep sleep, she thought of a wild ocean and a raging storm and a wildly tossing ship she claimed not to remember.

Julian turned his face from the intrusive morning sun and buried his nose in the soft and fragrant hair that fell across his chest and neck. Hair. He opened one eye, and saw the sun gleaming on red strands. He took a deep breath, and his lungs were filled with Anya. Wild and sweet-smelling and arousing Anya. His forbidden wife, the temptation of a lifetime.

She slept on her side. Her head rested on his shoulder, one leg—bare since the nightshirt she wore had ridden up to her hip—entwined with his, and her arm rested familiarly across his midsection. Her breathing was deep and even and peaceful. He lifted the hair that covered half of her face, to see that last night's terror no longer showed there. He was taken with the notion that if he kissed the freckles on her nose he would find them sweet.

He had never slept with a woman in his arms, and the experience was quite disturbing. Anya's body skimmed and pressed and intertwined along one side of his own, and the sensation of flesh to flesh was more than he could bear. He should extricate himself at once and leave Anya to sleep, peaceful and alone.

But he didn't move. Half asleep and vulnerable, holding her for a while longer seemed more important than his principles. Besides, there was nothing wrong with enjoying the warmth and comfort of an-

73

other human being's presence. As long as they went no further. He closed his eyes and almost drifted off again. A sleeping man could not be condemned for taking liberties with his own wife.

A return to sleep eluded him, and he was nagged by doubt. Stubbornly, he pushed those doubts aside. He knew he was right in his convictions. Studies had shown conclusively that chastity was best for mind and body. It wasn't as if he loved Anya madly and could not tear himself away from her. He had known her for less than a month, and while he had come to like her, anything more was out of the question. What he felt for her was lust, nothing more. Common lust. And he knew from experience that with lust, which might be pretty and exciting when one was caught in the throes of it, there was always a price to pay. A high price.

One of the things he most liked about his wife was her honesty. She might not be able to express herself in a proper way, but she also never lied. Well, except for that moment last night when she'd tried to tell him she was not afraid. But her lie had been so obvious, and so quickly rescinded that he forgave her that one transgression.

Some women were much better liars than Anya. Consummate liars. Demons of deceit.

The woman at his side squirmed and moaned. Her leg lifted, skimming along his and lifting his nightshirt. The activity beneath his nightshirt belied his insistence that he did not want this woman in his bed. He closed his eyes. He was only human, after all.

74

Anya was waking, thank goodness. Her body stirred slightly, her breathing changing. In a moment she would realize where she slept and crawl out of the bed. Surely she would.

But she didn't. Eyes closed, breathing deep and even, she shifted her head until it rested on his chest and her soft breasts pressed against his ribs. She sighed, curling herself around him. Her warm breath touched him through the linen. Her body, from end to end, was unbearably soft and sweet. He throbbed and ached, wanting her. Needing her in a way he had never needed anything.

She continued to move—an inch here, a subtle shift there—until she practically rested atop him. Her nightgown, the nightshirt she had confiscated from him on his first night in the house, rode up almost to her waist. Her hair spilled across his chest, and he buried one hand there, hoping to wake her as his fingers threaded through the red locks, moving so gently he knew he likely would not. Like it or not, he was not ready to give her up.

And she was right there. Her femininity so near to the evidence of his desire. Her body and his so close to coming together, that with a shift of his hips he could be inside her. More than anything—

"Good morning." She purred like a cat as she lifted her head and looked down at him. And smiled. Everything in him tightened, some part of his mind spun out of control. For a moment, a long, terrifying, oddly beautiful moment, he felt the beast Anya said slept inside him. And then she yawned and rolled away.

Julian yanked up the coverlet to conceal the embarrassing tent his nightshirt had become, and Anya sat up and lifted both arms above her head. He watched her stretch and come awake, and it was an amazing sight. He wanted her, still, but dammit he should not—could not—have her.

When she laid her eyes on his face, she smiled. It was not one of her blatantly brazen come-hither smiles, but one of the real, open grins he had come to love. To like, he amended. To like.

"Thank you," she said softly, and he knew the words did not come easily—or often—to her luscious lips. "I do not know why lately I am so afraid of storms. They have come to the island all my life, and I have never before shuddered at the sound of thunder."

Julian took a deep breath and tried to compose himself. Outwardly, at least. Inside he was dancing. Exploding. Falling apart. But his voice and face remained calm. "If you'd like, we can discuss what has happened since you returned home. Perhaps we can discover the reason for your newfound fear."

Anya's smile faded. "Perhaps I do not want to know."

"If you do not understand the fear, you will never be rid of it."

Anya reached out to him. Her soft fingers lightly brushed his cheek. "You need to shave, *marido*."

It was her way of neatly changing the subject, and Julian allowed her to get away with it. "I imagine I do."

"And your hair is such a mess." She very briefly

76

and lightly ruffled his hair, using both of her hands. "You probably should have a haircut, but I like it as it is."

"I usually get so lost in my research that I don't even think about getting a haircut when I should. Sometimes Aunt Helen will remind me."

"I like it as it is," she said again, and he believed her.

If she continued to look at him like this, he might never cut it again. He wished he could tease Anya about her messy hair, that he could casually run his fingers through the red strands without being overcome with the desire to ravish her.

Anya's eyes were so open and real. He was struck with the notion that she would never lie. That she was incapable of deceit. What a rare woman she was, if that were true.

"I have not always been kind to you," she said, "as you have been to me. You are a good man, Julian DeButy."

No, I am a common man, inches away from attacking my wife. "I try to be."

"Last night you were . . ." Her eyes went a little misty. "Wonderful. How can I ever thank you?"

He should take advantage of this opportunity and ask her to stop trying to seduce him. Or to quit throwing things when she did not get her way. Or to come back into his arms and help him break all his promises to himself. He might ask her to wear clothing when they were alone, to quit smiling at him, to stop smelling so good. But he didn't.

Linda Jones

"No thanks are necessary. I'm just glad to see that you're feeling better this morning."

Anya bound from the bed. What magnificent legs she had! They seemed to be made for bounding. And . . . other things.

"I am feeling much better. Shave and get dressed, and we will go down to breakfast together. I am starving!"

When she was gone, Julian collapsed back onto his bed.

One amenity of her new home Anya had learned to love was the bathtub. Large and deep and situated in its own room on the second floor, it was Anya's idea of decadence. There were fat towels and scented oils and hot water, and she could sit in the tub for as long as she wished.

Julian usually bathed late at night, after Anya had gone to bed. She suspected he did so in the hopes that she would leave him be. And she had, up until this point.

The night before, when he had held her as the storm raged, something had happened. Her husband had comforted her, tried to take away her fear. That was the action of a kind man, a man who cared, at least a little, for his wife. He could have accepted her assurance that she was not afraid and sent her back to her room, but he had not. Instead he had held her, sheltered her.

She had begun to lose hope where Julian was concerned. He did want her, but he was doing his best to prove that his blasted morals were stronger than his desire.

But something had changed as he had held and comforted her. They were closer than they had been. They were one step closer to being man and wife in truth, as well as in name.

So tonight as he bathed, she opened the door on the cozy room where the tub was located and stepped inside, wearing nothing but his confiscated nightshirt and a smile.

Julian almost jumped out of the water, then thought better of such a move. Anya tried to peer beneath the water, as nonchalantly as possible, and Julian laid his washcloth across it. The cloth floated and obscured her view. "What are you doing here?"

"I have come to wash your back," she said sweetly.

He held aloft a long-handled brush made just for that purpose.

"But is it not a wife's duty to see to the well-being of her husband?"

"Of course, but . . ."

"I am trying to be a good wife. Truly, Julian." She knelt beside the tub and whisked the washcloth from the water.

She was tempted to look blatantly, reach beneath the water, and arouse him. But Julian was not affected by such open advances. Physically he would respond, but his bloody brain always interfered. No one had ever taught her subtlety, when it came to seduction, but she was certain she could learn.

"Lean forward," she said, scooting to the side so she could take the washcloth to his back. Oh, and a fine back it was; muscled and lean, hard and shapely, the way a man's back should be. She gently worked the washcloth up and down his back, and eventually Julian relaxed.

"Soap," she said simply, offering one hand. He complied, depositing the bar of soap on her palm. She worked up a nice lather and continued. Sometimes she ran the cloth all the way up to his neck, adding a touch of lather to the ends of his hair. Then she would wash down his spine, allowing her hand to dip beneath the water.

"You are my favorite teacher," she said softly. "You teach me new things without making me feel stupid."

"You are many things, Anya," he said lowly, "but stupid is not one of them."

She gave a half-smile to his back. "I have felt stupid often since coming here. The other tutors, they despaired of ever teaching me anything. Grandmother never said I was stupid, but I see that look in her eyes, sometimes. That look that tells me she is disappointed that I am not more like Valerie."

"You have your own attributes, Anya," he said kindly. "I'm sure your grandmother does not compare you to Valerie."

She raised the washcloth to his neck and made small circles with her fingers, watching the lather build on his skin and creep into his dark hair. "What attributes?" she asked lowly.

Julian hesitated. Had he been lying? Perhaps she had no attributes at all. But then he cleared his throat. "You're intelligent, I can see that well. No wonder your other tutors failed. They probably tried to treat you like a child."

"They did," she said, glad he admired her intelligence, but not particularly satisfied.

"And you have . . . a spark."

"A spark? I do not understand."

"You have such a wonderful vivaciousness within you. It needs to be tamed," he added quickly. "But not erased."

She smiled. Vivaciousness was good.

"And you are . . ." He stopped, as if he had choked on a word.

"I am what?" she prodded.

"Beautiful," he confessed in a low voice. "Quite beautiful."

Pleased with his answer, Anya worked the soapy washcloth across Julian's back. "You have many fine attributes yourself."

"There's no need . . ." he began.

"You have a kind heart," she interrupted. "I knew that when I first met you. Truly kind hearts are rare, and should be treasured."

He mumbled something that might be "thank you," but she couldn't be sure.

"And as I said you are a marvelous teacher. The finest I have ever known." Her hands worked deeper into the water than it had before, her washcloth covered fingers barely brushing his backside.

"I'm sure my back is clean, Anya," Julian said testily.

"And you are beautiful," she whispered. "Julian, the Beauty."

"Men are not supposed to be beautiful," he protested.

"But you are." She was so tempted to continue her exploration beneath the water, to touch her lips against Julian's wet neck and back, to snake her arms around his wet body and push him a little further. But enough was enough. She tossed him the washcloth and stood. "There now. Your back is wonderfully clean."

Again he muttered something unintelligible.

"Good night," she said sweetly.

Julian stood at the top of the stairs and stared at the unimpressive swirl of gold chain and the small attached ornament that sat on the palm of his hand. It was a silly idea, really. Anya had more jewels than any woman he knew, and many of them were quite elegant. Grand, even. This trinket would be nothing to a woman like Anya.

He was about to stuff the necklace in his pocket when she came up behind him, moving quiet as a cat. "Good morning," she said sweetly. Too sweetly. That innocent tone usually meant she was up to something.

"Good morning." He closed his hand, making a fist around the necklace.

Anya missed nothing. "What do you have in your hand?"

"Nothing," he said, offering his arm to escort her to breakfast.

She took his arm and they descended the stairs. Good heavens, even dressed properly Anya looked like no other woman he had ever known. Wild. Free.

And not nearly as fearless as she would like everyone to believe. Her reaction to the storm proved that
to him.

"Actually," he said as they reached the foot of the
stairs, "it's not exactly nothing." He opened his fist
and displayed the plain necklace.

Anya wrapped one finger around the delicate
chain and lifted it slowly. The pendant, a gold rose,
swung between them. "It's very pretty," she said
softly.

"It was my mother's," he explained. "My Aunt Helen gave it to me when I turned twenty. She said I
might want to give it to my wife, one day."

Anya lifted her head and looked him dead in the
eye. "It is for me?"

"It's not fancy," Julian said quickly. "You probably
won't care to wear it." Her tastes were much more
extravagant, especially where jewelry was concerned.
"But Aunt Helen said my mother always considered
it a kind of good luck charm." He dropped his eyes.
"My father gave it to her soon after they married."

"They died when you were young?" she asked
softly.

"I was nine when my father died. My mother
passed on a year later."

Anya held the necklace high, so the gold rose
swung between them. "Do you have many remembrances of her?"

Julian's mouth went dry. "Only this."

"And you give it to me?"

"I thought you might like a good luck charm of

your own," he explained. "Something to hang on to when storms come." He wouldn't always be here to comfort her. Like it or not, there would come a day when Anya would be on her own. Something so simple as a lucky piece was not too much to offer.

Anya held the necklace aloft, offering it to him on the end of a slender finger. Of course, she wanted nothing to do with something so simple as a hand-me-down pendant. She grinned as he took the necklace from her, then spun to present her back.

"You will put it on me?" she asked.

For some reason, Julian felt relieved that she was not returning the gift.

"Of course." His fingers didn't fumble much as he draped the necklace around Anya's neck and worked the clasp. He told himself that it only made sense to give the geegaw to Anya. He reasoned that it wasn't as if he'd ever take another wife, and besides, a lucky charm might actually bring Anya a little comfort, one of these days.

When she turned to face him again, she laid her hand over the small gold rose that sat high on her chest. "Thank you," she said with a softening smile.

"It's nothing, really," he said too quickly. "I can't very well wear it, and it simply makes sense—"

"*Marido,*" she interrupted. "My teacher would tell me that the proper response to 'thank you,' is 'You are welcome.'" She licked her lips. "Thank you."

Julian took a deep, calming breath. "You're welcome."

* * *

The arrival of Julian's books, two days after the big storm, changed everything. Anya was so relieved to have something new to read! In the following three weeks, each afternoon after a family lunch, Julian and Anya retired to their sitting room to read. In the privacy of their shared room she shed her conventional clothing, but she always covered herself with well-placed brightly covered scarves. Julian seemed not to mind, anymore, though in those early days he did not mind because he rarely looked in her direction.

They had been married almost six weeks. He was proving to be much more steadfast than she had anticipated.

His library was wonderful. *Too* wonderful. Anya hardly knew where to start. She spent an entire afternoon arranging his books on the bookshelf Grandmother had moved to their sitting room for that purpose. All the medical books were placed on one shelf, the tales of travel on another. The bottom shelf was reserved for Shakespeare. So much Shakespeare!

On this warm June afternoon, Anya sat on the floor and tried to decide what to read next. Julian sat in the rocking chair in the corner, his nose buried in an anthropology book.

She felt a little guilty for trying so hard to seduce him in their first days of marriage. It had been wrong, she supposed, to try to control him by appealing to his libido. It had not worked, so she did not feel too guilty, but she did feel a little pang of regret now and then.

Her fingers skimmed over the leather spines of the books on the bottom shelf, but her eyes were on her husband. In the weeks since the storm, he had not cut his hair. Dark and thick, it fell over his ears and curled about his neck. Now and then Grandmother would suggest that he get it trimmed, and he always said he would take care of the matter. He never did. Sometimes Anya thought she saw a hint of a wild man in him, when they were walking in the garden and the wind ruffled his hair, or when he briefly—so briefly—looked at her just so and her heart skipped a beat. Her imagination was suffering from the reading of too many novels, or so the author of one of Julian's ridiculous brochures would suggest.

To thank Julian for being so kind to her, Anya had desisted in her plan to seduce him, since he seemed to hold his chastity in such high regard. She thought he was grateful for her change in attitude, but it was difficult to tell. Sometimes . . . sometimes she allowed herself to believe that deep down he really wanted her to seduce him.

He lifted his eyes from the book and smiled at her. "What will you choose next?" He always took such an interest in her reading material, and had forbidden her nothing.

"*Much Ado About Nothing,* I think," she said.

He placed his book in his lap and gave her his full attention. "I saw a notice in the newspaper this morning. *Romeo and Juliet* will be performed at the Wilmington Theater next week."

"Theater?"

"The play will be acted out by performers. Have you ever been to a performance?"

She shook her head.

"Would you like to go?"

"Yes."

"Then we will go."

Something terrible had happened to her, and this horrific thing had happened so gradually she had not known it was coming until it was too late. She had always found Julian attractive, and taking him to her bed in order to achieve her goals had seemed like a fine idea. But lately she felt . . . different. She wanted him. She did not crave just any man, and she did not want Julian in order to control him. She simply wanted him. Sometimes she actually ached for him.

She had never ached for anyone or anything. Before being given to King Sebastian, she had been trained as a lover. All the older women of the village had shared their knowledge with her. They had instructed her. How to move, how to seduce. How to touch, where to touch. From the age of fifteen, when she had been chosen, no man had been allowed to speak to her. She had been protected, guarded and cared for. When the old king stepped down from the throne and put his only son in his place, she was Sebastian's gift from his father. A virgin who knew how to please a man. What more could a man want?

Sebastian already had a concubine, but as he and Emelda had been together for three years and produced no heir, the new king could not refuse his father's gift. And so he came to her. As king, he was

Linda Jones

entitled to as many concubines as he desired. Even if he took a wife, he would be allowed his pleasures.

Sex was a task. A not altogether unpleasant one, but a task all the same. It had never been, not even in the later days when Sebastian so rarely came to her, an ache. Or a joy. She had never dreamed of a man taking her. Touching her. Filling her. Until now.

Julian was unlike any man she had ever known. No other man would have soothed her during the storm, no other man would have held her without expecting something more in way of thanks. She fingered the gold rose that lay against her chest. A man who did not care for her at all would not give her something so precious. His ideas about marriage were maddening, his lessons on decorum and propriety were often annoying, and still she felt something new and different growing inside her. She had been taught all aspects of physical love, but no one had ever spoken to her of the heart. She had seen this kind of love, though, in a few couples on Puerta Sirena who at times seemed to need nothing and no one else but one another. Some nights she was teased with a fleeting memory of love she could not quite grasp.

She feared she was falling in love with her husband, and that was a terrible thing. When his task here was done and he left, he would break her heart.

A man like Julian DeButy would never love the Beast of Rose Hill. No matter how much she tried, how hard she wanted to be the kind of woman he could love, she knew she wasted her time. She had read his ridiculous books and pamphlets, she knew what his notion of the ideal woman was.

According to the pamphlets Julian read, the ideal woman should be meek, pious, and not too smart. She should be content to immerse herself in domestic duties, and she should have no personal desires—sexual or otherwise. If she did allow her husband to touch her, it should be grudgingly, and only for the objective of making a child. One pamphlet had even suggested that the dutiful wife should lie in her bed and think of something more pleasant than what her foul husband was doing to her. He, of course, was being unmercifully driven by that monster lust that a man could not control but a woman must. What hogwash.

Anya was not that woman and never would be. She had said it herself, on one of their first days as man and wife: He might transform her on the outside, but inside . . . inside she would not change. Julian knew that better than anyone.

Julian insisted that she not again disturb him while he was bathing. Her more perverse nature might have compelled her to disobey, but he had blushed so prettily as he had sent her packing that she had decided to obey. For now.

An overly warm day had sent him to the bath earlier than usual. They had spent much of the afternoon in the garden, talking about the books they were reading while Julian tried his best to reform her way of walking. He had worked up quite a sweat, and said he needed a nice, cold bath.

Anya, who always knew what she wanted and how to get it, was torn. She wanted her husband in her bed, but she did not want to drag him there. She wanted him to come to her of his own volition—not because she enticed him, not because she appealed only to what his damned pamphlets referred to as his baser instincts.

She wanted him to love her, but of course that was impossible. But surely he could want her enough to make their remaining days and nights together memorable.

Anya walked into the south parlor, where Valerie sat diligently poking her needle into an uncooperative piece of linen. Grandmother had tried to interest Anya in embroidery, but after attempting the chore for a grand total of five minutes, Anya had thrown the tangled results at Peter, very nearly stabbing the man in the eye with the needle.

Valerie lifted her head and sighed. "Oh," she said softly, "it's you."

In the past weeks, Anya had been remembering more and more about the first years of her life in this house. Flashes of memory she told no one about. One fact came through loud and clear: Valerie, whose father had been Anya's father's brother and whose mother had died when she was a baby, had been her friend. Not quite two years older than Anya, Valerie had been the leader. The two girls, and a slightly older and more annoying Seymour, had practically grown up together while their fathers had been at war, and then when the family had begun to rebuild itself.

So why did Valerie hate her so now? And she did hate. The emotion was unmistakable in her pale blue eyes.

Anya took a deep breath. "May I sit with you for a while? Julian is taking a bath."

Valerie narrowed her pale blue eyes suspiciously. "I suppose." She returned to her embroidery. Valerie was no more talented at the craft than Anya had been, and yet she continued to try.

Valerie was the perfect granddaughter. She was the kind of woman Grandmother wanted Anya to be. Demure, sweet, and usually silent.

"Why do you hate me?"

Valerie lifted her head and put her embroidery aside. "I do not hate you, Anya. . . ."

"You do." Anya cocked her head and studied her cousin carefully. Yes, Valerie was a little fat, but she was also pretty, blessed with fair hair, creamy skin without a single freckle, and very nice blue eyes. "Why?"

"I do not *hate* you," Valerie repeated. "But . . ."

"But what?" Anya prompted.

"You've turned this household upside down," the young woman said crisply, her spine straight and her nose just slightly in the air.

"I apologize. That was never my intention."

Valerie blushed bright pink. "And your behavior has been shocking."

"I am who I am. I cannot change who I have become to please anyone."

Valerie sniffled a little, as if she were suddenly on the verge of tears. "And you're not the same. I grieved for you, and then I find out you're alive after all these years . . . and you're not the girl I remember."

"Do you remember me?"

Valerie laid her eyes squarely on Anya. Yes, there were tears sparkling there. "Of course I remember you. You were like a sister to me. I loved you."

"You loved me?"

Valerie looked taken aback. "Of course I did." A long moment of awkward silence filled the air before Valerie continued, in an attempt to explain her confession. "We were children, of course. Not the same people we are today."

Anya studied her cousin, a woman who had been cold and distant since her return. Of course, upon that return, Anya herself had been less than hospitable. By the time she arrived she was already missing Puerta Sirena, and it had not taken her long to realize that she did not belong. But here and now she tried to piece together the memories that had been coming to her, lately. Like jagged pieces of one of Grandmother's puzzles, they were beginning to take shape. To fit together. To make sense.

"I do not remember much," Anya admitted. "But Valerie, I think I loved you, too."

Chapter Six

"Why do you have no patients?" Anya rocked once in her chair. She had placed it by the window, in the sun, and the afternoon rays warmed her bare shoulders.

Julian lifted his head from the book he was reading and raised his eyebrows as he settled his gaze on her. "I believe I have proven that I have infinite patience."

Anya grinned. "No, silly. *Patients*. Sick people. You are a doctor, why do you not treat sick people?"

This was her favorite time of the day. The morning was filled with breakfast with the family followed by lessons. How to talk, how to dress, how to walk. What to say, what not to say. Julian was most especially concerned with what not to say. But after lunch, another meal taken with the family, she and Julian retired to this room, where she traded her restrictive

93

Linda Jones

clothing for a couple of scarves and Julian slipped off his jacket. They read. Sometimes they talked about what they read.

Julian took a moment to consider her question. "I'm more interested in research," he said. "My grandfather was an anthropologist, and that's where my primary interests lie. While I did go to medical school and serve an internship, I have never attempted to set up a practice of my own."

"Why not?"

The question seemed to vex him, and he did not quickly come up with an answer.

"I know," she said softly.

"Oh, you do." Julian set his book aside and gave her *that look*. The one he gave her when she refused to do as he asked. The one he gave her when she lifted a vase and thought about throwing it at him. She had not thrown anything in weeks!

"You do not like sick people because they are imperfect. Like me."

"Anya, you are not imperfect."

She grinned. "I am perfect to you?"

"No. No one is perfect . . ."

"But you said . . ."

He lifted a hand to silence her. "It's ridiculous to suggest that the reason I don't see patients is because I do not like sick people."

"There is no reason to feel badly. I do not like sick people, either." She wrinkled her nose. "They are annoying, always coughing and asking for water and moaning and—"

"Anya!"

94

"Well, why do you not like them?"

His look faded, and she saw the man she had come to love. The real Julian. He tried to be stern, sometimes, but he was also kind. He never made her feel stupid, and he never lost his temper with her—unlike those horrible tutors who had come before him.

"They make me feel helpless," he admitted.

"But you are a doctor."

"And in my training I learned just enough to realize that I don't know nearly enough. God, that sounds awful. It makes no sense at all."

"It does make sense," she assured him.

"Research I can control," he added calmly. "No one's life is on the line. No one . . . depends on me to save them."

"Research is safer."

"I suppose."

"You would rather study the way other people live than to live yourself."

"I wouldn't go that far," he protested, but not very vehemently.

"I think you would make a very good doctor."

He laid his eyes on her, and her heart skipped a beat. "Thank you, but I don't agree."

"You would make a good doctor because you have a good heart and a warm soul."

He picked up his book and turned his eyes down to the pages, but she could tell he was not reading. Her observation had disturbed him.

"*Romeo and Juliet* tonight," she said with a grin. "I am going to wear one of the new gowns Grandmother bought me, but I refuse to wear that bloody corset."

"Don't curse, Anya," Julian said without lifting his eyes from the page.

"Corset is a very bad word. I apologize."

He smiled, but tried to hide it.

"You will wear one of your new suits?"

"I suppose."

Grandmother had bought them both many new clothes. More than they needed, but Grandmother said they must both dress well. After all, they were Sedleys. Anya had tried to tell her grandmother that they were not Sedleys, they were DeButys, but it had made no difference. She and Julian had been measured, pinned, poked, and prodded for days, and within a week the clothes had begun to arrive. They were still coming. Every couple of days new clothing was delivered. She much preferred the scarves.

"I like the gray suit," she said.

"I like the blue gown."

"Then I will wear it." She picked up her own book and opened to the page she had saved. It was a small book, written by a surgeon, about the treatment of bullet wounds during the War Between the States. "But I will not wear the corset."

Julian could fight wanting Anya, and he did. He fought every day. He was having a much harder time fighting the growing friendship between them. He liked her. She was honest and funny and intelligent, attributes any man might admire in a woman.

Sitting with him in the private Sedley box, she

watched the players on the stage with tears in her eyes. Her spine straight, she leaned forward as if she needed to be as close to the stage as possible. In many ways she looked like the other fine ladies there that evening. Beautiful, well-coifed, and well-dressed. Tonight the only jewelry she wore was an exquisite and terribly expensive sapphire pendant.

If he had remembered that the blue gown was quite so low cut, he thought as his gaze dipped downward of its own accord, he might have suggested that she wear the gold, instead. The blue gown was entirely too tempting.

Even though she dressed to suit her station, there were some things about Anya that were unique. No other woman had that hungry gleam in her eye, the insatiable curiosity that lit her face, the apparent joy and sadness she could not, or would not, hide.

She listened closely to every word of the play. While those in the boxes near them watched half-heartedly, some of them wooden-faced and fighting sleep, Anya gave the play her full attention. She smiled, she laughed, she gasped, and now she cried. One of the tears that had made her eyes gleam slipped down her cheek. Examining Anya's every move was so much more fascinating than watching the group of competent players as they neared the end of the story.

Without taking her eyes from the stage, Anya reached out and took his hand. She squeezed, holding on tightly as Juliet awoke, found her dead husband, and stabbed herself. More tears came, and Anya did not try to hide the tears or wipe them away.

So, as the play ended and she turned to him, Julian reached out and wiped them away for her. His hands brushed lightly over her damp cheeks as she sniffled. All around them people applauded, the noise rose and fell, then rose again as the primary players took a bow.

For a moment Anya looked at him in that way she had: with a bone-jarring honesty that seemed to cut right through his flesh. And then she turned her face away and took her hand from his and started to applaud vigorously.

As the applause died down and the lamps were turned up, Anya sighed and turned to him again. Her tears had dried, but her eyes remained a little puffy and red. "I knew how the story would end, I knew it was not real, and still I cried. It was so . . . so sad."

"It's a tragedy."

Her eyes widened. "Yes, it is! Oh, Julian, I like the theater best of all."

He couldn't help but smile at Anya as he stood and offered her his hand. She was a love goddess, concubine to a king, a practiced seductress. And still she could be so innocent. "We will come again, then."

"Yes." She stood, her hand resting so delicately in his, and returned his smile. "When I said I liked the theater best, that did not mean that I like you less."

"I know."

"And Valerie," Anya added quickly. "I am beginning to like Valerie very much." She lifted a hand to her hair. "See this silk rose? She said I could borrow

it, since it matches my dress. And I like Grandmother, of course. But I still do not like Seymour."
Her smile faded a little. "He has small eyes, and his
hair is too pale and thin. And he is mean."

"Mean? Did he say something hurtful to you?" Julian pulled Anya close as they exited the box. She fit
very nicely against his side, he couldn't help but notice. If Seymour was harassing Anya, he would have
to do something about it. The little man was a wea-
sel, and Julian didn't much like him, either.

"Sometimes I hear him say things about me," she
said in a low voice. "But I do not mind so much.
Seymour is mean to everyone. Even Peter and Valerie, his own sister. He is not mean to Grandmother,
though. I think he is nice to her because she has so
much money."

"I'm sure you're right." They joined the flow of
the crowd, down the stairs and through the lobby.
Ah, they'd have to wait for their carriage to be
brought around in this crowd. But it was a mild
night, not too cold nor too warm, and he didn't
mind waiting with Anya. They would surely find
something to talk about. They always did.

"If he ever says anything to disturb you, come to
me and I will take care of it," he said, sounding very
much like a husband.

"You are so sweet, *marido,*" Anya said, patting him
on the arm. "But I can handle Seymour. Last time
he called me a whore to my face, I showed him my
knife and threatened to cut off his—"

"Anya," he interrupted in a whisper, afraid that in
the crush of the crowd someone would overhear.

Linda Jones

Then his outrage won out over his modesty. "He called you a whore?" Something entirely unpleasant rose up within him. It was more than indignation, it was pure white-hot fury.

"It happened long ago," Anya said softly. "Before we were married."

Julian found he didn't care when the transgression had occurred. Seymour needed to be taught a lesson. And to think, he had been insisting that Anya treat the odious man with civility and dignity. When they got home . . .

"Julian!"

His heart froze and his spine went rigid at the sound of that familiar feminine voice coming from directly behind.

"Julian DeButy," she said again when he did not immediately turn to greet her.

He released Anya, turned around, and faced Margaret. Of all the women in the world, why did *she* have to be here tonight? It had been such a nice evening, until now. Seymour and Margaret had ruined a perfectly lovely excursion.

Anya turned with him, and took his arm again. She laid her wild eyes on Margaret. "Julian, *cher*, who is this woman?"

Margaret was not a great beauty. She had honey-brown hair, dark brown eyes, and a passably pretty face. The neckline of her deep green gown was slightly more modest than Anya's, though she was so tightly corseted her waist was unnaturally small and her breasts looked like they were attempting to break free. Yes, she was a fairly attractive woman,

100

nothing particularly special on the outside . . . and she was the one who had made him swear off women forever.

Instinctively, Anya hated the woman who had called Julian's name. Anya trusted her instincts, and the way the woman stared and smiled and . . . the truth hit her like a thunderbolt. They had lain together, Julian and this woman. She knew it in her heart, she knew it in the depths of her soul. It was as real as the breeze that washed over her face as they stood outside the theater where a moment ago she had been so happy.

"Anya, this is Mrs. Margaret March, an . . . old friend from home. Margaret," Julian added, looking slightly pained, "what are you doing in Wilmington?"

"I have a cousin here," Margaret replied, her eyes pinned to Julian's face. "She and her husband are over there, visiting with friends they ran into as we exited the theater. When I saw you I just had to come over to say hello." Her smile widened. "I'm here for an extended visit."

"Lovely," Julian said, almost choking out the word.

"Perhaps I'll see you while I'm here?"

"We're quite busy," he looked down at her. "This is my wife, Anya DeButy."

Margaret nodded and smiled, but Anya knew a friendly gesture when she saw one. This ogre of a woman despised her. "How utterly charming."

Anya replied in French, using some of the old King's best insults. It made her feel much better to

101

call the woman who had once slept with Julian a stinking bow-legged ogre.

"She doesn't speak English?" Margaret asked, turning her gaze to Julian once again.

"Of course she does." Julian gave Anya a censuring gaze.

He had told her, so many times, how to properly greet. She really should practice now. He would want her to smile and say hello and tell this odious creature how pleasant it was to make her acquaintance. She could not. The idea of being civil to a woman Julian had touched as he refused to touch her was impossible.

And then the woman laid her hand on Julian's arm, leaned in, and whispered. "Do call on me while I'm visiting. I miss you."

Anya leaned toward the cozy pair and whispered, in English so there would be no misunderstanding, "Touch my husband again and I will cut out your heart and feed it to you as you take your last breath."

The woman stepped back with a satisfying expression of horror on her face, raising a delicate hand to her chest as if that lily-white fist might protect her. Anya barely brushed her fingers against the knife she wore beneath the folds of her gown.

All around them, people talked about the play they had just seen. They visited, laughed, and preened. No one seemed to notice the little drama that was taking place in their very midst.

Julian took a firm hold on her arm. "Anya, please," he whispered.

She lifted her face to her husband and pinned her

eyes on him. "Please what? Please do cut out her heart? Please do not?"

"Julian," Margaret said, regaining her composure quickly. "Wherever did you find this . . . this little savage?"

Julian glanced over his shoulder to the line of conveyances in front of the theater. "That's our carriage. Thank God," he added in a lowered voice.

They made their escape through the throng, and Julian assisted Anya, a bit too forcefully, into the carriage. One glance out the window revealed that Mrs. Margaret March watched with great interest as Julian took the seat next to her.

As their carriage took off, drawing away from the theater, Julian sighed and ran his fingers through his long dark hair, mumbling something too low for Anya to understand.

"Did you really wear your knife to the theater?" he asked.

"Yes." Did he think she would leave the house without her weapon?

"It is entirely unacceptable—"

"She was your lover," Anya accused. The confines of the carriage were dim, but the moonlight lit the interior well enough for her to see her husband's face.

"Don't be . . ." he began, and then faltered. "That's not—"

"I have never lied to you," she interrupted. "And I do not believe that you have lied to me. Do not start now, Julian. You do not seem to be very good at it."

103

Linda Jones

He turned so that his face was mostly in shadow, and looked down at her. "Yes, you're right. But I was very young, and foolish, and I had not yet studied the debilitating effects of the physical relationship."

Anya snorted.

"Don't do that," Julian chastised lightly.

"Tell me about her," Anya insisted.

Julian sighed. "I don't see why—"

"We have a long ride ahead of us, and I want to know. We are married. There is no reason for you not to tell me all about your intimacy with that horrid woman."

"I'd rather not," he replied coolly.

"If you asked me to tell you all about my time as King Sebastian's concubine, I would comply."

"I have never asked."

She scooted over, just a little, so her hip rested against his. "Why not?"

Julian ran his fingers through his hair again, made a noise no more polite than her snort, and mumbled beneath his breath.

"I could not understand you," she whispered.

"I do not want to know," he said succinctly. "There, now I've said it. It makes me a little insane to think about your blasted king. I most certainly do not want to hear details about your time with him."

Anya dropped her head against Julian's arm and smiled. He was jealous. She rubbed her cheek against the warm fabric of his gray suit and snaked her arm through his. "I simply want to know what she did to you to make you take a vow of chastity."

"She didn't . . ." he began.

"Do not lie to me," Anya insisted softly. She was quite comfortable, her head resting on Julian's shoulder, his arm entwined through hers. "How long ago did you know her?"

"It's been almost two years."

She smiled. "So long ago. Yes, you were much younger then. Young and foolish, I believe you said." Her smile faded. "Did you love her?"

Julian squirmed.

"Do not lie," she said again.

"I thought I did," he said softly. "I was wrong, of course."

"Of course," she whispered. Oh, she wanted Julian to love her. It was a silly wish, as most wishes were. No matter how hard she tried, she would always be much too unrefined for Julian.

"Did you . . . love your King Sebastian?" he asked, almost reluctantly.

"No," she answered quickly.

Julian's answer was a low grunt.

"What happened?" Anya asked.

Julian shifted, placing his arm around her and pulling her a little bit closer. "It's rather sordid, Anya. I hate to subject you to such things."

"I am a savage, remember?" she said, a hint of anger coloring her voice.

"You are not," he said, cupping her cheek in one hand and forcing her to look him in the eye. "You are a far better woman than Margaret March could ever be."

"And yet you loved her."

He returned her head to his shoulder, perhaps so

105

she could not see his face, and tightened his arm around her. "I thought I did. She was a widow, grieving for the loss of her husband just a year earlier."

"She is young to be a widow."

"Her husband was much older, and in ill health. And wealthy." He sighed. "I thought she was the ideal woman. Decent, kind, soft-spoken, modest—"

"Yes, yes, I see." Anya cut him off, wishing to hear no more of Margaret's virtues.

"We became friends, and then, when we . . ."

"When she invited you into her bed," Anya supplied when he faltered.

"I thought immediately of marriage," he said quickly. "But whenever I mentioned making her my wife she said it was too soon after her husband's death. I believed her, and for almost a year we were . . ."

"Lovers," Anya snapped.

"One afternoon I decided to surprise her with an afternoon visit. I carried with me flowers, and an engagement ring I had saved for months to buy. At the time I was working in a hospital, and saving all I could so I could support her. I had even spoken with another doctor, one with an established practice, about joining him."

"But you do not like patients."

"I was willing to do whatever it took to . . ."

"To have her," Anya once more supplied, with more than a hint of dejection.

"She was not alone that afternoon," he finished softly. "I will not bore you with further details, but my eyes were rudely opened. She was not the woman I had thought her to be."

"And so you decided never again to touch a woman?" She had wondered why a man like Julian would subscribe to such ridiculous notions. Now she knew. The horrid woman had hurt him, and chastity was his way of making sure he was never hurt again.

"When I was with her I lost all ability to think clearly," he confessed. "My desires blotted out my brain. I should have known what she was like. If I had been thinking clearly I would have seen the truth of her deception."

"Now I am glad I called her a stinking bow-legged ogre," Anya said angrily.

"That's what you called her?"

"If I ever see her again, I will call her much worse."

He seemed to relax. "If we are fortunate we will never see her again."

Anya snuggled against Julian's side. She liked it there, even if that ogre of a woman had ruined their evening. "Your problem is that you do not know what love is."

"And you do?"

"No. Not really. Sometimes I remember . . ." Her heart pounded too hard, and she pushed back those teasing memories. "According to Shakespeare, love usually ends badly."

"Not always," Julian argued, not very convincingly. "You enjoyed *The Taming of the Shrew.*"

Anya shook her head. "Yes, but it was not a happy story. Petruchio treated Katharina terribly."

"I suppose," Julian said in a low voice.

"He . . . he tortured her mercilessly, and then insisted that she *kiss* him."

"I wouldn't call it torture," he argued.

Julian had married Anya with every intention of taming his bride, but he would never treat her badly. She knew that with all her heart. Of course, he had also never insisted that she kiss him. . . .

"I would."

"You shouldn't confuse fiction with reality," he said sensibly. "And if we're going to discuss Shakespeare, we should discuss the play we saw tonight."

" 'Thus with a kiss I die,' " she quoted in a whisper.

Julian sighed, displeased with the turn the conversation had taken. "Next time we will choose a happier play," he said softly. "A comedy."

Anya was undeterred. Her mind kept turning to lips, to kissing. " 'And lips, O you the doors of breath, seal with a righteous kiss a dateless bargain to engrossing death!' "

"Love doesn't always end in untimely death," Julian insisted. "Not even in fiction."

"Fiction is easier to understand than reality," Anya said, snuggling closer to her husband. "It's less complicated, and there's a clear beginning and an end. In real life love is a muddle, and that is especially true here. In truth, the ways of love in this place are maddeningly puzzling!"

"Puzzling how?"

"On Puerta Sirena, there are no lies. No hiding. No pretending. Before marriage, it is perfectly acceptable for a man and woman to lie together, if they both desire to do so. Here it is forbidden. On my island, it is acceptable for a young man and a young woman to *fardini* without commitment."

"Fardini?"

"To lie together for the pleasure they can give to each another."

"Oh." He squirmed uncomfortably.

"After marriage, a husband and wife are sworn to be faithful to each other. It does not matter who or what came before, it only matters that they choose each other for life."

"So on Puerta Sirena, Margaret would not be condemned for taking more than one lover?"

"No, but she would be beaten for lying."

"Really?"

Now it was Anya's time to squirm. "No, but she *should* be beaten. I would certainly ask that she be punished."

They became silent for a long while. All she could hear was the rumble of the wheels on the road, the steady clomp of the horses' hoofbeats, and Julian's heartbeat. It all worked together in a strange sort of rhythm, and almost lulled her to sleep. But she could not sleep.

"Did you kiss her?" she whispered.

"Anya . . ."

"Did you?" She unconsciously fingered her gold ring.

The wheels turned, the horses plodded onward, and Julian's heart continued to beat.

"Yes," he finally said.

Anya sighed. "On Puerta Sirena, it is permissible for a man and woman to seek out and satisfy their most passionate desires without restraint. *Fardini.* But a kiss . . . a kiss is reserved for the expression of love."

Julian squirmed. "A kiss can be very intimate, in the right circumstances."

"The needs of the body and the needs of the heart are not always the same. A kiss is an expression of love from the heart. It is a promise, a most sacred vow."

"I didn't know that."

Anya tipped her head back and looked at Julian's face. He was so handsome, caught in moonlight, with his hair slightly mussed and his face turned to watch the passing fields as they made their way out of the city. "Is it very nice?" she whispered.

"Is what nice?"

"A kiss."

Julian glanced down. When he looked at her like this she knew he desired her. He did not want to desire her, but he did. It was a passion he had been fighting since the day they had met. He had fought well and hard.

Now that Anya had met Margaret, she knew why he fought so hard. A woman had deceived him, and he was afraid of being deceived again. Worse, in his mind Margaret had made a fool of him, and Julian DeButy was not a man to be made a fool of. He would not allow that to happen again.

"A kiss," she repeated. "What is it like?"

"You know perfectly well," he said, his voice deep and rough.

"I do not know." She looked at his mouth, studied the lines and the tempting swell. He had such fine, well-shaped, firm lips. "I have never been kissed."

Chapter Seven

A man could only take so much. *I have never been kissed.* For the past four days, every time he looked at Anya he heard those whispered words, lightly accented and touched with wonder! *I have never been kissed.*

He had been tempted to kiss her there and then, as the carriage carried them home, but he had not. He had been tempted to kiss her a hundred times since, but he had not. A man could not live in this condition, surely. He was aroused more often than not, haunted by erotic dreams, and his nerves had been stretched to the very limit. A dropped dish in the kitchen had sent him jumping out of his chair, just last night. Valerie's occasional twittering laughter made him want to shout for her to shut up, and Seymour's very presence made his fingers itch and his hands ball into fists.

Linda Jones

Since he had not been sleeping well, he'd actually fallen asleep that afternoon, a book in his lap and a silk-scarf-clad Anya seated on the other side of the room. Her scarves were not sufficient lately to quiet his nerves. A voluminous tent made of wool dwarfing and disguising her body would not have been sufficient to quiet the passion that danced within him. She was more tempting now than she had been when she so blatantly tried to seduce him.

Waking and finding her gone was an unpleasant surprise. He had opened his eyes expecting to find her where she had been when he'd dozed off. No, not expecting. Anticipating. Julian slipped on his jacket and headed downstairs. He presumed he would find Anya in the south parlor with Valerie, but Valerie perched on the sofa all alone and stitched on her sampler. Julian searched the room quickly without stepping in, and Valerie never knew he was there. If so, she likely would not have uttered a curse word she'd surely learned from Anya as she yanked at her tangled thread.

In the foyer, Julian closed his eyes and listened. Anya was never quiet. Surely he would hear her, the jewels she wore clanking, her throaty laughter calling to him, her soft voice sending chills down his spine. He heard nothing.

A disquiet settled in his stomach. A woman like Anya could get into a lot of trouble, unsupervised.

He found Peter dusting the library, but no Anya poking through the books she loved. Peter was more observant than Valerie; he became aware of Julian's presence immediately.

112

"Have you seen my wife?" Julian asked sharply.

"No," the butler said, continuing to dust. "Have you checked the south parlor?"

"Yes."

"She's not in your rooms?"

"If she were I would not be searching for her."

Peter raised his eyebrows, just slightly, at Julian's sharp tone.

The man who was butler, and more than butler, didn't seem at all like a servant to Julian. He was surely no more than forty years old. He was fit, though Julian never saw him engage in physical activity. There was a touch of gray at his temples, but the silver only made him appear more dignified. Why was the man here? He could surely engage in more satisfying endeavors.

"I'm . . . a little worried," Julian confessed, in way of an apology.

Peter allowed himself a soft smile. "Before you arrived, when it was this quiet in the house I knew Miss Anya was on the Captain's Walk."

"The Captain's Walk? I didn't know she liked to go up there."

Peter shrugged. "She said she could see the ocean from the walk. I suspect she misses it," he added in a low voice.

"Do you think so?"

The butler dropped his dusting rag and turned to face Julian. "Anya was always an impulsive child. Not undisciplined, mind you, but she always possessed that stubborn streak. When she wanted something, she wanted it *now*. Back then she didn't throw things," he said with a soft smile. "But she definitely thought about it."

"I didn't know you had been here that long."

"I moved here in '65, right after the war. Anya was five years old, and a handful even then."

"She doesn't remember much about her life here, before the ship was lost."

Peter's smile faded. "I know."

"She should, don't you think?"

The butler nodded.

Over the past two weeks, Anya had told him that she was remembering bits and pieces of her old life here. There were flashes of her mother, her grandmother, her cousins. But she remembered nothing of her father. Even seeing his portrait did nothing to stir her dormant memories. Even more disturbing was the fact that the omission did not bother Anya at all. Apparently she did not want to remember her father.

Julian ran up the stairs to the second floor, hurried down the hallway, and took the narrow stairwell that led to the small observatory on the third floor, two steps at a time. He opened a narrow glass-paned door and stepped onto the slim Captain's Walk that encircled the observatory, one hand quickly finding the wrought-iron rail that separated the walkway from the roof. Anya was not there.

"What are you doing?"

His head snapped around, toward the sound of that familiar voice, and there she was . . . far from the wrought-iron rail, seated on the roof with her legs tucked beneath her and the scarf that usually bound her breasts clutched in one hand and catching the breeze. It whipped around her, as did her unbound hair.

His heart jumped into his throat. "What are you doing on the roof?"

She lifted her hand, the one with the scarf fluttering in it, and pointed. "I can see the sea best from here. There are so many ships." Her hand dropped slowly. "And I want to go home."

One hand cautiously on the rail at all times, Julian stepped to the corner of the Captain's Walk that encircled the observatory. "You are home, Anya."

She turned her head and looked at him. Wild red hair caught in the wind danced around her face, the sun touched her bare skin. "No, I am not home," she said softly.

"Come here," he said, offering his hand to her.

Anya ignored him, returning her gaze to the faraway sea once again.

Julian slipped off his jacket and tossed it across the wrought-iron rail. He took off his shoes, not trusting the slick soles against the sloped roof. He brushed his hair out of his eyes and loosened his collar. God help him, he was about to choke.

Throwing the first leg over the rail was no problem. Tossing the second over and releasing the rail was a challenge, but he accomplished it with only a muttered and very mild curse. He took careful steps across the roof, his arms held out for balance. Only once did he look down, into the garden. It was a mistake he did not repeat. When the wave of dizziness had passed, he pinned his gaze on Anya and kept it there. If she knew he was coming to her, she gave no sign.

It was with great relief that Julian placed himself beside her, sitting down and feeling, for the first time since he'd climbed over the wrought-iron rail, relatively secure.

"What's wrong?" he asked.

Anya tipped up her face. The sun caught her freckles and the copper lights in her wild red hair. It also glinted on the gold of the necklace he had given her, the only jewelry she wore today. She squinted against the sun, and still he could see the brilliant blue-green of her eyes, eyes as deep and brilliant as the sea itself. "There is a party this weekend, Grandmother says, and we must go."

"Parties are lovely," he said in his most soothing voice. "Most women get quite excited at the prospect of a social gathering."

"We must spend the night there, at this woman's house." She pouted, her lower lip trembling, and he couldn't help but think—*I have never been kissed . . .* "And Grandmother says I should wear a corset."

"We will discuss that later. I'm sure she'll understand your objections if we present them rationally." His eyes were drawn to the shape of her breasts, the nip of her waist. "Besides, you don't need a corset the way some women do."

"Why not?" She laid her eyes on him, and for a moment he actually forgot that he was sitting on a roof.

"You have a lovely figure," he said, his heart catching in his throat.

"Do I?"

"You know very well that you do." He managed to sound only a little testy.

Her severe expression softened, and she almost smiled. "I still do not want to go. An entire weekend, and I imagine I must remain properly dressed at all times!"

"Of course."

"And I must spend the entire weekend visiting with women who will not like me."

"What makes you think they will not like you? You're utterly charming, and if you use the manners we've worked on and refrain from throwing things when you do not get your way, you will be a smashing hit." He grinned.

She shook her head. "I am different and I will always be different. I might try to be one of them, but women like your Margaret will always be there to remind me that I am not."

He hated hearing Anya refer to that woman as *his* Margaret. "Not everyone is cruel."

She returned her gaze to the far-off sea. He followed her gaze. Ah, yes, the view from there was lovely, and it was as if they sat apart from the world. Higher. Distanced. And all alone. It was not an altogether unpleasant thought.

Everything was smaller from this view, and the rest of the world became insignificant. Beautiful, yes, but unimportant. Julian's heart rate slowed.

"On Puerta Sirena," Anya said, her eyes remaining fixed on some faraway view, "I was also different. For as long as I can remember . . . different. No one else

117

had red hair, and sometimes people would want to . . . to touch it just because they had never seen such a thing before I washed onto the beach. Everyone else had families. Parents, sisters and brothers. And I was always dismayed because I got spots on my skin instead of turning a lovely brown."

"Freckles," Julian said.

"What?" She looked up at him.

"They're not spots, they're freckles."

"I know. Grandmother gave me a cream to make them go away, but it is not working."

He pinned his eyes on the light sprinkling across her pert nose. "I rather like your freckles," he said softly.

"You do?"

"Yes. They're . . . charming."

Anya flipped the hair off one shoulder and presented it to him. "I have freckles here, too."

"I know," he choked.

She laid a hand on her shoulder, pointing at one particular freckle before dropping that hand down. "And here," she said, pointing to the valley between her breasts.

"Yes." His eyes followed the progress of her hand. His mouth went dry and . . . oh hell, not here! How was he supposed to maneuver off the roof with his manhood erect and his heart about to come through his chest!

From the roof—one of Anya's favorite places, Peter said—very little seemed important. What people thought, what they expected . . . it was so easy not to care about the rules that other men made and enforced. It all seemed very small, at the moment. Why had he thought that discipline so damned important?

I have never been kissed. I have never been kissed. Julian heard the words echoing in his head until they drowned out everything else. In some part of his brain, he knew exactly what was happening. He was losing a battle, perhaps the war itself. His desire was so much more important than his determination not to let a woman touch his heart.

He took Anya's chin in his hand. If he kissed her, she would think it an expression of love. A kiss meant more to her than the body she had offered in the days following their wedding.

But he wanted that kiss at this moment more than he'd ever wanted anything. He wanted it with the summer warmth on his face and the wind in his hair and the sunlight making Anya positively sparkle.

She tipped her head, as if she knew what was coming. Her lips parted slightly, and so did his.

Perhaps he did love her. He had certainly never felt this way about any woman. Margaret didn't hold a candle to Anya, and she never would. There was, truly, no woman in the world quite like his wife.

His lips moved slowly and unerringly toward hers. Her eyes drifted closed. The world closed in, and Julian no longer cared that he was sitting on a roof far off the ground. In fact, he no longer realized where he was. He only knew that Anya had never been kissed, and he was the man to show her how it was done.

"Julian," she whispered when his lips were no more than an inch from hers.

"Yes."

The wind whipped around them. They were miles from anyone, from everyone. Nothing else mattered but . . .

"There you are!"

His head popped up and around. Valerie stood at the railing that encircled the Captain's Walk, an idiotic smile on her face as she waved enthusiastically. "Julian, you have a visitor."

"A visitor?" he snapped, ready to strangle Anya's cheerful cousin.

"A Mrs. Margaret March. She said she was an old friend."

Anya cursed in French and stood too quickly.

"Be careful."

She glared at him, then dropped the fluttering scarf she'd been holding into his lap. "I believe you need this more than I do, husband. It would be quite embarrassing, I imagine, for your lover to realize that you desire your wife."

"Margaret is not my lover," he hissed.

"Well, she is here for you."

"I didn't invite her," he said as Anya stalked away, moving without care around him and across the sloped roof. "There's no need to be angry at me."

She responded in curtly delivered Spanish. He didn't know what she said, but if her tone was any indication she had just dismissed all his teachings on decorum.

"There's no need to curse."

Anya climbed over the railing to join her cousin. "I cannot believe that you would kiss a woman like that."

"He kissed her?" Valerie asked, raising an outraged hand to her ample breast.

"Yes!" Anya snapped.

"It happened a long time ago." Julian still was not ready to stand and make his way across the roof—which seemed much higher off the ground than it had when he'd crossed it in order to rescue Anya.

Anya, who apparently didn't need to be rescued.

"I will keep her company until you join us," she promised with a demonic smile.

"No!" Julian stood quickly, and Anya's scarf caught the wind and flew away, drifting brightly across the roof and down into the garden.

"Perhaps we can compare spots." With that, she turned and entered the observatory.

Valerie cast an indignant nose-in-the-air glance Julian's way, sniffed, and followed her cousin; and Julian hurried, as fast as he dared, after them.

Anya had never experienced jealousy. She had not loved Sebastian, so she had never minded that he seemed to prefer his first concubine, Emelda. Until Julian, Sebastian had been the only man in her life, so she had nothing else with which to compare this newfound rage.

For a moment, on the roof, she had actually thought Julian meant to kiss her. Ha! He saved his kiss for women like this one, a tightly corseted, false-faced, tittering *puta*.

If not for Valerie, she would have run straight from the roof to the north parlor, where Margaret waited. Valerie had insisted that Anya don a proper gown and fix her hair. One softly whispered argument had won Anya over. *Don't give her a reason to make fun of you.* Anya had dressed quickly, and Valerie had styled her hair. By the time Anya stepped into the north parlor Julian was already there, talking softly and politely to the hussy he had once kissed.

Margaret's eyes cut Anya's way as she entered the room. The sparkle Anya saw there was not laughter or happiness, it was a jealousy like her own. No, Anya amended as she crossed the room to stand beside Julian. The jealousy she herself felt was fueled by love. Margaret's anger was ugly. No love lurked there.

"Mrs. DeButy," Margaret said, not bothering to rise from her seat in Grandmother's favorite velvet chair. "How lovely to see you again."

Liar. The word was on Anya's lips, but she did not allow it to escape. Julian had been drilling these blasted manners into her for two months. He would be furious if she forgot them all now. "A pleasure to see you again, Mrs. March."

Julian took a deep breath and let it out slowly, in a sigh of relief, perhaps. Relief that she had taken the time to dress? Or that she had not yet threatened to cut out Margaret's heart?

"What a charming accent you have," their guest said insincerely. "When I told my cousin that I had met you, she shared the story of your homecoming.

It's quite fascinating." Margaret wrinkled her nose. "But she did not know how you came to meet and marry Julian. I'm sure that's just as fascinating a story." She waited for a response, eyebrows lifted and ears perked.

"It is not so fascinating," Anya began. "We simply . . ."

Julian grabbed her arm and pulled her close. "Met and fell instantly in love," he said quickly.

Anya glanced up at her devious husband. He looked down at her and pleaded with his dark eyes. "Yes," she said softly. "Very simple."

When Anya looked at Margaret again, she saw the widow's face had grown harder. Her mouth was set in an unappealing line, her eyes were narrowed. "How charming."

Anya might have spent more of her life on a remote island than off it, but she was no simpleton. Julian was using her to make his old lover jealous. If he really cared for her she might not mind so much, but he did not. This marriage was a task to him, a chore, and she had been a fool to allow herself to fall in love with him.

If she did not love Julian, she would tell Margaret that their marriage was a pretense. That he had never touched her, that in two months he would be gone. But she did love him, so she said nothing.

She did love him, but she would never forgive him.

Margaret began an inane diatribe on the weather. Julian nodded politely, as if he hung on every word.

123

His eyes were on the odious woman, he nodded and agreed with every word she said.

Anya reached out to grab the figurine that sat on the table by the window. She did not even have to step to the side to reach it, it was simply . . . there. Before she could cock her arm back, Julian's fingers closed around her wrist. Margaret, studying the portraits in the parlor as she talked about the unbearable heat, did not notice.

With a surge of something that felt like relief, Anya smiled as Julian took the figurine from her and placed it out of reach. So, he had been watching her all along, out of the corner of his eye. He certainly did not want his wife to embarrass him in front of his *puta*.

Anya's eyes fell on the vase of roses that sat on a long table behind the couch. She took a step toward it, but Julian wrapped his arm around her waist and pulled her close to his side. This Margaret did see, but to one who did not know of Anya's penchant for throwing things, it might seem like a gesture of devotion.

"Do come sit with me," Margaret said, her words small and tight. "When you stand before the window that way the sun hurts my eyes when I look at you."

"Certainly." Julian took Anya's arm and led her to the couch, where he sat close beside her.

"Now, what does your cousin's husband do?" Julian asked.

Margaret replied with great vigor, telling them all about the businesses her cousin's husband owned. She could not have said the man was a successful shopkeeper. No. She had to give them endless details of each and every shop.

The more Anya watched and listened to Margaret, the more she hated the woman. Julian had loved her. He must still, if he was so anxious to make her jealous. He likely did not care at all that Anya herself was experiencing the new and unpleasant emotion.

Anya fingered the knife she wore at her thigh, tracing the shape beneath the fine fabric of her gown and thinking of ways she might make use of the weapon. Julian clamped his hand over hers, and Margaret jumped. The harlot actually blushed.

Julian kept his hand there, firmly over hers. Instead of pushing him away, Anya lifted and threaded her fingers through his. And she smiled. Ah, if he wanted to make Margaret jealous, she could be quite accommodating.

When Anya twisted just slightly and reached for the vase behind the couch, Julian tensed and started to pull her back. He relaxed when she plucked a single perfect yellow rose from the vase and twirled it between her fingers.

She brought the flower to her nose and took a deep breath. The scent was lovely, the petals soft. Margaret droned on about imported fabrics.

With the scent of the rose filling her, Anya very casually lowered the bloom and allowed the petals to brush her lips, her chin, and then her throat. The hand that remained clamped over hers stiffened. Julian cleared his throat.

Anya's hand swayed to the side, and she very nonchalantly stroked the petals of the rose against Julian's throat. Up to his chin, then down to the starched white of his collar. To the side and sweeping to brush just beneath his ear.

Margaret stumbled over a difficult word. Anya suspected the word was *and* but could not be sure.

Julian's free hand jerked out and snatched the rose away. His cheeks blushed pink, and he swallowed hard.

Margaret almost regained her composure. At least she did not stumble over her words for a while. She finished the tedious tale of shopkeeping and began to tell them all about her cousin's children.

God above, Anya did not want to sit here and listen to the sweet tales of babies. She would never have her own, so she had no patience for charming stories of other children. It only reminded her that she was, to Julian and to every other man, incomplete as a woman. Imperfect.

She turned her head, reached up to sweep away long strands of Julian's dark, wind-brushed hair, lifted her face, and sucked his earlobe into her mouth.

Julian did not move away. His earlobe remained in her mouth, then caught between her teeth. "Anya," he groaned softly.

Margaret shot to her feet. "I really should be going."

Anya released her hold on Julian and stood to smile at their guest. "Yes, you should. We have things to do. I am supposed to say it was very nice of you to stop by."

Margaret went white. "It was my . . . pleasure." She

turned panicked eyes to Julian. "It was good to see you again. Congratulations on your . . . marriage."

"Your strumpet is very good," Anya said brightly. "She says that as if she means it."

Margaret spun on her heel to leave, and Julian made as if he intended to pursue her. Anya's hand fell on a small porcelain bowl that sat on the table at the end of the couch, and she sent it sailing. It broke against the doorframe with a satisfying crash, and Julian stopped in his tracks.

"You will not follow her," Anya seethed. In the distance, the front door closed behind their visitor.

Julian turned slowly, and with one look at his face Anya took a step back. She had never seen him so angry. "I was only going to see her out and apologize for your atrocious behavior."

"Do not apologize for me."

"Someone has to!"

Anya circled the couch, intent on that vase of roses. Julian ran into the room and they met at the vase. Both of her hands closed over the rounded porcelain. Julian's larger hands covered hers.

"What were you thinking?" he seethed.

She lifted her eyes and stared at him over the yellow roses. "I was thinking that if you insist on lying to make your whore envious of your new love, we should at least make her believe that the lie is true."

His anger faded, but he did not release her or the vase. "I apologize," he said softly. "I don't know what came over me."

"I do. You loved her and she hurt you, and now you want her to think that you do not hurt anymore.

127

But you do. You must. Otherwise you would not have thought to lie." Her eyes burned. "You would not have cared so much. You must still love her."

"Anya." Julian, no longer angry, took his hands from hers and lifted them to her face. "I don't . . ."

With Julian's stilling hands away from the vase, Anya lifted the container and quickly dropped it to the floor. It landed with a loud crash and splattering of water and roses. In the distance, Peter cursed.

Julian closed his eyes and dropped his hands from her face. "Go to your room," he ordered softly.

Anya, who would have loved to storm to the sanctuary of her room if he had not ordered her to go, planted her feet and placed her hands on her hips. "No."

"I said—"

"No."

Julian reached for her, and in an unexpected move he lifted her easily and in a smooth, sweeping motion tossed her over his shoulder. She felt dizzy for a moment, as she hung there in such an undignified manner.

"I do not have the fortitude to argue with you now," he said in that damned sensible voice of his.

She dangled from his shoulder as he carried her to the stairs. "You . . . you . . ." There was no English word strong enough or angry enough for the way she felt at this moment. She used the language of Puerta Sirena, the language that came to her almost as easily as English, to curse her husband. To insult him.

She salted her dialogue with a few words in Italian,

and a few in French. He never slowed his step, and Anya bobbled as Julian all but ran up the stairs with her suspended from his shoulder.

Growing angrier with each passing second, she reverted to the language of her island home as Julian threw open the door to her room.

And in that language he would never understand she told him, angry tears in her eyes as he carried her into the room and dumped her onto her own bed, that he was the only man in the world who could break her heart, and for that she would never forgive him.

Chapter Eight

It was too late to run for the roof, Julian thought as the carriage rumbled down the road. They were on their way to the party Anya had been so dreading. The plan was to travel that day and spend the night at the home of one of Elizabeth Sedley's oldest friends, the woman who was throwing this summer party. Planned activities would fill the day and night the next day, and on Sunday everyone would travel home.

The Sedley servants had been given a holiday. Hilary and Betsy had each gone to spend the weekend with their families. Even Peter had taken off, telling Mrs. Sedley that he would pass the time at a friend's home in Wilmington. He seemed as anxious to get away from the house as Anya was to remain in it.

Julian was mightily tempted to run for some sort of escape. For a while it had seemed that Anya was taking to her lessons quite well. But lately she had been reverting to her old ways, and he had no idea what she might do next. It would be a disaster of major proportions if she decided to saunter down to breakfast wearing only her scarves and a melange of jewelry. And if she decided to throw a vase or nibble on his ear . . . would he be quick enough to stop her?

She had been very quiet in the past few days. He didn't like it, he didn't like it at all. A quiet Anya was rather like a volcano. It wasn't a matter of if she would erupt, it was only a matter of when. And how.

Julian rode in the carriage with Anya, her cousin, and her grandmother. Seymour had chosen to ride a horse, a method of travel Julian would have preferred. But he needed to keep a close eye on Anya. There was no telling what she might say in his absence.

"William Mathias is going to be there this weekend," Valerie said, a wide smile on her face. Oh, how her attitude had changed in the past few weeks. She had been so sullen, in the beginning. But she and Anya had mended some fences, and the cousins were becoming quite close.

"That William Mathias is a rounder, and if he expresses an interest in you, you must remember that he is only attracted to your money," Mrs. Sedley said curtly, and with an unintended cruelty. "The Mathias family never did recover financially from the war. As a Sedley you must always remember your position."

Valerie's face fell, and she turned her forlorn gaze

Linda Jones

out the window. Not a word of argument passed her lips.

But Anya was not about to let the incident go. "How do you know this William Mathias is only interested in Valerie's money?"

"We don't know, Anya, but we must assume . . ." Mrs. Sedley said gently, as if she were talking to a child.

"Perhaps he is interested in her bosom."

Mrs. Sedley gasped, and Valerie blushed from the exposed skin above her modest collar all the way up to her pale hairline.

"Anya," Julian said gently. That gentle rebuke should be enough.

It was not. "But this is family. You said I could say some things to family that I cannot say to strangers."

"That is true, but . . ."

"Is it not important that we know if William Mathias likes Valerie for her money or her bosom?"

"We don't know that he likes her at all," Mrs. Sedley said tightly.

"Valerie must have many beaus," Anya said with a smile. "She is beautiful and usually very sweet."

Valerie wrinkled her nose. "I'm too chubby, and not nearly as pretty as you."

"You are a very pretty girl, and you are not chubby," Mrs. Sedley snapped. "You just haven't gotten rid of all your baby fat, yet."

"I'm almost twenty-three," Valerie whispered. "I don't see how this can be baby fat."

Julian wished he could disappear. Crawling out the window seemed a perfectly reasonable option.

132

"The fat is what makes her bosom so magnificent," Anya said.

"Would you please not say the word *bosom* again?" Mrs. Sedley snapped.

"Of course, Grandmother," Anya said sweetly, and then she turned to Valerie. "You must introduce me to this William Mathias. I think he must like you for your *tete*."

"Anya!" Mrs. Sedley snapped.

"I did not say bosom." Anya turned to Julian. "You will ask him."

"No!" Valerie shouted, all but coming out of her seat.

Julian stared with admiration and wonder and complete bewilderment at his wife. "There is no proper way to ask a man if he cares for a woman because of her fortune or her . . . feminine assets."

"I guess that is true. At least I know why you married me," Anya said coolly. "For a ship and a few sailors, you became my husband and teacher. I never had to wonder why, or if, you cared for me. Take heart, *querido,* your time is speeding past quickly. In less than two months you will be finished with your arduous task."

Mrs. Sedley cleared her throat and began to tell them all about the home of her old friend, Katherine Mansfield. She was quite thrilled about the weekend, in spite of William Mathias's presence and the excitement of never knowing what Anya might say or do next.

Anya pretended to listen, so Julian stared at her. He stared intently at the set of her chin and the

133

gentle shape of her lips. At the way her hair would never quite behave. If he leaned forward, just a bit, he would be able to see the fire in her eyes, a flash of sea-green flame that was so much a part of her.

She was right. His days with the Sedleys were flying past. His time there was more than half over.

And he was not ready to go.

She cut him a quick glance, and he saw the trace of fear in those magnificent eyes. Instinctively, he took her hand, and she quickly threaded her fingers through his.

Anya lifted her head from the pillow, awakening with the sun as she often did. She was still tired, though. She had not slept well in this strange bed, in this strange house. Her eyes slipped from the soft daylight at the window to her husband, who slept in a padded chair in the corner of this large room. His trousers had been loosened, his linen shirt and undershirt had been removed and tossed aside.

She had been so angry with him, of late. Most of the time she was not certain why. He annoyed her, as he had in those early days, and he was never out of her thoughts.

Whenever she became too annoyed, she remembered the way he had held her after the storm, the way he had held her even though she insisted she did not need to be comforted. He said he married her for his ship and sailors, that there was no tenderness in their arrangement. And yet, at times she did see affection in him. Affection he fought with every breath he took.

Poor Julian, he had almost turned green last night when he had realized that they would have to share a room. Why had he not thought of that before? There were a number of guests staying for the weekend. Grandmother and Valerie were sharing a room, and Seymour had passed the night with the youngest son of the house, a fact that did not please him. Of course, little pleased Seymour.

She rolled quietly from the bed, trying not to wake Julian. He had been miserable since the day his hussy had called upon him. Perhaps he had suffered long enough for his crimes of the past. He could never suffer enough for breaking her heart, but as he had not done so on purpose she would not make him agonize any longer.

She crossed the room, her hands skating down the nightshirt she wore. The maid who had packed her trunk had included two new nightgowns, but not the softly worn garment she had taken from Julian. She wore that nightshirt every night; it was one of her small comforts.

Julian had not protested at all when she had confiscated his other nightshirt last night. In fact, he had not seemed at all surprised.

Moving cautiously, she knelt down in front of her husband. In the complete relaxation of sleep, he had fallen back and allowed his legs to fall apart. She rested nicely between his thighs.

He did not love her. He did not plan to stay. But why could they not be truly together in the time they had left? She wanted him to be a true husband, just

135

for a while, but he had been resistant to her initial advances.

Because he was a man who did not take what he wanted without reservation. His life was filled with reservations, with rules and morals. One of the rules he lived by was apparently that it was possible to have too much fun. That if something felt too good it must be immoral. Some nights her body ached for his, and she saw no reason why he could not put an end to that ache.

But gently, she had decided. Very gently.

She could wake him with a stroke to the bulge in his trousers, but he would not appreciate that. Not yet. He would likely come out of his chair with a shout that would wake the entire household, if she were so bold.

Besides, she wanted more from Julian. In the early days of their marriage, she had attempted to seduce him seeking two things: pleasure and a way to buy his affection and loyalty. But now she wanted more. And she was suddenly sure that there truly was more to be had.

"Julian," she whispered, laying her hands on his thighs.

He made a deep moaning sound and turned his head to one side. Anya raised up and placed the flat of her hand on his chest. Here he was bare, firm, nicely muscled, and a sprinkling of hair dusted his chest. Her fingers danced, teasing him, and he took a deep breath and moved again. Just a little.

"Julian," she whispered again.

"Anya," he responded lowly, still more asleep than

awake. His hand covered hers, there on his chest.

She rose a little bit higher, so her body leaned over his. "Julian, wake up."

His eyes fluttered open and his sleepy gaze fell on her. For a moment that gaze was utterly wicked, and then he realized that this was not a dream and his dark, hooded eyes cleared.

"Is something wrong?"

"No." She backed up slowly, took his hand, and stood. "But you should sleep in the bed for a while."

"No," he protested. "You can have it."

"I will not sleep anymore, but it is too early to be prowling about a strange house. You sleep in the bed, I will sit here."

"Are you sure . . ."

She leaned slightly forward and grinned. "I want you rested enough to dance with me tonight. You cannot be sleeping well in this chair."

Julian mumbled his assent and rose, and Anya released his hand. Still half asleep, he headed for the rumpled bed. In a delightful boyish and charming way, he fell onto it and moaned in satisfaction as he grabbed a pillow.

Anya gave him a few minutes, which was all he needed to fall back into a deep sleep. She crossed the room, covered Julian with the coverlet, and after watching him sleep for a moment she crawled into the bed with him.

Julian's body was warm, long, and strong and crying out for hers—whether he knew it or not. She snuggled against him and sighed, and in his sleep his arms encircled her. *Yes, this is nice,* she thought as she closed her eyes.

He came awake slowly, feeling content in spite of the dreams he'd had. Dreams about Anya, again. He buried his face into the pillow, searching for relief from the bright light that streamed through the window and pulled a sleeping Anya against his chest, where she cuddled and sighed.

One eye drifted open. What was she doing here? Hell, he was so tired he didn't care. No wonder he'd dreamed that Anya had stripped off that nightshirt and climbed atop his willing body to ride him, her breasts and hair swaying, her body wrapped around his. It had been a dream, hadn't it? He lifted the covers and peeked beneath. He still wore his trousers, and Anya still wore the nightshirt. Pity.

"Anya." He shook her lightly and tried to set her body away from his. "Wake up, Anya."

She smiled and purred but did not wake up. Her leg lifted and hooked over his hip.

One glance at the window told him it was late morning, long past the time the festivities had been slated to begin with a large breakfast in the opulent dining room downstairs. "Anya." He shook her a little more forcefully, and she finally opened her eyes.

"Good morning, *caro,*" she said huskily.

"I thought you said you did not need any more sleep."

She sighed and worked the muscles of her lithe body, stretching like a cat. "I did not think I was tired at all, but soon after you fell asleep I dozed off in the chair for a few minutes. Then I woke up and I was so chilly."

"It's July. It is not chilly."

"Not any longer," she said, not at all chastised. "You are quite warm." She tilted her head and smiled at him, as if she wasn't doing this on purpose. This was no vulgar grab or titillating dance, but it was seduction all the same.

"We should have been downstairs quite a while ago."

"I know." Unconcerned, she laid her head down again, snuggling against his bare chest. "When the maid came to wake us, I sent her away."

"I didn't hear a thing."

"You were sleeping so soundly I did not dare to wake you. But she did bring us coffee and biscuits, in case you are hungry."

Julian lifted his head and saw the silver tray beneath a carafe and plate of biscuits on the table by the chair where he had slept for a few early-morning hours. For most of the night he'd sat in that uncomfortable chair and watched Anya sleep. He'd watched the rise and fall of her chest as she breathed, the expression of peacefulness as she rested, the gentle sway of her body as she'd moved in time to a dream. Studying her every move was painful, but it was a torture he could not make himself end.

"It is all cold by now, I imagine," Anya said with a yawn.

"The maid was in this room," Julian said.

Anya hummed an affirmative answer.

"And you were . . . here."

"Of course." Anya lifted her head, all golden skin and tempting freckles and wild red hair. "I told her to be quiet, as you had had a strenuous night and needed your rest."

"Strenuous?"

"All that unpacking," Anya said sensibly. "The maid seemed to understand just what I meant."

"I'm sure she did."

"You would have been proud of me," Anya said with a smile. "I was very polite. I thanked her, and when she tripped over your shirt and almost dropped the coffee, I did not call her a clumsy idiot."

"What did you call her?" Julian asked suspiciously.

"Nothing. I simply suggested that she be more careful, lest she hurt herself."

"Very good," he mumbled.

He could not leave the bed, not yet. And Anya showed no indication that she might be leaving soon. She collapsed onto the bed and closed her eyes. "This is a wonderful bed," she said. "So soft. Do you think it would be rude if we spent the entire weekend right here?"

"Extremely rude." Though it didn't sound like such a bad idea. "We have already missed breakfast, though."

"We may soon miss lunch," Anya countered with a smile.

Sometimes his wife made him think that perhaps he was wrong. Wrong about . . . everything. Anya was not like Margaret, not at all. What little deceit she practiced was so apparent it couldn't be labeled deceit at all. She did not have a conniving bone in her body. As for the physical relationship . . . maybe the theories were incorrect. Perhaps, just perhaps, there would be nothing wrong with following his natural instincts. He had fought those instincts for more than two months, but with every day that passed he lost a small battle. He wanted his wife. He craved her, dreamed about her, became sure, in some heated moments, that he needed her in order to survive. Maybe the "experts" were mistaken, just this once.

He rolled up and placed his hand on the opposite side of Anya, effectively trapping her beside him. She looked up at him as if she had no idea what was on his mind.

"You are very beautiful in the morning," he said softly.

"So are you."

"Somehow I doubt that."

She reached up and touched his cheek. "You need a shave, your hair is mussed, and your eyes are dreamy. It is the one time of the day that I can clearly see the beast within you."

No doubt.

For once in his life, he didn't want to think about what he was doing. He just wanted to follow his instincts and feel deeply, the way Anya felt. This was the wrong time, the wrong place, and still . . . it seemed right. Very right. More right than anything he had ever known.

Anya's hand remained on his face, gently caressing. He lowered himself slowly, his eyes on her lips.

Linda Jones

He was drawn there like a fly to honey, like a moth to the flame. Like a beast to the prey that patiently waited to be devoured.

The hand at his face drifted through his hair, as Anya's arm encircled his neck. Everything between them was about to change. Everything.

He closed his eyes and groaned when the sharp knock sounded at the door. A moment later it flew open, and Valerie stormed in.

"There you are! Are you sick? Why weren't you down for breakfast? It's almost time for lunch!"

Julian pushed himself up and away and Anya sat up, a smile on her face. "We overslept."

Valerie, a woman he was learning to dearly hate, didn't even have the decency to blush. "Well, hurry up. William Mathias is here."

"Ah, the man who is in love with your bosom."

Now Valerie blushed. "I want to know what you think of him. Hurry."

"I will be right down," Anya promised.

Julian had a feeling he would not.

When the door closed behind an excited Valerie, Anya turned to Julian. "I suppose I should go meet this man."

"I suppose."

"We cannot have Valerie taken with a man who loves her for her money." A shadow crossed Anya's face. Perhaps she was remembering that Julian himself had married her for a ship and a handful of sailors. "It is much better for a woman to be loved for her bosom."

She began to leave the bed, but Julian stopped her

142

with his hand on her wrist. Obediently, she turned to silently ask him what he wanted. Eyes wide, lips parted, she waited.

"I just thought that perhaps this would be a good time to tell you that I adore your bosom."

She smiled. "Do you?"

"I most especially like the freckled parts."

"Then I shall use Grandmother's cream only on my nose."

"Throw Grandmother's bloody cream away," he said huskily. His hand tightened on her wrist.

"You said bloody."

"Yes, I did."

Anya didn't crawl, she threw her body back onto the bed and hovered over him. She took his face in her hands, tilted her head, and moved her lips toward his. "Tell me if I should stop," she whispered when her mouth was almost on his.

"You'd better not stop," he whispered. And if Valerie came to the door again, he was going to borrow Anya's knife and make good use of it.

Anya laid her lips on his, softly, with innocence and emotion. Her eyes drifted closed. Her lips moved, very slightly raking over his.

Julian placed his hand at the back of her head, so she could not move away. His fingers speared through her hair and he held on for dear life as she sucked and nibbled and he answered in kind. He parted her lips with the tip of his tongue. She moaned, deep in her throat, a sound of pure, sensual pleasure that almost sent him over the edge.

Her body was close to his, but only their mouths

touched. It was enough. It was miraculous. He had never known a kiss could be so powerful.

He released her, because if he didn't do it now he might never be able to let her go.

"Now I have been kissed," she whispered, kneeling over him. Her face was more radiant than usual, the color in her cheeks and the sparkle in her eyes high and bright.

"Yes, you have."

"I do hope it will not be my last kiss."

"It won't be. Trust me."

He traced the line of her jaw with a lazy finger, needing to touch her, not yet ready to let her go.

"I did not know I would feel a kiss through my entire body," she whispered. "Julian, I felt it in my toes and at the top of my head."

"So did I."

"No one ever told me a kiss was so wonderful."

"I'm a little surprised, myself."

Anya rolled from the bed with the most satisfied smile on her face. "Oh, why must I meet this William Mathias now?"

"Because you love your cousin and will not allow her to be mistreated."

"Yes," she said, twirling about until his nightshirt floated around her body like a cloud. "And I love you." She stopped twirling and laid her eyes on him. Her smile faded, became uncertain. "I love you, *marido*."

Before he could answer she turned away and reached for the washcloth at the bath stand with one hand and began to unbutton the nightshirt with the other.

"Anya," he said, leaning back in the bed to watch. He would not run and hide, no more. He would not pretend he did not want his wife to distraction. That time was past.

"Yes?"

"Look at me."

She turned to face him, the nightshirt unbuttoned to her navel, wild hair spilling around her shoulders. And he was not bothered, because for the first time he knew that she was his, now and forever. The freckles, the bosom, the temper and the knowledge of endless curse words in every language known to man.

"You are worth so much more than a ship," he said. "More than a thousand ships. More than a thousand ships and a cargo of gold in each of those ships and ten thousand sailors to sail them." In truth, she was priceless.

"Thank you," she said softly.

"Any man would consider himself incredibly lucky to have you as a wife," he continued, trying as he spoke to come up with just the right words for this extraordinary moment.

She smiled. "Are you trying to say that you love me?"

So simple, so frightening. So true. "Yes."

Anya flew to the bed, jumped on to join him, and took his face in her hands to kiss him again. Quickly. Too quickly.

"You know," he said when she moved away again.

"I'm quite sure this William whoever-he-is is a fine man who loves Valerie for her bosom."

"Are you suggesting that we stay in this room for the rest of the day?"

"Yes." What was he thinking? "No, of course not. Your grandmother would not be pleased."

"It is not my grandmother I am thinking of pleasing."

He was about to agree with her when Valerie knocked on the door again. "Are you ready yet?" she called.

Julian's eyes scoured the room. "Where's that knife?"

Chapter Nine

Anya drifted through the day in a dream, a strange warmth at her center, an odd happiness bringing a permanent half-smile to her face. In many ways she had been right about Julian. He did want her. There was a beast within him waiting to be set free.

But she had been wrong, too. Julian loved her. He cared for her in the way a man might care for a woman with whom he would spend a lifetime. She had never thought he could, or that he would truly love her. She had only hoped, on rare occasions.

There was so much more to loving a man than she knew. She had thought she knew everything, that there was nothing new to learn . . . but there was much to learn, she suspected. There was pleasure, yes, and that was good. But there was something else. Something elusive that could not be so easily identified, or learned.

She was a love goddess who knew nothing of true love. She would learn, though. Julian would be her teacher in that subject just as he had been her teacher in so many, more ordinary, matters.

Her first kiss had been so magnificent, she had to force herself not to search out her husband during the day to ask for another. That kiss had started a warmth brewing within her, a heat that shone hot like the sun and soft like the moon. That heat needed to be tended, stoked and fanned like any other flame. It was Julian's fire to tend.

But Katherine Mansfield's idea of a party included a tremendous lunch followed by sending the men off to hunt while the women napped and then made themselves beautiful for the evening's ball.

Anya had hoped that she and Julian would have some time together this afternoon, as they usually did. But he was out hunting some kind of bird with William Mathias and Seymour and a handful of others, while Anya paced and watched Valerie attempt to sleep on the bed. A bed she and Julian would share that night.

"I can't sleep," Valerie said. Wearing only her chemise and petticoat, she stretched out stiffly on the bed. "Why is it that we are expected to nap, even now? We didn't nap when we were children. We pretended, when Grandmother insisted, but even then . . ."

Another memory came to Anya in a flash. She had sneaked into Valerie's room, when they were both supposed to be napping. She had crawled into Valerie's bed and they'd pulled the covers over their heads to whisper. Sunlight had shone strangely through the tented coverlet, coloring everything red. She did not know what they had whispered about, and it had surely not been important. But she remembered giggling, and then lying down and trying to be quiet when Peter opened the door to check on Valerie.

The butler had sneaked in and peeked at the wiggling bed, had been fooled into thinking that Valerie was asleep, and had left quietly. Or maybe he had not been fooled at all.

"We did not always sleep," Anya said softly.

"No, we didn't." Valerie sighed dramatically. "And I certainly can't sleep now! I'm much too excited. We'll just talk for a while. Tell me, what did you think of William?"

Anya had not had an opportunity to meet William Mathias. Valerie had pointed him out to her at lunch, but he had been seated at the opposite end of the table. After lunch she had attempted to approach the man, but every time she tried Valerie pulled her back. Anya had decided her cousin was a little bit terrified of this William Mathias.

"He is very handsome," Anya conceded, "though not as handsome as my Julian."

"He's taller than Julian," Valerie said defensively.

Anya shot a sharp glance at her cousin. "By no more than half an inch, surely. And Julian's dark hair is much nicer than your William's short, pale hair."

"Yes, but William is wider in the shoulders."

"I do not think so."

149

Linda Jones

Valerie smiled. "Shall we agree that they are both fine men?"

"Yes, we shall." Anya went to the window. She searched the grounds, but saw no sign of the men. Hunting. Ha! Julian would rather be here, with her. She knew it.

"He spoke to me after breakfast," Valerie said in a dreamlike voice.

"What did he say?"

"He asked after Seymour."

"Oh." Anya wrinkled her nose.

"And then he asked if I would save him a dance this evening." Valerie's smile widened. "I said yes, of course."

The ways of romance in this place were strange, to Anya's way of thinking. On Puerta Sirena, if William and Valerie were attracted to each other they would spend time together. If they both desired, they would lie together. After a short time, they would know if what they felt was real.

Here men and women were so hesitant. They danced around each other, they were polite and cool and nervous. No wonder Julian had been so slow to come around! He did not know what it was like to be honest with his own desires, to speak without reserve, to follow the call of his heart and his body.

But he would know, one day. He was learning quite well, just as she was learning to listen to her own heart. And when he came back from hunting, Anya was going to kick Valerie out of this room, pushing her into the hallway in her chemise and petticoats, if necessary.

There was a soft knock on the door, and then it opened. Grandmother stuck her head in and grimaced, before stepping into the room and closing the door behind her. "Anya, you're still dressed. Didn't you take a nap?"

"I was not tired."

"Valerie?" Grandmother turned her head to her elder granddaughter and lifted her arched eyebrows.

"I slept quite well, for a little while," Valerie lied.

"Well, come along, you two. Katherine has loaned us the use of one of her maids, and everything has been set up in our room."

Valerie jumped up and began to dress quickly. Anya did not know if Valerie was eager to please Grandmother, or anxious for the approaching ball. Perhaps both.

"I will wait here for Julian," Anya said.

"No." Grandmother shook her head. "Everything is arranged."

"I will wait here."

Grandmother sighed and paced while Valerie dressed. "This will be your first formal event," she said softly. "We do so want to make an impression."

"Julian will help me dress."

"Good heavens, that will not do." The older woman crossed the room and faced Anya. They were almost eye to eye, though Anya stood a little bit taller. Perhaps an inch, perhaps less. Grandmother could look very determined, when she wished to. "Besides, can you imagine the look on your husband's face when you come down the stairs in that gold satin gown I purchased for you? With your hair

fixed and the sapphire pendant around your neck?
I promise you, the sight of you walking down the
stairs will take his breath away."

Anya was suddenly interested. "Are you sure?"

Grandmother smiled. "I chose well for you, when
I picked Julian, didn't I?"

"You did."

"I thought so. At first I had my doubts, but
lately . . ." The elderly woman smiled coyly. "I see the
way you two look at each other."

"You bought him for me," Anya said accusingly.

"Yes, I did. I bought him for the price of a ship
and the financing of his research he loves so dearly.
But he will stay for another reason entirely." Grandmother laid a small, soft hand on Anya's arm.

"Because he loves me," Anya said softly.

"Yes. When I first thought of Julian, I hoped you
two might suit. I had no idea if you would or not,
but . . . I did hope."

"And when I come down the stairs dressed as you
say I must be dressed for this evening, I will take
Julian's breath away?"

"I promise."

It was a rather pleasant thought.

Julian had been expecting to find Anya waiting in
their room when the hunt was over, but the chamber
had been ominously empty. He loved her, he wanted
her, but Anya on the loose could be a disastrous
prospect.

The servant who had laid out his evening clothes
had assured him that his wife was in a room down

the hall with her grandmother and cousin, getting ready for the ball. Julian DeButy was never rash, he was not an emotional or spontaneous man. But it took all his resolve to dress for the evening without storming down the hall to knock on every door until he found the room where Anya was preparing herself for the evening. Not because he was worried about what she might do on her own, not because he thought she might embarrass herself if left unattended. He wanted to hunt her down because he needed her with him. He wanted to lay her on the bed where they'd kissed and make love to her until neither of them could move. It took every ounce of resolve he possessed not to hunt down his wife and carry her into this room they shared.

Julian had won that battle and now he stood, his collar tighter than it should be and his every nerve on end, waiting at the foot of the stairs. Where the hell was she? All around him people mingled and laughed and drank champagne. Those guests who had not been invited to spend the weekend but would attend the ball arrived one after another. Overly friendly and much too loud greetings filled the air, as he stood at the foot of the staircase and waited impatiently.

He tapped his fingers against the railing, then paced a while. William Mathias, who had turned out to be a very nice fellow, walked by every two minutes or so and asked if Julian had seen Valerie yet.

Finally, after an excruciating half hour, Julian was able to say "yes," and point to the top of the stairs.

William lifted his eyes, swallowed hard, and went

red in the face. Even his ears blushed pink. Valerie walked down the stairs, and even Julian had to admit that she looked lovely. Her embellished pink gown was more low cut than usual, her hair more elaborately styled. She had been corseted so tight her waist was small and her breasts were prominently displayed.

If the expression on William's face was any indication, he did not admire Valerie for her money.

Mathias did manage to regain most of his natural color before Valerie reached the bottom of the stairs. Anya's cousin smiled then, at William and then at Julian. "Anya is almost ready," she said sweetly. "She'll be right down."

Julian nodded, as William mentioned the grand buffet to Valerie and took her arm to lead her there.

A minute passed. Two. Where was his wife?

A rustle at the top of the stairs made him look up. Mrs. Sedley stood there, resplendent in matronly plum. She made her way down the stairs with a satisfied smile on her face. "Anya will be down shortly," she announced as she reached the bottom of the stairway.

So he had heard. If Mrs. Sedley was smiling, he could be relatively certain that Anya would not come down the stairs dressed in silk scarves and all the jewelry she could lay her hands on.

Mrs. Sedley greeted an arriving friend and walked away with a swish of fabric. Julian lifted his head to watch the top of the stairs and wait. He didn't have to wait long.

Was this woman really his wife? God in heaven,

she was gorgeous. Anya smiled and hesitated at the top of the stairs, gold fabric swirling around her legs, softly curling tendrils of red hair barely touching her bare shoulders. Somehow her grandmother had talked her into wearing a corset, and the effect was startling. His heart got caught in his throat. His fingers itched. And then she started to descend, with her own style of grace. Each step was a seduction, and the brilliant smile she gave him was real and for him alone.

Her transformation was perfect. His wife was the ideal melding of the naked savage he had married and the fine lady she was by birth. He lifted his hand as she came near, and when she was able she took it, laying her soft, golden hand in his and wrapping her fingers around his palm.

"You are beautiful," he said.

"Thank you," she said softly. "So are you."

"I will be the envy of every man here tonight." He glanced at her exposed cleavage. The corset had elevated her already bountiful breasts up and out, making them look as if they were about to spill over.

"Grandmother wanted to cover the freckles with a white powder," Anya whispered, "but I would not allow it."

"Good."

"When you look at me like this, I tremble down deep," she said, just as softly.

His eyes caught hers and held them. He had fought her for months, but Anya forced him to think with his body and his heart instead of his brain. She made him look deep within himself, at his own desires and failings. Margaret had hurt him, and he had been determined to never again let something so common as lust rule his life. But this . . . this was more than lust. He brought Anya's hand to his lips and kissed her knuckles.

"How utterly charming."

He turned toward the grating voice, barely lifting his head. Anya's smile died. *Speak of the devil.*

The newly arrived Margaret, long out of mourning, wore red. Her gown was every bit as low cut as Anya's, and yet . . . she simply looked vulgar. "I did not know you two would be here," she said.

"Mrs. Sedley and Mrs. Mansfield are close friends."

"I didn't know that."

Julian wondered if Margaret would have come to the ball if she'd known he and Anya would be in attendance. He had once been drawn to Margaret because she could appear to be the ideal woman— when it suited her. Her deceit went so deep, it was as much a part of her as Anya's frankness. Margaret had pretended to be the woman he wanted and needed, in order to gain his affections. Anya never pretended. Deceit was beyond her. For the first time, he felt truly lucky that Margaret had betrayed him. A lifetime with her would be miserable, for any man.

Out of the corner of his eye, he saw Anya's free hand flutter over her thigh. Surely she was not wearing that knife! What was he thinking? Of course she wore the knife. If she would not leave her room without it, he should have known she would not go so far from home unarmed. This could be disastrous.

He drew his wife to his side. "If you'll excuse us,

I'm starving. I hear the buffet is very well laid out."

Margaret simply raised her eyebrows. Anya glanced over her shoulder only once, probably to see if the other woman followed, and as they entered the dining room she muttered a string of words in some foreign language. French, he thought, though her voice was too low for him to be certain.

From the tone of her voice, he was quite sure he didn't want to know what those words meant.

The presence of the bitch in red, Julian's *puta*, ruined what should have been a perfectly wonderful evening. Anya tried to take her husband's advice and ignore the woman. After all, there were more than sixty people there, and Margaret March was only one.

Anya did ignore the crone, but she could not forget that the woman was close by. How could she? When the harlot's voice was shrill and raised above the rest, and then that flash of red caught Anya's eyes everywhere she turned, it was impossible to pretend Mrs. Margaret March did not exist.

Anya tried to think of other things. Valerie was so happy, and William Mathias paid very close attention to her. After watching them dance once, Anya had no reservations about the man. He definitely loved Valerie for her bosom; his gaze had rarely strayed elsewhere.

Julian never left her side. They had eaten, though with the bloody corset strangling her she could not eat much, and they had danced. Julian said it was improper for them to dance together so often, but he would not allow any other man to hold her, or to have the view their closeness afforded. Perhaps the corset, painful as it was, was a worthwhile sacrifice. Just for this evening.

She adored the way Julian held her when they danced. They had practiced, in the south parlor at home, but something between she and her husband had changed since those particular lessons. The air around them sparkled, she was sure of it. Her heart beat steady and hard, but every now and then something in her stomach fluttered. Desire. Anticipation. Love. Love, most of all.

She adored the way Julian looked at her. Tonight the beast lurked in his dark eyes, eyes as possessive as the arms that held her.

He leaned down and whispered in her ear. "I suppose we could retire early."

"Yes."

"Your grandmother is standing near the ballroom door. As soon as she moves, we'll sneak out."

Anya tilted her head and smiled at her husband. "Have you ever *sneaked* anywhere before?"

"No."

"I thought not." He was so straightforward, so diligently honest. One would not think he had a devil-may-care bone in his body.

"But the alternative," he revealed softly, "waiting until the wee hours of the morning when the party is done, is impossible."

"You want me," she whispered.

"More than I've ever wanted anything."

Anya glanced toward the doorway, where Grandmother stood. When would she move away? To dance, to eat, to visit with an old friend. Finally, she spotted Mrs. Mansfield and moved to the other side of the room.

"Grandmother has departed from the doorway."

"Good." Julian took her arm, and they turned toward the wide doorway. Their escape was going well, until an agitated red-faced young man came up from behind and grabbed Julian by the shoulder.

"Dr. DeButy," the intruder said breathlessly. Anya recognized him as Katherine Mansfield's youngest son, James, the one Seymour had been rooming with during their stay here. "Would you please come with me? One of the maids has burned herself."

"I'm not really . . ." Julian began, protesting, but James turned and ran back to the kitchen, and he had no recourse but to follow. "I'll be right back," he promised.

Anya sighed and searched the crowded room for a familiar face. A friendly face. She knew so few of these people. Grandmother was seated on the opposite side of the room, with her good friend Mrs. Mansfield. They seemed to be having a pleasant conversation, and Grandmother even tapped her foot in time to the music.

Seymour was also on the other side of the room, a fact Anya noted as if minding the location of a poisonous snake. She had no desire to speak to Seymour any more than she had to. She had noticed her cousin and Margaret March dancing earlier in the evening. They were a well-suited couple: two vipers.

Finally she caught a flash of Valerie's gown, a pale pink, and headed in that direction. Anya wanted to tell her cousin that Grandmother had been right. She had taken Julian's breath away. The corset, while painful, was perhaps a useful contraption after all.

As she drew closer, stepping around the edge of the crowded dance floor, she saw that Valerie stood with a small group of people. William Mathias was there, standing very close to Valerie, as well as a number of others. They seemed to be crowded around someone or something of great interest. As Anya came closer a few in the group laughed, though Valerie did not.

When she was close enough to see the flash of red through the crowd, Anya's heart leaped in an unpleasant way. She would rather pass the time speaking to Seymour than to listen to Margaret March prattle on! She knew how deadly dull the woman's idea of conversation could be.

The music ended, and suddenly there was a lull, a long moment of silence. A voice rising from the crowd filled the room. "She was a king's whore and a savage. Anya DeButy might dress in a fine gown and speak with a charming accent, but she's still and always will be a whore and a savage."

In an instinctive move, Anya's hand fell over her concealed knife. And then it dropped. Her heart was suddenly heavy, the joy she had felt when Julian held her was gone. She did not care what a woman like Margaret March thought of her or said about her. What hurt, what broke her heavy heart, was that Valerie stood there and listened, and said nothing in

Anya's defense. She did not laugh like the others, and her face had gone pale . . . but she said nothing.

Someone noticed that Anya stood within earshot, just as the orchestra began to play again. Then another person saw her, and then another. The throng parted, until Anya and Margaret could see each other and a short corridor formed by well-dressed revelers stretched between them.

Heart in her throat, Anya stepped through the pathway, past the shocked people who watched with great interest, as if this were a play, a show for their entertainment.

Margaret glared at Anya, a feral gleam in her eyes. "Did I say something that wasn't true?" she asked calmly. "Are you going to call me a liar?"

"No," Anya said softly.

"Poor Julian. I did think better of him. Didn't he know that it wasn't necessary to marry you in order to get you into his bed?" Margaret's eyes hardened. "Tell us, Anya, did you really run about the house naked when you first arrived? When Seymour told me I scarcely believed it, but . . ."

"Yes," Anya said, cocking her head to watch Margaret's face. Where was the evil that should be so evident? She moved closer, snaking through the crowd that closed behind her until she was trapped in the midst of these curious, shocked, titillated people.

"What is the difference between a king's whore and a prostitute who will sell herself to any man who walks by?" Margaret asked.

Anya stopped when she stood no more than a foot

away from Margaret. "I do not know. Perhaps you can tell me."

Those who did not know of Margaret's less-than-virtuous behavior might not catch Anya's meaning, but the widow herself certainly did. Her face went red and her hands formed small fists. "You are a despicable person, and you must've tricked Julian into marrying you." She no longer tried to hide her anger. "You are no better than an animal. Surely you don't think your husband truly cares for you. I understand your grandmother is going to pay Julian a tidy sum for taking you. I wonder if it's enough to make up for the sacrifices he's made. Good heavens, for a respected physician to marry the Beast of Rose Hill, the sum must have been great."

The corset choked Anya, and she was close to tears. Tears! Her eyes burned, and she felt the growing moisture gather there. Weeping for *Romeo and Juliet* was not a sin, but to allow this woman to make her cry would be.

Anya cast a quick, condemning glance to a pale Valerie. If anyone were to say bad things about her, Anya would come to Valerie's defense without a second thought. She would fight for those she loved. It did not matter what Margaret March or these other people thought of her, it did not matter that they thought her an animal, that they knew her husband had been purchased at a high price. But Valerie stood there and said nothing, and that was what hurt Anya's heart.

"I am going home," she said softly. She turned and pushed her way past a squealing young lady in a yellow gown and a tall skinny man who was so anxious to get out of her way that he almost knocked down the lady standing behind him.

"Anya," Valerie called softly.

But it was too late.

Chapter Ten

The kitchen maid's burn had been blessedly minor. Julian had applied a bit of salve, offered a few calming words and a neat bandage, and once that was done the young servant finally quit crying. It had been the hysterical tears that made James Mansfield panic, not the severity of the injury.

Julian searched the crowded ballroom for Anya, certain his eyes would fall upon her right away. That red hair, that gold gown. The almost tangible energy that radiated from her. A disquiet settled in his stomach when he did not see her immediately. He loved her. He wanted her. He was still not sure what she might do next.

When he finally decided Anya was not in the room, a scene on the other side of the room caught his eye. Valerie. Surely she knew where Anya had gone. He was halfway across the room, weaving past and around the dancers, when he realized that Valerie stood toe to toe with Margaret. Neither of them appeared to be happy.

"You should be ashamed of yourself," Valerie said, her cheeks blushing bright pink and her hands working nervously. A quiet and seemingly supportive William Mathias stood at her back. "Anya is a sweet, wonderful woman who suffered a horrid tragedy in her childhood."

Margaret looked down her nose at the plump, fair-haired Valerie. "No matter what the cause, she is exactly as I described her, a . . ."

"Julian!" Valerie caught sight of him and rushed away from Margaret while the widow was in mid-sentence. "You must stop her."

"Margaret?"

"Anya! She left. She said she was going home."

Julian's heart lurched. He knew that, more often than not, home to Anya was a place far away from North Carolina. Everything had been going so well. What had happened to make her run this way? All that mattered now was stopping her before she went too far. He headed for the door, not even glancing at Margaret as he passed her. Valerie kept up with quick steps, and Mathias was right behind her.

"Tell her I'm sorry."

"For what?" Julian's eyes were on the front door.

"Tell her I'm not brave like she is, but . . . but that I did defend her after she left." Valerie sniffled. "I should have said something sooner, I know. I'm such a coward."

"You are not," Mathias said, reaching out to place

a hand on Valerie's shoulder. "You were quite brave."

Julian stopped with his hand on the front door-knob. His instinct was to run after Anya, but he needed to know exactly why she had run. "What happened?"

Valerie's trembling lips hardened. "It was that awful Mrs. March. She said terrible things about Anya."

"Such as?"

"That . . . that she was an animal, and that she was a king's . . . a . . ." Valerie looked pleadingly up at her suitor, and Mathias leaned forward to whisper the vile word into Julian's ear.

Julian's fingers twitched, and a ball of fury joined the worry in the pit of his stomach.

"And she told everyone that Anya used to wander around the house without clothes, and that Grandmother . . . bought you for her."

Julian groaned. Not this. Not now. "She can't have been gone long."

"Just a few minutes."

He burst through the front door and onto the lawn. Carriages and drivers crowded the well-lit driveway. Torches burned bright in the night. Julian headed for the nearest driver.

"Red hair, gold dress," he snapped.

The man pointed to the road, and Julian cut through the grass. Once on the road, he ran. The lane was narrow and lined on either side by a well-kept white fence and lush fields. His heart pumped hard, and not from the exertion of running. What if he didn't find her? If any woman would be brave enough to strike out on her own, to walk away without looking back, it would be Anya. She would have no second thoughts about sneaking aboard a ship bound for parts unknown, and then demanding that they take her home. Home to Puerta Sirena. The thought of actually losing her made him run faster.

He hadn't gone far before he finally spotted her. There was enough moonlight to illuminate the narrow road, to shine upon Anya's gold dress and her copper hair, as she stalked down the road ripping pins from her elaborate coif and shaking her red tresses down one strand at a time.

"Anya," he called as he ran after her.

She must be able to hear. He was certainly close enough, but still she did not answer or turn around to acknowledge him.

"Anya!" He ran faster. She didn't slow her step, but she didn't run from him, either. He finally caught up with her, wrapped his arms around her waist, and spun her around.

He expected to see tears, and he did. A few drops hung in her eyes and glistened in the moonlight. He expected to see anger, and he did. Fury shone in those tearful eyes as surely as the moon did. He had not expected his own heart to break when he saw her face, but it did.

"You don't have to run," he whispered.

"I do. I am going home." She tried, not very vigorously or successfully, to shake him loose.

"Margaret is a vindictive, vicious person, and you should not allow her to upset you."

"Vindictive and vicious mean the same thing," she

Linda Jones

said, pouting slightly. "And your *puta* did not upset me. It was . . . it was . . ." Her lower lip trembled.

He had heard enough of the story to know what troubled her. "Valerie?"

The tears in her eyes dripped down her face. "She just stood there and let that awful woman talk about me as if I had no feelings, as if she cared nothing for me."

"Valerie did defend you, after you left," Julian interrupted. "She was giving Margaret a piece of her mind when I discovered you were gone."

"Truly?"

"Valerie asked me to tell you that she's sorry she took so long to speak up in your defense, but that she does not have your bravery. She does love you, Anya."

Anya slipped out of his arms and stepped back. "I am glad to hear that, but it changes nothing."

"I'd say it does."

"All the things Margaret said about me? They were true." Anya spun in the moonlight, as if she were dancing all alone. Pagan and wild and beautiful, she seemed to pray to the moon. "I do not belong here."

"That's not true."

"It is true. It does not matter that I love you, that I sense something wonderful just out of reach, that for a while I thought this place was home." Anya stopped spinning, lifted her skirt, and very deftly slipped the knife she wore at her thigh into the palm of her hand. "For all my threats, I have never harmed anyone," she said softly. "I have never committed murder, until tonight."

"Anya . . ." Julian stepped forward quickly, but he was not quick enough.

With a quick, precise motion, Anya slipped the tip of the knife into the bodice of her gown and drew it downward. The sound of fabric ripping, tearing in two, was loud there, so far from the house and the noise of the party. "I am tired of pretending to be someone I am not. For you, Julian, only for you would I go so far."

"You are not pretending. You are . . . my wife."

The gold fabric hung over her untouched chemise and corset, flapping lightly in the summer breeze. "Am I? I do not know who I am anymore. On Puerta Sirena, I knew. There was no question. I knew my place, and no one ever questioned it."

"The king's mistress," he said softly. "A goddess of love." He had tortured himself wondering about this damned King Sebastian. About the training of a love goddess. How many men had touched Anya? What kind of training did a love goddess undertake? Some nights it was like torture, as he wondered. As he imagined.

He no longer cared. "It doesn't matter who you were, or who your family expects you to be, or even who I expect you to be."

She slipped the knife beneath her chemise and ripped down once again. The fine linen, decorated with silk ribbons, was cut in half, and the ragged ends fluttered in the breeze. "I am tired of pretending." She began to cut at the corset, a tougher chore than slicing through the gown and chemise. She worked, and as she did the tears began to fall again.

Linda Jones

"Stop it," Julian said as he neared her.

"No. It is choking me. It is not who I am."

In a move she did not expect, he deftly took the knife from her. "You're going to hurt yourself."

She shot him an accusing glance. He studied the knife for a moment, before turning her about and gently pushing what remained of her gown off her shoulders. With a surgeon's precision, he slipped the tip of the blade beneath the bottom corset cord that laced up her back. He worked the blade upward, slicing through one lace after another. The corset came looser with the popping of each string, and finally fell free when the last one was severed.

"Better?"

Anya turned, lifting her face to him. "Yes."

Julian shook off his jacket and put it around her shoulders, covering the tattered gown and her exposed breasts. Anya stood there, unmoving, as he placed her arms through the long sleeves, rolled them up to free her hands, and then buttoned it closed.

"Do you still want to go home?" he asked softly.

"Yes."

"I will take you."

"But—"

"Don't argue with me, Anya," he said, guiding her to the side of the road and almost forcing her to lean against the white rail fencing there. "I'm going to borrow Seymour's horse, tell Valerie to collect our things tomorrow before they head back and your grandmother not to worry, and then I will be back to collect you and we will go home."

A strange look passed over Anya's face, something childlike and strikingly poignant. "Do you promise?" she asked softly. "Do you promise that you will come back?"

"Yes."

"Hurry."

For much of the journey on horseback, Anya rested her head against Julian's chest and pretended to sleep. The ruse was not necessary, as he did not seem to want to talk any more than she did.

Of course he did not want to talk. What was there to say? Everything Margaret had accused her of was true, in a distorted way. It all came down to one truth. She did not belong here.

Julian might feel an attraction for her, but surely he did not love her. She had successfully used her body to win him, but what did she really have? His love? No, it was only desire. He simply did not know the difference. She had been foolish to think otherwise.

"We're home," he said softly.

Anya lifted her head to look at the depressing, sprawling brick mansion lit by eerie moonlight. "This is not my home."

"Of course it is."

"It is very dark."

Julian steered the horse toward the stables at the back of the property. "It's empty, with all the servants gone for the weekend. They'll return tomorrow afternoon."

"I do not like this place," she whispered.

171

Linda Jones

"It's a fine house."

"Yes, but I do not belong in it." She hugged close the coat Julian had put on her. "It is a cold, lifeless place, filled with lies and false promises."

"I have never lied to you," he said defensively.

"And when you leave?"

He did not deny that he would, one day too soon, leave. It had been his intent from the beginning. "Your grandmother and Valerie both love you very much. Peter seems to be very fond of you. And Seymour . . ." Julian shrugged and Anya felt it, the subtle shifting of his warm, solid body against hers. "I don't imagine Seymour likes anyone, much."

It was not what she wanted to hear. "When you leave here, would you take me home?"

"Anya, you are home."

"This is not home," she whispered.

They reached the stables and an eager boy, surprised to see them, ran out to take the horse. He held the reins while Julian dismounted and then lifted his arms to assist Anya as she left the saddle.

"Everything's in good order, sir," the boy said. "I checked around the house just before sunset."

"Very good," Julian said, taking the lantern the boy offered.

They walked to the house, the dimly lit lantern hanging from Julian's hand, his free arm around her waist. Was he afraid she would run even now? She was tempted. Very tempted.

But Anya did not run. She leaned into Julian and took the comfort he offered. "I will go without you," she promised.

He sighed, but did not seem surprised. "I wish you would give your family another chance."

"They are not my family." *You are my only family.* She felt that, wanted to say it, but did not. "I have been too long away from this place for them to be my family."

Julian opened the door that led them into the north parlor, a rarely used room she had never cared much for. There was no color, here, no life. In the moonlight the room seemed full of ghosts. She and Julian had married here. She had not loved him then. In fact, she had not known him. Not really.

"You must be hungry," she said as they left the dark parlor behind. "We had a long ride."

"I am a little hungry," he confessed. "Should we raid the kitchen and see what we can find?"

The thought of the staid Julian DeButy raiding anything brought a smile to Anya's face. "A wonderful idea."

He placed the lantern on the oaken table in the center of the large kitchen, and they foraged until they had bread, jam, and apple cider. Instead of going into the dining room to share their simple meal, they sat at the oak table where the servants took their meals.

Anya liked the kitchen. Even now, it was warm and welcoming, in a way the rest of the house was not. The bread and jam sat well on her stomach; the cider was sweet and cool. "I have an idea," she said, pushing her mug and napkin away. "I could go with you." She could stay with him until the passion between them expired, and he realized that he did not love her. It would be enough, she decided. His passion would satisfy her love for him, for a while.

"Go with me where?" Julian asked as he finished the last of his late-night meal.

"Wherever you go," she whispered, terrified that he would immediately dismiss her suggestion as foolish. "I can be an anthropologist, too. I know many languages, and might be of great help to you."

"I get the feeling," Julian said in a teasing voice, "that most of your impressive linguist abilities are phrases only salty sailors will respond to."

"Perhaps, but I have a good ear and am a very fast learner."

Julian pushed his own mug away, stood, took the lantern in one hand, and offered her the other. "If you had made that suggestion a month ago, perhaps even a week ago, I would have thought you'd lost your mind."

She smiled as she placed her hand in his. So far, this sounded like a "yes" to her.

"And taking a woman to the kinds of untamed places I intend to travel, well, most will say it's madness."

"What do you say?"

"I say your idea would solve my most immediate problem."

"And that problem is?"

They stepped into the dining room, and Julian placed the lantern on the long, bare buffet. He very gently spun her around and took her face in his hands. "The very thought of leaving you behind, that's my problem. How am I supposed to choose between the career I have sought for so long and the woman I have found?"

"You do not have to choose." She rose on her toes and laid her mouth over Julian's, telling him again, in this most eloquent way, that she loved him. And for the moment, it was enough that he thought himself in love with her.

His lips parted slightly, and she shared his breath for a moment before pressing her mouth firmly to his. His arms crept around her, and he pulled her close. Her hands snaked around his waist and up his back, her fingers dancing against the fine linen that covered the muscles there. Feeling his warmth, arousing him and herself with the gentlest of touches, she allowed herself to caress as she pleased.

She had never known such pure heat, such a searching need. Without taking her mouth from his, she slid one hand along his arm until she reached his wrist, and then pulled his hand up and around and placed it against her chest.

When she released Julian's hand, it crept unerringly into the gap of the jacket she wore, to caress her breast gently. He found and stroked the nipple that hardened at his touch, and deepened the kiss.

Nothing that had happened on this night could spoil the moment. Julian wanted her; she knew it well. And she wanted him, in a way so powerful and inescapable it surprised her. She had been taught control, seduction . . . she had not been taught to handle a power that shot through her body like lightning.

175

Their mouths parted, and she laid hers against his neck, tasting the salty skin there, sucking lightly on the inviting flesh.

"I never knew I could feel like this," he whispered.

"I know."

"I'm spinning out of control."

"So am I. Is it not wonderful?"

Julian's hands slipped between their bodies and unbuttoned the jacket she wore, his own jacket. With a push, the garment fell from her body and pooled on the floor.

Cool night air chilled her exposed skin, but Anya did not stay cool for long. Julian placed his hands at her waist and lifted her off her feet, spinning her around and placing her so that she sat on the edge of the table. His arms encircled her, his hands stroked her back, and once again he returned his attention to her breasts. First with his fingers, and then with his mouth.

Her head fell back, her fingers twined through Julian's hair as he suckled one nipple, drawing it deep into his mouth. Fire traveled through Anya's body, sparks and flames of a potent urgency that Julian fanned with his mouth and hands.

"I need you," he said as he lifted his head and looked into her eyes.

"I know." She reached between their close bodies, raked her hand down, and caressed the stiff manhood beneath his trousers. "And I need you." Could he feel her tremble? Did he know that she had never felt his kind of craving before? It was more than a craving. She would not survive unless he came to her. Now.

They kissed deeply while she stroked the ridge in his trousers. Julian moaned, and she caught that moan with her parted lips, tasted it with her flickering tongue. She returned that telling moan as she began to unfasten his trousers.

He pushed her farther back on the table, and she listed back and back until she was lying there, the polished walnut a hard bed. Julian followed, crept ever forward and up until he towered above her. Her legs crept around his, bringing him closer. Closer.

Inch by inch, kissing and touching all the while, they moved until they were completely on the table. As he straightened his body, Julian kicked something that went rolling and then crashed onto the floor.

It surprised them both enough so that their lips parted.

"Never fear," Anya whispered breathlessly. "They will think I did it."

Julian smiled at her, and she reached up to unbutton his shirt. A difficult task, since he was so close—since he was atop her. Still, she continued until she was able to tug the shirt off.

"There," she said, as she tossed the shirt aside. She ran her hands along Julian's muscled chest. Pressed her breasts against his flesh.

There was an opening in the crotch of her drawers, drawers she would not have worn had Grandmother not been there to insist. With a slight shifting of her body, Julian could be inside her. She

Linda Jones

wanted that, wanted it so much that her body arched toward his in silent invitation.

But she also wanted this first time for them to be right. Perfect. She wanted flesh to flesh along the length of their bodies. "Julian?"

"Yes?" he moaned, his body moving unerringly toward hers.

"Undress me."

He did as she asked. It would have been simplest for them to leave the table, shed their clothes, and then come together again. But that would not do. Bit by bit, dropping kisses as he went, Julian removed her torn gown and what was left of her underthings. Their bodies never moved far apart. She removed the knife and scabbard from her thigh and carelessly tossed them aside. Julian rolled down her stockings and tossed them aside. Soon all she wore was the sapphire pendant around her neck.

That done, it was his turn. The unbuttoned trousers had to come off. His own underthings. Those shoes and socks. The diligent chore continued, frenzied and still deliberate, until they lay, bare body to bare body, along the walnut table.

Her skin was sensitive, reacting in a surprising way to Julian's simplest touch. A finger here, a tender kiss there. She ran her own fingers down his arm, then turned and lifted her head to lay her mouth against the delicate skin at Julian's inner elbow. He moaned, and dropped his head to her neck, where he proceeded to devour her.

His manhood brushed against her most intimately, and she rose up in invitation, her hips sway-

178

ing, a moan breaking free of her parted lips. Julian barely touched her, and still that gentle contact evoked the most powerful sensation she had ever experienced.

She slipped her hand between their bodies and guided him to her, inside her.

A heartbeat later he rocked forward to slowly fill her, quelling the need she had experienced and firing another to life. He moved slow and deep, so deep. She whispered to him, speaking the words that came to her, husky, tender words she could not contain. Some French, some Spanish, a few words in the language of her island. Words for which there were no suitable substitutes.

She had never known such raw power. Julian filled her, cautiously, fully, so slowly she could not breathe until he was buried deep, as deep as possible. Then he withdrew just as slowly, stealing her breath again. And then again he pushed to fill her, and then again he almost left her. Each stroke was perfect, and she had been right. There was more. Julian was a part of her body and her heart. His soul and hers changed as he made love to her. Their very souls mingled, as deeply as their bodies did. Nothing she had ever been taught could have prepared her for the intensity of this moment.

Julian began to move faster, and so did she. Their rhythm was quick and instinctive, as their bodies and souls ruled their minds and hearts. He drove deep and held himself there, and she shattered, crying out and arching into him, feeling and savoring the shudders that wracked his body as he found his own completion.

He collapsed atop her, his head buried in her hair, his heartbeat pounding against hers. Sweat glistened on his body and hers, shining in the light of the single dim lantern Julian had carried from the stables.

They lay there for a while, out of breath and wonderfully entangled, Julian's long body resting protectively over hers. Anya stroked his long dark hair, ran her foot up and down his leg, and sighed contentedly. More than once.

Finally, Julian lifted his head and looked down at her. "Anya, we're on the dining room table," he said as if he'd just realized where they had made love.

"Yes, we are."

"Naked." He seemed to be protesting, but his half smile gave him away.

She slithered her body against his. "Yes."

Julian began to withdraw, but she tightened the leg that was wrapped around his and pulled him back. He didn't seem to mind.

"You are a wonderful lover," she whispered. "A magnificent husband."

"I love you," he said.

She wanted, so much, for that to be true. No one had ever loved her this way. No one ever would. No one but Julian. "I love you, *marido*."

"But we really shouldn't . . ." he began.

Anya reached up and laid her hands on her breasts. Her fingers flicked over the nipples. Julian's hooded eyes followed her progress. "I loved the way you put your mouth on my breasts. Your tongue. Your lips." Her husband, her lover, began to grow hard inside her. "I did not know I could feel so much, that I could desire a man the way I desire you." She rotated her hips gently. "I desire you now."

"Anya," Julian said as he lowered his head to brush his mouth across her breasts. One and then the other. He suckled one nipple deep, then lifted his head to look her in the eye. "We can't." His hips swayed, apparently of their own volition.

The fever within Anya began to build again. "We can."

Julian barely moved inside her. His body rocked into hers, his flesh raked along her own sweat-covered skin. "But we just . . ." he protested weakly.

"We *can*," she said, once again wrapping one leg snugly around his and lifting her hips.

Julian began to slowly withdraw, but before he left her body completely he surged forward to fill her again. She felt his gentle surrender, tasted it in his sigh. "Yes, we can," he said, before he captured her mouth with his.

Chapter Eleven

Julian groaned and pulled the covers over his head, and Anya's, as morning sunlight crossed their faces and interrupted their sleep. Well-deserved sleep.

But it was too late. Once he began to awake there was no turning back. Awareness crept slowly in, though Anya slept on, peaceful and beautifully satisfied.

He held the coverlet over their heads, allowing only a small amount of the morning sun to creep inside. Anya still wore a pink flush of love on her beautiful cheeks. Her brilliant, mussed hair spread across his pillow, and her warm, bare body rested against the white sheets she slept upon. She was, in fact, a vision.

Julian reached out and touched a wayward strand of hair. Last night he had willingly put aside the beliefs he had embraced for the past two years. He had tossed his prim ideals away for the joy of loving his wife. He should be feeling at least a little bit of regret, perhaps even guilt. He felt nothing but satisfaction. Love and happiness and the certainty that this was right, no matter what the greatest medical minds of the nineteenth century preached. Twice on the dining room table and then again in this bed could only be called excess, the kind of excess that he had once condemned as unhealthy.

But Julian wasn't concerned. His common sense won out over the massive number of pamphlets he had collected. Loving his wife would not make him ill, it would not drain or damage him in any way. If anything, he felt more energized this morning than he ever had.

If he allowed himself to question his own beliefs, he might admit that it was Margaret who had driven him to a life of chastity. That, with his heart broken, he had forced himself into a position where it would never again be in danger. But he didn't want to analyze his feelings at the moment. He just wanted to watch Anya sleep. He just wanted to touch her and watch her come awake. His fingers crept across the pillow to caress her shoulder, and she purred in response. Her eyes fluttered open, she set them on him, and smiled.

"Good morning," she whispered as she rolled over and into him, her arm draping across his waist as she lifted her head and kissed his neck. Lightly, the lips lingering and arousing.

Dropping the covers so that the sun touched them once again, he pulled her tighter against his body, gently cradling the back of her head and pressing his other hand against the small of her back. "Good morning, my love," he whispered into her wealth of red hair.

"I do so adore the way you look in the morning, *marido*," she murmured. "With your hair wild and your beard coming in and your eyes still filled with last night's dreams." She sighed, seemingly contented, and kissed his throat again. "Did I tell you last night that I like your bed much better than mine?"

He smiled. "I believe you did."

"Did I tell you that you are a magnificent lover?"

"Yes."

"A continued vow of chastity would be a tragedy for one so gifted," she teased. "Such a gift should not be wasted."

Her hand slipped down his side until it rested on his hip. How was it possible that already he wanted her? The rest of the world faded, and nothing else mattered but the way Anya felt in his arms.

"Did I tell you," he said softly, "that I love you?"

"Yes, you did." She brushed her cheek against his shoulder, nuzzling, aligning her body to his inch by inch. "It is what I wanted more than anything, for you to love me as I love you."

His blood thrummed and his body grew warm. His manhood had been erect and ready since the moment Anya had awoken and smiled at him.

The kisses she feathered across his neck grew more ardent. Her hand was no longer content to rest on his hip, but traveled and teased. His own hands would not be still. They explored her soft flesh as she explored his. After the night before there should be no secrets, nothing to discover . . . and yet they were still discovering.

With a gentle shove Anya pushed him onto his back. She followed, her leg sliding over so that she straddled him and her head rested on his chest for a moment as she kissed his flat nipples. She raised her head slowly, strands of wildly disheveled hair partially covering her face until she lifted her hands and forced the curling locks back. The sun shone on bare flesh. Warming, illuminating sun. Anya was a vision to undo any man, her rounded breasts lifting with each breath she took, her mouth lushly inviting, her eyes hooded with sleep. And what a shape she possessed!

"Last night you made love to me," she said. "This morning I will make love to you."

"Anya . . ." His protest died an easy death as she manacled his wrists with her fingers, lifted his hands, and laid them on her breasts. The flesh beneath his fingers was giving, warm, and silky. With her hands remaining over his, Julian cupped her breasts and flicked his thumbs over her hardened nipples. She closed her eyes in response and moaned low and deep as she dropped her hands.

She began to move atop him, teasing, torturing. It was an undulating dance, and as her body moved, barely touching his, he lost all rational thought and thought only of the way his body felt. Of how he wanted her. Every nerve was exposed, on fire.

Finally she reached between their bodies and

guided his manhood into her slick body. Slipping into her welcoming heat was a pained relief. She took him in, nurtured him, stroked him. Her body rose and fell slowly. Too slowly. The breasts he caressed swelled with each deep breath she took. Eyes closed, she continued to dance atop him, taking him deep, rising up slowly until he was barely inside her, then plunging down to take all of him before rising up again. His hips rose and fell in time with hers as they found their own rhythm.

Without warning Anya added something new; a twist of her hips that almost sent him over the edge. It was subtle, and jarring, and erotic. She licked her lips and lowered herself slowly and twisted again . . . in the opposite direction.

His body no longer knew what to expect, and what was left of his tenuous control faded fast. But Anya's control left her, too. She began to move faster, more frantically, her body undulating above his. Julian grasped her hips in his hands and held himself deep inside her, and with a final twist Anya cried out and found release. He came with her, with a growl of his own, spurting his seed deep into her body, giving over to the pleasure he had denied himself, and her, for so long.

Sated, Anya lowered her head to his shoulder and relaxed, going boneless against him. "My beautiful beast," she said softly.

Julian almost argued with Anya. He was no more beast than she was. He was just . . . a man. A man who loved his wife. He turned his head and found her lips with his.

*　　*　　*

The family had returned, and so had the servants. She and Julian no longer had the house to themselves. But nothing, not even dinner with Seymour, could ruin Anya's mood. She was too happy. Had she ever been so content? No. She had not.

Valerie had been silent since her return, probably wondering if Anya was still unhappy about the previous night's betrayal. If Valerie had truly defended Anya, even belatedly, then there was no betrayal. Anya's friendly smile across the table seemed to soothe Valerie's frazzled nerves instantly.

When Anya smiled at Betsy, as the maid placed a plate of fried chicken on the table, the girl flinched. Of course, Betsy knew fried chicken was not Anya's favorite. Still, Anya was surprised at the girl's reaction. She had not thrown anything at the servants in quite a while.

When Anya muttered a demure thank-you, Betsy backed away with a suspicious expression on her face.

"Anya, dear," Grandmother said, picking at the vegetables on her plate. "You seem very happy this evening." Was that puzzlement in her voice?

"Of course I am happy," Anya said in her sweetest voice. "We are all home, and I have been blessed with a wonderful family who loves me, as well as a kind husband who has a very great penis."

Seymour spewed wine across the table, and Grandmother turned quite red.

Julian almost choked on his first bite of chicken.

187

Anya ignored the others and began to pat her husband soundly on the back.

"Anya," he croaked when he was able to breathe again, "you can't say that."

"But my family does love me," she protested. "Do they not? And you are most definitely a kind husband who has a great—"

"Anya," he interrupted forcefully.

Of course. Again with the body parts. "You did not mind when I told you so last night."

"You said no such thing," he protested lowly.

One glance around the table told her that everyone present was listening intently. "I forget that you cannot speak French."

Julian shook off his disapproval and the discomfort from choking on his dinner, and Anya smiled at her family. "Of course I am happy," she said again. "Last night Julian and I made love right here on this very table."

Her grandmother brought a hand to her forehead and swooned. Seymour removed his hands from where they had been resting on the table, as if he'd just discovered that his fingers rested in boar dung.

"Anya," Julian whispered in warning.

"Twice," Anya finished with a smile. "Like wild animals."

Julian took her hand beneath the table and squeezed. "Anya. That's enough."

Anya turned loving eyes to her husband. "But this is my family. You said I could say things to family that I could not say to others. That they would rejoice with me in good times and cry with me in bad times. Did you not say that?"

"Yes, but—"

"So why should they not rejoice in our love as we do?"

Julian turned his head and lowered his mouth to her ear. "Some things are private. Just for the two of us and no one else. I'll explain later. For now just . . . eat your chicken."

She gave him a come-hither smile. "I would rather nibble on—"

"Anya!"

With a sigh, she returned her attention to the family. Grandmother was quite pale, and she fanned herself furiously with the silk fan she wore at her waist on warm days. Seymour had backed his chair up slightly, folded his arms over his chest, and scowled at the table. "I can never eat here again," he muttered.

Valerie sat across from Anya, wide-eyed and not at all disturbed. "What's a penis?"

"It is—" Anya began.

Grandmother stood. "That's enough." She turned narrowed, accusing eyes to Anya.

"That is not the proper name? I found it in one of Julian's books." She cast a smile at her pale husband. "The one you hid behind the poetry because you thought I would not look there."

"I know the book," he mumbled.

Anya returned her attention to Valerie. "It is another name for—"

"I said *enough!*" Grandmother commanded. Then,

189

Linda Jones

with a hand to her forehead as if she were faint, she retook her seat. "Valerie will learn of such things when the time is right."

"When will that time be?" Anya asked.

"After she is married," Grandmother said with a curt nod of her head. "It is a husband's place to teach her."

"To teach me what?" Valerie asked, still innocently unaware.

Anya was truly horrified. "You would send her to a husband unprepared?"

"It is the way things are done, Anya," Grandmother said testily.

"It is *wrong*," Anya insisted. "Every woman deserves a proper teaching before marriage."

"We are not savages," Seymour chimed in, his nose in the air.

Anya laid her eyes on her least favorite cousin. "I would disagree." She looked at Valerie and smiled. "I will teach you."

"You will not!" Grandmother insisted.

"Teach me what?" Valerie almost shrieked, finally displaying her exasperation.

"The ways of a man and a woman," Anya answered, over the protests of her grandmother and her husband.

Valerie smiled. "Oh, you mean kissing. But I still don't know what a pe—"

"Valerie!" Grandmother shouted. With her strong voice she took command of the room. "There will be no more discussion of any kind at this table. Everyone will eat *silently*."

Julian breathed what seemed to be a sigh of relief.

Anya picked at her chicken for a few moments, after the room fell silent, and then she leaned into her husband. "You really do have a great—"

"Not now," he interrupted.

"Later, then," Anya agreed with a smile. "After I have a nice long talk with Valerie."

Julian leaned his head back on the sofa, closed his eyes, and sighed. Anya was determined to have that talk with Valerie, even though Elizabeth Sedley was just as determined that her elder granddaughter remain innocent until she was properly wed.

There had been a time, not so long ago, when he would have agreed with Mrs. Sedley. Right now he found himself sympathizing with Anya's position. How many women had been terrified on their wedding night, and all because they were unprepared? There had to be a happy medium between love goddess and untouched, untaught innocent.

"There you are."

Anya's exasperated voice brought a smile to Julian's face. "Just dozing," he admitted as he opened his eyes and lifted his head. "I didn't get much sleep last night, you know."

"I know." Anya didn't sit beside him, but perched on his knee and draped her arms around his neck. His arms went around her waist. "Neither did I, but what sleep I did get was marvelous."

"Did you have your talk with Valerie?"

"No." Anya rested her head on his shoulder.

191

Linda Jones

"Grandmother is guarding her as if I wish to do her harm."

"Perhaps in your grandmother's eyes what you want to do will cause harm."

"I would never harm Valerie."

"I know."

"But I will have that talk with her soon. I cannot allow her to marry her William Mathias without the proper teaching."

He did not like to hear Anya speak of teaching, not knowing what form her own teaching had taken, but he understood her need to protect her cousin from the unknown.

She relaxed in his arms, and sighed deeply. "Grandmother has Betsy scrubbing down the dining room table as if we did something wrong there. How can something so beautiful be a sin? How can love be something you want to scrub away?"

"It isn't that simple," he said.

"Why not?"

"Intimate relations between a man and a woman are very complicated."

"They should not be. Sex is astounding and natural. There should be poems and songs written about intimate relations."

"I'm sure there are," Julian began.

"Not in your poetry books," Anya complained.

He smiled and pulled her close. "I wish I possessed your ability for absolute frankness. You say what you feel and take what you want."

"Why can you not do the same?"

She made it sound so simple. "It isn't the way

192

things are done here. We have rules. Too many
damn rules."

Anya lifted her head and smiled at him. "You
cursed."

"Yes, I did."

Anya reached down and laid her hand over the
bulge in his trousers. Her smile widened when she
found it, naturally, affected by her presence. "Do you
want me?"

"You know I do."

"Now?" Her hand stroked. "Here?"

"Anya, we no longer have the house to ourselves."

She did not desist. "Grandmother is guarding Valerie. They will come nowhere near me." She laid her
soft lips on his neck and suckled. "Seymour has ridden off to play cards with other scoundrels, and will
likely not be home before dawn," she whispered
when she took her mouth from his flesh. "Betsy is
scrubbing the dining room table, Hilary is upstairs
pressing the gown Valerie will wear tomorrow, and
Peter is sitting in the pantry sipping at a bottle of
Grandmother's best brandy. No one will catch us."

"But . . ."

His last protest died when she reached down and
began to unfasten the tiny buttons at her already low
bodice. He watched, fascinated, as her fingers unbuttoned three pearl buttons and then spread the
fabric so that the swell of her breasts was revealed.
Another half inch, and the coral darkness of her au-
reole would peek above the pale green fabric of her
gown.

"I did not know I could ache for a man," she whispered. "I ache for you."

Julian lowered his head and kissed the soft swell of skin above her bodice. He understood ache, in a way he never had before. His fingers pushed the fabric down so that the nipple of one breast was free, and took it in his mouth. Anya shifted so that she straddled him, and swayed into him like a gentle wave.

"We could go to bed early," he suggested.

"No. Here," she insisted.

"Someone might hear us," he protested weakly.

"Then we must be very quiet," she whispered. "Very, very quiet."

His body was screaming. How could he be quiet?

Anya was impossible to resist. He should know that by now. She unbuttoned his trousers, and he did not protest. When he snaked his hand beneath her skirt and found her leg bare, he was not surprised. She had come here with the intent of seducing him. And he was so easily seduced, now.

Thoughts of impropriety and fears of being caught left his mind and he laid Anya on her back. Hovering above her, his hand skimmed up her inner thigh. Such softness. Such wonder. He touched her intimately and she closed her eyes, parting her lips in a silent cry. She tilted her head back and into the brocade that had become her pillow, their bed, and gave into a soft half-cry, half-moan as he found the sensitive nub hidden in red curls.

She rocked against him and did some teasing of

her own, her hands gentle but not too gentle, her fingers moving firmly but tenderly over his length. Finally, as she shuddered deep, she guided him to her.

When he entered her, she opened her eyes and placed her arms around his neck and her legs around his hips. He made love to her, quickly, deeply, and she responded as she always did when he touched her. Immediately and intensely. There was a ferocity in the way they made love, something primal and fierce.

"Kiss me," she whispered hoarsely. "Kiss me or I will scream."

He latched his mouth to hers and caught her cry as she found fulfillment. Her body swayed up and into his, and he joined her. Their bodies throbbed and jerked and shimmered together. In time, in tune. Poetry and songs. Perhaps she was right about that.

Julian took his mouth from hers and reached down to straighten her bodice. "I can't believe we just made love on your grandmother's favorite sofa. Which is," he added as he helped Anya into a sitting position, "much too short for such an activity."

Anya allowed him to straighten her gown. There was nothing to be done for her mussed hair, though, or the flush on her cheeks, or those magnificent swollen lips. She looked well-loved, satisfied, and decadent.

"The couch might be too short, but we have a perfectly good bed upstairs."

He raised his eyebrows slightly and Anya leaned into him. "I know, you suggested that a while ago. But first I wanted to make love to you here, where I met you."

"If sexual excess is truly harmful, we are both doomed," he said half-heartedly.

"As long as we are doomed together," she whispered. "I love you."

He threaded his fingers through her hair. "I do love you, too," he confessed. "So much. I didn't know . . . I never expected."

"Is your love for me real?" she asked, her voice so low he could barely hear the words. "Sometimes I think it is. Other times I wonder, and that wondering makes my heart ache."

"You never have to wonder about my love for you, Anya. It's real. As real as anything I've ever known."

She kissed him quickly, and he sensed a relief there. He didn't want her to ever doubt him, but he didn't know what else to say to make her understand. Love was new to him, so new he was learning as he went.

They straightened their clothes as best they could, then crept to the door. As Anya had promised, no one was about. Hand in hand they slipped through the foyer and to the stairway, just in time to meet Peter. He seemed to be heading for the library.

The butler took one look at Anya and Julian, raking his eyes over them. There was no explanation, Julian knew, for their disheveled state, their desperately locked hands. Anya looked too well loved, and

Julian suspected he did, too. Peter groaned before turning wordlessly about.

"Peter, where are you going?" Anya asked curiously.

"Back to the pantry."

Chapter Twelve

It was more than three weeks before Anya had the opportunity to speak to Valerie alone. For those weeks Grandmother had been a vigilant watchdog, keeping a wary eye on her elder granddaughter. Anya waited patiently, and never again mentioned Valerie's lack of preparation for marriage. Grandmother apparently thought she had forgotten all about it. Ha.

She did not mind waiting. It had been such a wonderful time. Julian was her lover, in every way possible. They found pleasure in their bodies, of course, but there was more. Much more. Every day Julian seeped a little deeper into her soul, became more a part of her. His essence and hers mingled, until she knew she was not the same, and neither was he. She had been alone all her life, but now she knew that she would never be alone again.

Julian was sleeping soundly in his rocking chair when Anya slipped from their sitting room. He had not slept well the night before, she remembered with a smile as she walked quietly down the hall toward Valerie's room. He needed his rest this afternoon if he were to have strength for the night to come.

They were all supposed to be napping on this hot afternoon, but Anya found she could rarely nap. And if she remembered correctly, Valerie didn't care much for sleeping in the middle of the day, either.

Anya opened Valerie's door and stepped inside the pastel room. She closed the door silently behind her as Valerie sat up on the bed. As always, she was dressed in her chemise and petticoats for a nap. Anya was sure her well-placed scarves were much cooler, and more appropriate, apparel for such a warm day.

"I knew you would not be asleep," Anya said as she sat on the foot of Valerie's bed.

"I thought I would never get a chance to speak to you alone again," Valerie said with a small smile.

"Grandmother was quite vigilant," Anya agreed, offering her hand.

Valerie laid her hand on Anya's palm. "I never did get to apologize for my behavior at the party. I should have spoken up sooner. I just—"

"I understand," Anya broke in. "You were not taught to stand your ground. You have never had to fight for yourself or for anyone else."

"No, I haven't."

"I hope you never have to fight," Anya said, "but if you do you should know how."

199

Linda Jones

"I will try to be more like you," Valerie said softly.

Anya smiled and dropped her cousin's hand. "Do not try too hard. I do not think Grandmother could bear two of us. How are things with William Mathias?"

Valerie wrinkled her nose. "Grandmother won't let me see him." Her eyes shifted to the window, as if she could no longer bear to meet Anya's gaze.

"But . . ." Anya prodded.

"But I have sneaked out of the house to meet him, twice in the past week."

"Where do you meet?"

"Behind the stables, where we can't be seen from the house." Valerie braved a direct glance at Anya. "And you don't have to teach me anything about the ways of a man and a woman. I know everything, now."

"Oh, really?"

"William kissed me." Valerie laid two fingers to her lips.

"Just a kiss?" Anya asked.

"No, much more than a kiss," Valerie insisted. "A wonderful, marvelous kiss that made me feel like melted butter."

Anya shifted uncomfortably on the bed. This could be worse than she thought. "There is more than a kiss," she said softly, "between a man and a woman."

Valerie's eyes widened. "More?"

Suddenly, Anya was angry at her overly protective grandmother who would allow a woman to reach a fully grown age and still be completely ignorant. "Do you love him? If you kissed him you must."

"I do, but . . ." Valerie caught her bottom lip in her teeth and wrinkled her nose. "William says he loves me, but how can I know Grandmother isn't right? What if he only loves me for my fortune?"

"There are ways to be sure," Anya said confidently.

"What ways?"

"I will think of something." But first she had to make sure that if Valerie did wed William Mathias she would not get the shock of her life in the marriage bed.

"Making love," Anya began gently, "involves much more than kissing." She explained, in very simple terms, exactly how the act of love was performed. As she went on, Valerie's eyes went wide and her face turned pale as one of the white roses in the garden.

"I . . . I don't believe you," Valerie finally said, lifting her chin. "You're making this up to pay me back for not defending you at the party. Well—"

"I am not making anything up," Anya inserted gently. "And I forgave you many days ago for your silence." She could not hold a grudge when that night had ultimately given her Julian as a complete and loving husband.

"What you're telling me can't be true," Valerie whispered. "It sounds so disgusting!"

Anya smiled. "Making love is *not* disgusting. When you kissed your William Mathias, did you feel a stirring in your belly?"

"Well, yes," Valerie admitted.

"And did you feel a gentle throbbing between your legs?"

Linda Jones

Valerie blushed. That was answer enough for Anya.

"Making love is a hundred times more pleasurable, a thousand times. You will be amazed that such pleasure exists."

Valerie wrinkled her nose. "It just doesn't sound quite right. And . . . and it *grows*? How can that be?"

"You must trust me," Anya insisted. "And if you will allow me, I can teach you ways to pleasure a man that will make him your willing slave."

Reluctantly, Valerie was becoming a believer. "I don't know. What does a . . . one of those . . . what does it look like?"

Why did these people have such trouble mentioning body parts? Anya sighed. "I would ask Julian to show you his, but he is so shy about such things I feel certain he would refuse."

"I don't actually need to see . . ." Valerie began.

"Of course you do. It is long past time." Anya leaped from the bed, quietly slipped out the door, and ran down the stairs on bare feet. She knew where to find Peter. More and more he found solace in the pantry, sometimes with a bottle of brandy, sometimes with his head resting in his hands. It was almost as if he wanted to hide there.

The big house was silent, deserted. She met no one as she ran to the kitchen and the large pantry. As she swung open the door, Peter, who had been sitting on a stool at the back of the long closet, lifted his head.

"I was just straightening some of these shelves," he said quickly. "They're quite out of order."

"Come," Anya ordered. "Valerie and I need you."

Peter shot to his feet and followed her. "Is something wrong?" he asked, sounding truly concerned.

"No."

"I thought you had taken to wearing clothes, Miss Anya," he said with a hint of censure in his voice. "What is this?"

"It is too hot for petticoats and long skirts," she said as she ran up the stairs.

"Perhaps, but . . ."

"Never fear, I will wear a proper gown to dinner, so Grandmother will not be shocked."

"Thank goodness for that," Peter muttered.

He followed her down the hall, but Anya made him wait while she opened Valerie's door. Her cousin paced by the bed, a wrapper drawn over her chemise and petticoats. Anya grabbed Peter's hand and pulled him into Valerie's room, closing the door behind them.

Valerie went pale again. "Oh, Anya, this is really not necessary."

"It is." Anya glanced up at Peter. "Please show Miss Valerie your penis."

"What?" He turned as pale as Valerie and took a step back, toward the door.

In the past several days, she had tried to get her husband to supply her with a suitable name for this particular body part. Most of them were silly, and still, he said, not fit for use. "Your manly instrument," she said, in case he had not understood her. "Your manhood. Your—"

"I know what you mean," he snapped. "But really, Miss Anya, you have gone too far!"

"But Valerie has never seen one."

"As is right and proper."

Anya tried her most severe face on Peter. "You are a servant, and I command you to do as I say."

Peter leaned forward and into her. "I rocked both of you to sleep when you were ill. I have cleaned up after you two, worried tremendously, and stood guard in perilous times. And I will not display myself obscenely for your amusement."

"This is not amusing," Anya insisted. "It is *teaching.*"

"I did help you study your alphabet at one time, Miss Anya, but that is where my tutorial efforts end."

"It's all right," Valerie insisted. "I don't really want to see, anyway. I would just close my eyes."

Anya sighed. "I am only trying to help." She raised her eyes to a determined, stony-faced Peter. "Did you truly stand guard during perilous times?"

He actually blushed. "It was long ago. I should not have mentioned it."

"Now that you have mentioned it, I should like to know when this occurred."

"In the years after the end of the war, things were unsettled. Even here."

"I wish I remembered that time more clearly," Anya said. "Everything about my time here before the shipwreck is so . . . hazy."

"Once we hid in the stables," Valerie said, speaking quickly. "I had forgotten."

"As you should," Peter said in a quiet voice.

"Yankees were rooting through the house, and the three of us children hid in the stables, and Peter was there." Valerie smiled. "You made us move to the back of a very small room, and then you . . . you stood between us and the door with a six-shooter in each hand."

"I was only doing my duty," he said shyly.

"And I was not afraid," Valerie said softly. "Because I knew you would not let anyone hurt us. How could I have forgotten that?"

Anya wished she remembered more than the indistinct flashes that came to her. Of course, Valerie was two years older. It was only natural that she would remember that time more clearly. "Since you are a hero," Anya said, "I will not insist that you display yourself for Valerie's teaching."

"Thank you so much," Peter said, more than a hint of sarcasm in his voice.

"But could you round up some modeling clay for us? I think I should like to try my hand at sculpture."

"Good God," Peter mumbled as he turned and laid his hand on the doorknob.

"Grandmother always says I should take up a hobby," Anya answered innocently.

Waking and finding Anya not where he'd left her always sent Julian into a kind of panic. The first place he looked for her was the roof, but she wasn't there. Thank goodness. Just as he was about to exit the Captain's Walk he saw them. The sight was enough to make him stop and stare. And smile.

Anya and Valerie were huddled over a small table

Linda Jones

in the garden. They sat there, each of them in a pale pastel dress, and pursued what looked to be some kind of craft. When they laughed, he smiled. The two of them looked like summer flowers, seated among the other blooms.

It was good to see them spending time together. They should be close, and they hadn't had a chance to visit properly since—His smile faded—since Anya had offered to teach Valerie about . . .

Julian ran down the stairs. The quickest way to the garden was through the north parlor. Peter, standing there watching, blocked his exit.

"Pardon me," Julian said as he brushed by the butler.

"You don't want to go out there, sir," the servant muttered.

Julian ignored the butler and made his way through the garden, past the fragrant roses in every shade imaginable. Anya's back was to him, but he had a clear view of Valerie's face. The plump girl was apparently fascinated by something on the table. She leaned forward, watching the workings of Anya's hands. Her eyes were wide, her lips parted in wonder.

Anya heard him coming and cast a glance over her shoulder. She smiled widely. "*Caro*! I thought you would sleep the day away."

Valerie looked up at Julian, squealed, and placed both hands over her face, covering her eyes. The flesh behind those hands went quite red.

"Anya, what are you doing?" he asked as he stepped closer.

"I have taken up sculpting," she said innocently.

"That's . . ." He was about to say *lovely*, when he stepped to the side and saw the "sculpture" she had both hands wrapped around. "Very phallic," he finished.

"Thank you," she said as she began to very lightly reshape the large object in her hands.

"I have to . . . do something," Valerie finished brightly, rising from her seat with her hands remaining over her face. She left without so much as glancing at Julian.

Anya continued to shape the phallus before her, searching for perfection with her pale, soft hands. She had fashioned a life-size, erect model of manhood. Hmm, perhaps a bit larger than life-size.

"If you wanted to take up sculpting, you might have started with a . . . bunny rabbit or a small vase," he said, not quite choking on the words.

"But Valerie needed instruction, and Peter refused to . . ."

"You asked Peter to assist in Valerie's instruction?" Julian asked, taking the shy cousin's vacated seat.

Anya's hands and eyes were on the molded clay before her. Her fingers worked up and down slowly. "I only asked him to provide a specimen. Valerie has never seen a—"

"Would you stop that?" he asked sharply.

Anya only smiled, and did not desist. "Stop what, *querido?*"

She knew exactly what she was doing to him, with her hands and that smile and the lewd—no, pornographic—sculpture. He should be offended. He

207

should be outraged. But he found her continued caress of the sculpture erotic, not obscene.

"You never did ravish me in the garden," she said absently. "Our marriage will not be real until you do."

"And why is that?"

"The ritual is not complete until you have chased and taken me." She closed her fingers around the sculpture and stroked downward. "I cannot believe you do not know that. It is a tradition as old as man, *mi amante.* The husband claims his wife, he makes her his in a way as old as time itself, with his body. He shows his wife his love, his strength, and his possession." Her fingers danced up the sculpture with slow deliberation.

"My love," he said with surrender, "you are trying to kill me."

"Never."

He took a deep breath and shook off the line of thought his mind had taken. "You really must not instruct Valerie against your grandmother's wishes."

"I cannot allow her to marry thinking the only way a man and wife express love is through kissing and holding. Until today she had no idea what would happen when she goes to the marriage bed."

"None?"

"None. She did not know how a man is made, how a husband and wife fit together. Is it right for her to go to marriage completely ignorant?"

"Of course not, but if your grandmother wishes—"

"Grandmother is wrong." Anya smiled. "Now Valerie knows what to expect of her husband, when she takes one. In the coming days I will teach her all the ways to please a man."

"I don't think that's wise," Julian said softly. "Our society frowns on a woman being . . . too well-taught."

"Do you frown on me?"

"Of course not," he said gently. "But you were raised in another place. When Valerie marries, her husband will have certain expectations."

"He will expect her to be ignorant?"

Julian sighed. "Yes, I'm afraid so."

Again, Anya stroked her fingers down the length of her sculpture. "My way is better."

"I'm beginning to think you might be right," Julian said softly.

He caught sight of Elizabeth Sedley exiting the house by way of the north parlor entrance. The woman smiled widely and approached. "What are you two doing out here?"

"I have taken up sculpting," Anya called brightly.

Julian panicked. He reached across the table, grabbed the clay phallus and tossed it as far into the garden as it would go. It made an ungodly noise as it fell through bushes and then landed on the ground with a thud.

"What was that?" Mrs. Sedley asked.

Anya, learning a bit of tact after all this time, smiled and said sweetly. "A bunny rabbit. However my efforts were not to my husband's liking." She smiled at him, wicked and happy. "He is such a perfectionist."

* * *

Linda Jones

Julian reclined on the bed, waiting patiently for her as she undressed.

"Valerie didn't look directly at me all through dinner," he said. "Nor did she look at Seymour or Peter."

"She is shy," Anya said, turning to face her husband as she removed her gown. "In a day or two she will accept what she has learned and will no longer be afraid."

She never ceased to marvel at Julian's beauty. She liked him best this way, with an evening beard coming in, his hair ever longer and mussed, and without a stitch of clothes on his fine body. She had found the wild man, and she did own him. And she did love him.

"At least she will not be terrified when she marries her William Mathias."

"Do you really think they'll marry?"

She shed the last of her clothing and joined her husband in their bed—wearing nothing but the necklace he had given her, her precious good luck charm. "I do. She is worried that perhaps he only loves her for her money, but we have found a way to discover if this is true or not."

He looked suspicious. "And how will you discover this?"

"When Mathias asks Valerie to be his wife, she will tell him that if she marries him Grandmother will cut her out of the family fortune."

"She will lie," Julian said softly. "I thought you didn't approve of lying."

"It is a very small lie," she said, a kernel of unease

210

rising within her. "And the truth will ease Valerie's heart."

"If it is the truth she wishes to find."

"Do not be so dismal," she said, leaning into him until her bare body lay against his. "Of course he loves her. He has kissed her many times."

"Anya, here a kiss does not have the same meaning as it does on Puerta Sirena." He settled his hand in her hair, in a comforting gesture. "Some men kiss many women, and it means nothing to them."

She began to doubt her plan. "Do you think William Mathias is one of these men?"

"No. He seems very nice, but . . . one never knows."

"Are you one of these men?" she asked, placing her face close to his.

"You know I'm not."

"I know." She kissed him tenderly, and he returned her kiss. "There was a time when I despaired because I had left my home behind, but I despair no more. I am happy because I found you, Julian. My home is wherever you are."

She reached down and caressed him, molding him as she had molded the clay statue he had tossed away, stroking his length with loving fingers. For a man who had once denounced excess, he was quite willing to be led astray.

Lightning flashed and thunder boomed, and Anya was drowning. Salt water filled her mouth, went up her nose, covered her face. When her head broke above the water she took a deep breath that filled her lungs before the sea pulled her down again.

This happened again and again, until she knew she would drown. And then her head broke the water again and she saw him.

"Daddy!"

He swam hard, fighting the sea and the storm to reach her. It seemed she waited forever, but then he was there.

"Baby girl," he said as he swept her up and into his arms.

Anya hung on, throwing her arms around his neck and clinging to him. Wet, hurting all over, she clung to her father. She would never let go. Waves pounded them, tried to suck them down.

Already the storm was dying, moving away from them. The ship was in shambles, those who couldn't swim had been pulled down or swept away. Some had gone down with what was left of the ship. The only living person she could see was her father. She wouldn't let go.

He snagged a part of a large crate that floated on the water and pulled it toward them. "Here you go, baby girl," he said. He tried to sound calm but his voice shook as he helped her crawl atop the crate. "I want you to wait right here."

"No!" she screamed. "Don't leave me."

"I have to go back for your mama."

"Mama." Anya's eyes scanned the ocean, looking toward what was left of the ship. She was too far away to be sure, but she thought she saw a flash of her mother's favorite pink dress, the one she had been wearing when the storm had come.

She wanted her mother, but she was so afraid to be left alone. "Take me with you."

"I can't," her father said. He hauled himself partway up her makeshift raft, cradled her head, and kissed her cheek with his wet, cold lips. "You'll be safer here, and I can swim faster without you." He winked at her, as if nothing was wrong. "I love you, baby girl. I'll be right back with your mama."

"Promise?" she cried as he pushed away from the raft.

"Promise," he called as he moved farther away.

She watched him swim away toward what was left of the ship. The skies cleared, the storm leaving as quickly as it had come, and Anya squinted, straining to see her mother and father amid the waves. And she waited. He had promised he would come back. He promised.

Anya came awake with a start, as the thunder of the present time rumbled above the house. Her body quaked, she felt cold all over, and now she knew why.

"He didn't come back," she whispered. "He didn't come back."

Julian rose slowly beside her. "It's just a storm, my love. Everything's fine." He wrapped his arms around her and lay down, cradling her gently.

"He didn't come back," she whispered against his chest.

"Shhhh." Julian stroked her hair. "It's just a nightmare. I'll protect you."

She raised up and looked down into his sleepy face. "Promise you will never leave me."

"Of course," he said, still more asleep than awake.

"Say it," she insisted.

"I promise, on all that is holy, that I will never leave you."

Anya lowered her head to rest her cheek against Julian's chest. She had wanted to remember, but now she wished she had not. She wanted to run down the stairs and confront her father's portrait in the hallway. He had left her. He had promised . . .

She remembered every detail of that face, now, and she knew she was not recalling the portrait. The small scar he'd gotten in the war, that was not in the portrait. The brilliant blue of his eyes was more gray in the painting she saw and ignored every day. And downstairs, framed and lifeless, he was somber. She remembered the way he smiled.

The remembrance of love that sometimes teased the corners of her brain . . . it was *them*: her mother, her father. The way they had loved one another, the way they had loved her. Her father had swum to his death, attempting to save his wife. Anya had not seen them drown, but she knew they had gone down together.

Remembering hurt. She did not want this pain, she did not want to remember. Anya shut her eyes tight and wished for sleep. And she wished that when she woke in the morning she would forget that she had remembered.

Chapter Thirteen

It was a bit of a shock to wake and find Anya gone. She usually slept well past sunrise, content, warmly cuddled against his side.

Julian jumped from the bed and dressed quickly. Good heavens, more instruction for Valerie! The cousins had probably conspired to wake at the crack of dawn and continue with their lessons. Without stopping to shave or comb his hair, Julian hurried into the hallway. Would they be up on the Captain's Walk or ensconced in one of the quiet downstairs rooms? Thanks to last night's storm there was surely water standing on the Captain's Walk, so he sprinted down the stairs.

And found Anya standing in the foyer, alone, demurely dressed, and staring up at the portrait of her father while her fingers mindlessly caressed the gold rose that dangled from her neck. The expression on her face was so solemn his heart lurched in his chest. "Anya?" he said softly.

She turned around and gave him a smile that did not have her usual radiance. "Good morning." She studied his disheveled condition and the smile became more real.

"Is everything all right?"

She returned her gaze to the portrait. "I do not feel well," she confessed. "And I had the strangest dream last night."

He vaguely remembered waking to find her in a nightmare, pulling her close, and going back to sleep. "You don't feel well? What's wrong?"

She laid a hand on her stomach. "I feel as if I eat anything it will come right back up."

If he didn't know it was impossible, he might optimistically think she was with child. He'd never cared much for children, but the idea of Anya's babies was quite nice. Julian shook off the fanciful thought. He would take Anya, knowing they would never have children, over the most fertile woman on the planet.

"Perhaps some toasted bread . . ."

"I tried that," she said with a wrinkling of her nose. "It came directly back up. Peter was most annoyed."

"I can imagine."

She turned her back on the portrait of the father she did not remember, and came to him. She didn't stop until her arms encircled his waist and her head rested against his chest.

"I am never ill," she whispered. "I do not like the

roiling in my stomach. You are a doctor. Can you make it stop?"

"I'll see what I can find," he promised. "Perhaps you should lie down," he suggested, leading her gently for the stairwell.

"Will you lie down with me?" she asked.

"If you'd like."

They climbed the stairs slowly, arm in arm. Anya really did seem to be ill, and that concerned him. She was sluggish, pensive, and that was not like her at all. Perhaps she had eaten something bad. He tried to recall what she might have eaten the day before that he had not.

"I want you to hold me," she said as they reached their bedroom. "That will make the queasiness go away, I am quite certain."

"I was thinking of peppermint tea," he teased, "but I think I like your remedy better."

They undressed and crawled into bed, and Anya rested her head against his shoulder, breathing deeply and snuggling there where she fit so well. "It was just a dream," she whispered.

He stroked her hair. "Yes, it was." He wondered if her fear of storms would ever completely subside. "Just a dream."

"And you will never leave."

"I will never leave."

Anya breathed deep and almost instantly went to sleep.

Anya knew that she must be very, very ill. She, who had never been infirm in her life, had been sick for

Linda Jones

an entire two weeks! Throwing up every morning, exhausted and sleeping every afternoon. It was horrid. And she knew quite well how her husband detested sick people!

Julian had been very kind to her, though, wiping her face with a cool cloth when she was nauseated, sitting or sleeping with her in the afternoon. Fortunately for them both, she usually felt quite well at night. Fortunately for her, there had been no more storms, no more dreams.

Lunch was over, and she sat in the garden alone. Already she was tired, and looking forward to a nice long nap. She sighed as she looked out over the roses. So many roses. Such a beautiful day. And all she could think of was sleep. A nap! She was quite disgusted with herself.

"My love," Julian said as he approached, "you should not be sitting in the sun. The heat isn't good for you."

"I like the heat," she said, lifting her face to catch the rays. "I like the sun."

When she lowered her face and opened her eyes, she was surprised to see a smile on Julian's face. A smile! He had been worried, in the first few days of her illness, but in the past two days he had been oddly cheerful.

"I am sick, and you smile at me," she said, pouting.

Julian sat in the chair next to hers, reached out and took her hand. He threaded his fingers through hers and held her hand tightly. "I do not think you are sick."

"Not sick! I am ill every day. I am tired in a way I have never been before. I am—"

"With child," he interrupted.

It was cruel of him to tease her this way. "You know that cannot be."

"I know you *believe* it cannot be," he argued. "Who told you that you were barren?"

"King Sebastian's mother, Queen Carola," she said. "Poor Sebastian, every woman he chose for his bed was unable to give him a child. It was a curse, his mother said. Repayment for some sin he committed in another life."

Julian's smile faded, just a little. "And how many women did Sebastian choose for his bed?"

"There was his first concubine Emelda, then me, then Isabele—"

"Anya," Julian interrupted sharply. "Did it ever occur to you that King Sebastian might be unable to father a child?"

Her eyes widened at the suggestion. "Impossible. Sebastian is young and strong, a virile, handsome king. To suggest that he might be unable to sire a child is ridiculous."

Julian gritted his teeth, just a little. "How young or strong or handsome a man is has nothing to do with fertility. Anya," he said, taking her hand and squeezing it. "When was the last time you had your monthly flow?"

She screwed up her nose. "I can't remember, exactly. A couple of weeks before Katherine Mansfield's party, I think."

219

"Anya, the Mansfield party was six weeks ago," Julian said.

Her heart lurched, but she was afraid to hope that he might be right. "If you are correct and I am going to have a child . . ." She looked deep into his dark eyes, trying to read his thoughts. There were moments when she was sure she could do just that. "You said you did not care for children."

"I will care for ours," he assured her. "In fact, I find that I am quite excited by the prospect."

"Really?" she smiled, no longer feeling so tired. "Do you think it is truly possible that I am with child?"

"I'm quite sure you are," he said. "Trust me, Anya. After all, I am a doctor."

"A doctor with no patients," she teased.

"I have one patient, now," he said, tugging on her hand and assisting her to her feet. "No, I have two," he said. When she stood beside him, he placed the palm of one hand over her belly.

"You know," he said as they walked toward the house. "Since you are with child, modern medicine dictates that we abstain from marital relations until well after the birth."

"Hogwash," Anya responded. "Even when I am large with child, there are positions that will accommodate us."

"But . . ."

"It was part of my teaching, *querido*. Do you think I would ever do anything to harm our child?" *Our child.* Those words made her heart swell.

"Of course not," he conceded.

"But perhaps you should be especially gentle with me," she added softly.

"You know I will."

Mrs. Sedley and Valerie were both ecstatic when they heard the news. Seymour was his usual dour self, and actually choked on his brandy when Anya said she'd like to have at least a dozen children.

The entire family congregated in the south parlor. Peter had been standing in the doorway when the announcement was made, and though he tried to disguise a smile and maintain his severe image, he didn't quite manage. There was a softening of his face, a brief half-smile.

This new development changed everything. They couldn't possibly travel, not with Anya in her delicate condition, and not with a newborn baby. Julian's plans would have to be changed, drastically. So why wasn't he disappointed? Why was he so unexpectedly filled with joy?

Anya, once she accepted his diagnosis, was radiantly happy. She had truly thought herself to be barren, since the amazingly manly and handsome King Sebastian couldn't possibly be unable to father a child. Julian tried, most diligently, not to think about that damned king, but now and again the man popped into his mind. He had rather hoped the king was short, skinny, and bow-legged. But according to Anya's wide-eyed description, King Sebastian was none of these things. He was young, and strong, and . . . virile.

When the excitement from their news died down

and Anya had been heartily hugged by her cousin and her grandmother, Valerie stepped forward to make an announcement of her own.

Head high, cheeks flushed pink, she said, "William Mathias has asked me to marry him."

Anya squealed and hugged her cousin. "I knew he loved you for your bosom," she said brightly.

"William Mathias?" Seymour asked with a twist of his small mouth. "He doesn't have any money."

"We don't need money," Valerie said as Julian stepped forward to offer his own congratulations.

"That's easy to say when you have plenty," Mrs. Sedley said tightly. "Valerie, I forbid you to marry this man."

Valerie's bright smile faded quickly. "You can't do that. I'm twenty-three years old and perfectly capable of choosing my own husband."

Mrs. Sedley's face hardened. Her spine went rigid. "If you marry William Mathias, you will do so without my blessing or my money."

Elizabeth Sedley managed the family fortune with an iron fist, and she had no qualms about using her power. Julian's estimation of the woman dropped several notches as she stood there and threatened her granddaughter.

Valerie's head dropped and she stared at the tips of her shoes for a moment. Mrs. Sedley sighed in relief, and Seymour started naming his well-to-do friends who might make suitable marriage material, if Valerie were looking for a husband.

Anya remained silent, her eyes on Valerie. She wanted to speak up—she was almost bursting to ar-

222

gue—but she kept her mouth shut, gripped her hands into small, tight fists, and finally whispered. "It is time," in a voice so low only Julian could hear.

Valerie lifted her head and sniffled, but she leveled her steady gaze on her grandmother. "I'm sorry you don't approve, Grandmother. But I am going to marry William, with or without your blessing."

Elizabeth Sedley took a deep breath and narrowed her steely eyes. "We'll see if your William is so anxious to wed when he finds out you will be going to him without access to the Sedley fortune. When he breaks your heart, I don't want you to come crying to me."

"He will not break my heart."

"No, I will not," a steady voice called. They all turned toward the doorway, where William stood, an almost smug-looking Peter standing behind him.

Mathias smiled at Valerie. "You could have waited for me," he chastised gently.

She smiled back. "Anya shared good news, and I was so anxious to share mine that I couldn't wait any longer."

Mrs. Sedley was not about to stand down. "Mr. Mathias, I have protected my granddaughter from fortune hunters since she was of a marriageable age."

"For that I thank you," Mathias said serenely.

"This is not an idle threat," Mrs. Sedley said tightly. "If you disobey me and marry without my blessing, you will leave this house with nothing."

Mathias wrapped his arm through Valerie's and pulled her close. "Valerie thought you might react that way. We have discussed it, and are in agreement."

"And that agreement is?"

"We don't need your money. We love each other and will elope tonight."

Seymour smiled and stepped forward. "I wish you both all the happiness in the world," he said, shaking Mathias's hand and hugging his sister.

Mrs. Sedley turned pale.

"You will visit often?" Anya said, stepping forward to also hug her cousin.

"Yes, and you must come to visit me. William's farm is not that far away."

"A farm," Mrs. Sedley scoffed. "If you loved Valerie, you would not take her from the comforts she knows to a farm."

William smiled. "I might not have a fortune, Mrs. Sedley, but Valerie will always have a roof over her head, food on the table, and a husband who loves her dearly. She seems to think that will be enough. I'm sorry for you if you don't agree."

Not accustomed to being spoken to so candidly, Elizabeth Sedley blushed for a moment. Then she turned purple.

Mrs. Sedley and Seymour remained in the south parlor while William and Valerie made their way to the door. Anya followed, and Julian stayed close behind her.

"Oh, I will miss you!" Anya said.

"We will visit often," Valerie said. "But I will miss seeing you every day, too."

"I suspect that Grandmother believes you think

she's bluffing," Anya said in a lowered voice. "But when she realizes that you and William are truly in love, she will open her arms to you again."

"I hope so. I don't care about the money, though. She's always held it over my head like she was dangling a carrot before a horse. But I don't need it, not if I have William."

Valerie looked radiantly happy, and so did William. Julian didn't know how Mrs. Sedley could doubt that they loved each other.

"Miss Valerie," Peter called as he hurried down the stairs, "I'm glad I caught you." A stuffed tapestry bag hung from his right hand. "I took the liberty of packing a few of your favorite things. A couple of dresses and your mother's ruby necklace, along with a few other personal items."

"Thank you, Peter," Valerie said as William took the bag. She leaned forward and went up on her tiptoes to kiss the butler on the cheek, bringing a bright red blush to the older man's face.

"It's a pity I never had Betsy teach you to cook," Peter said, trying to sound completely cool and professional. "That skill might come in handy now that you are going to be a wife."

Valerie smiled widely. "I can learn to cook." She cast a meaningful glance at Anya. "I'm going to make a *very* good wife."

William and Valerie made their escape, Peter headed for the pantry, and Julian placed his arm around Anya's waist. "Darling, what was that last fairly wicked glance from Valerie all about?"

"*Cher*, there is much more to being a good wife

than cooking. Why, I cannot cook at all and you do not seem to mind."

"I did tell you to desist in your lessons, did I not?"

"I believe you did."

"And of course, you would never disobey me."

"They were very minor lessons," she explained. "A move she might try, a position she and William might both enjoy, the most effective way to touch a man's—"

"Anya!"

"Well, they are both virgins. It seemed a shame to send them off to the marriage bed with no instruction at all."

Julian sighed. "William will be shocked."

Anya grinned. "William will be most pleased with his new wife."

They headed for the parlor and the unpleasant confrontation that awaited them. "Of that, I have no doubt," Julian muttered.

The next morning, Anya left Julian sleeping and crept down the stairs. She was starving! She had never been so hungry in her life. She found Grandmother in the dining room, having her own breakfast of eggs and ham. Anya took a chair near her grandmother and when Betsy asked what she wanted to eat, she asked for everything in the kitchen. With a smile Betsy, who had no doubt heard the good news, hurried off to comply.

Last night, after Valerie's departure, Grandmother had been livid. For a few volatile minutes she had blamed everyone for her eldest granddaughter's desertion. Then, in her own fanciful way, she had convinced herself that Valerie would soon return, her foolish marriage set aside. Anya had not argued with her grandmother. Not yet.

Grandmother put her fork aside and smiled. "It does my heart good to see you so happy," she said sincerely.

"Thank you," Anya said. "You are very kind."

The woman's blue eyes went misty. "I have waited so long to see this house filled with laughter and children again. I hope you and Julian really do have a dozen children."

"Seymour will not be pleased," Anya said with a small smile.

"Seymour needs to find himself a wife and have a few children of his own. Perhaps then he would grow up."

Betsy arrived with the first course: tea and sweet bread. Freshly prepared ham and eggs and biscuits would follow, she promised. "Seymour seems quite worried that Julian and I will create a brood that will take over the Sedley mansion."

Grandmother sighed in contentment.

"Of course, as soon as the baby is of an age to travel, the three of us will set out and begin Julian's studies." Oh, the sweet bread was delicious.

"You can't travel with a baby," Grandmother said sternly. "You must stay here. I had hoped Julian would stay, too, but if he must travel, you and the baby will live here until he returns."

Anya shook her head. "Thank you for the offer, but I could not bear to be separated from my hus-

227

band for such a length of time." It would be physically painful, she suspected, to watch Julian sail away for parts unknown. "No, we will go with him."

"Perhaps he could be persuaded to stay here and take up his own medical practice."

Anya broke off another piece of sweet bread and popped it into her mouth. Heaven. She had never liked food so much! "No," she said after she swallowed. "He does not like sick people."

Though he had been wonderfully kind to her, and she had been sick for weeks. She was feeling much better today. Julian had said the sickness would pass, and she hoped this was a good sign of days to come.

"Have you and Julian discussed this?"

Anya shook her head. "I know my husband well—I know what he wants."

"I see," Grandmother said softly. "I will so hate to see you leave."

"But we will visit," Anya said brightly. "As often as we can. And there will be other babies. I do not think Julian will want his children born around the world. We will come home to have our babies here."

Grandmother gave her a tight smile. "If you have very many children, you will have to quit traveling and stay in one place. You can't just . . . drag them around the world like little vagabonds."

"Why not?"

The conversation ended when Betsy appeared again, this time bearing a large plate of hot food. When the plate was set before Anya, she lifted her face to smile. "Thank you, Betsy. You are such a wonderful cook."

The woman seemed surprised, but pleased.

When Betsy returned to the kitchen, Anya laid unsmiling eyes on her grandmother. "You must accept Valerie and William. You must give them your blessing."

"I will not," Grandmother answered sternly. "Valerie deserves better than a . . . a farmer."

"But this farmer loves her so much. Can you not see it when he looks at her? William does not care about your money. You should have seen that last night."

"He thinks I'll relent." The older woman nodded her head sharply. "I'm tougher than he thinks."

Anya lifted her head. "Did you plan to buy Valerie a husband as you bought Julian for me?"

"The situation is very different."

"Of course it is. Valerie does not need to have a man bought for her, as I did."

Already, grandmother was shaking her white head. "I only did what I thought was best."

"And I thank you," Anya said softly. "I thank you for the gift of love. If not for you, I never would have met Julian. I would not have known love, and I would not be carrying a child. Love is the grandest gift of all."

Grandmother's expression softened.

"Valerie found her love in a different manner, but it is love all the same. You must forgive her for defying you, and you must also understand that she would be miserable without the man she has chosen. If you love her, you will be happy for her."

"It's not so simple."

"It is," Anya said softly. "It is just that simple."

Chapter Fourteen

She had lost Valerie not much more than a week ago, she did not want to lose Julian, too!

"Take me with you," she pleaded as he rushed about the room, throwing a change of clothing and a comb into a bag. The letter he had just received was lying on the bed. His aunt had taken ill, and a letter came from a concerned neighbor.

"You shouldn't travel," he said sensibly.

She pouted. "You are always telling me what I should not do, and you are always wrong."

"Not always."

Anya plopped down on the bed. Something she did not like welled up inside her. Panic. Fear. This was the way she always felt when she knew a storm was coming. "I am afraid you will not come back," she said softly.

Julian stopped packing, laid his eyes on her, and

smiled softly. "You know I will return as soon as I can. No one else could drag me away from you now. My aunt raised me. I owe her more than I can ever repay, so I have no choice but to see to her well-being. I'll check on her, arrange care for her if necessary, and return to you quickly."

"I know," she said, "but I also fear. How long will you be gone?"

"A few days."

"How many is a few?" How would she sleep without him? What would she do if a storm came?

Julian sat beside her and cupped her cheek in his hand. "I will come back to you as soon as I can." He kissed her quickly. "You know I will."

"But . . ."

He jumped from the bed and pulled her to her feet. "Come with me." He led her out of the room, leaving his bag behind. He walked gingerly down the stairs, ever careful of what he called her delicate condition. Holding her hand, he led her through the north parlor and into the garden. He studied the roses there carefully, as if searching for just the right one. Finally he stopped before a yellow rosebush.

"I suppose you are wearing your knife, against my wishes."

"Of course."

"May I borrow it?"

Anya lifted her skirt and removed the knife from its sheath.

Julian shook his head as he took it from her. "How will I ever convince you that you do not need a weapon in your own home?"

He apparently expected no answer, as he leaned forward to cut a tight yellow bud from the bush. When he handed it to her, she took the stem between two fingers, careful of the thorns. "We will put this in water," he said, "and before the first petal falls I will be home."

"Promise?" she whispered.

"Promise." He offered the knife to her.

Anya laid her hand over his, and over the handle of the knife. "You should keep it," she said. "I will be home and safe. You might have need of a weapon on the road."

"The roads are quite safe," he assured her.

"Still," she said softly. "I will feel better if you keep it." She removed the sheath from her thigh and handed it to him. "I will sleep better at night knowing you have something of me with you."

"My love, I always have something of you with me."

His endearments always made her smile, even in sad times.

Back in the house, she put the rosebud in a slender silver vase, and placed it on a table in the south parlor. She was staring at the flower when Julian came back downstairs with his bag in hand. She did not see the knife, but she knew he wore it. Somewhere.

"My party is in two and a half weeks," she reminded him.

"I will be home long before your birthday. I'll be gone a few days, no more."

She wanted to ask him again to promise, but did not. He would think her silly. She thought herself

232

silly! Julian loved her, he loved their child. He would be home as soon as possible.

He would.

Julian had never given any credence to what was called the sixth sense, but as he took the North Road he felt as if someone watched. The hairs on the back of his neck stood up. His every muscle tensed. It hadn't been dark long, and with any luck he would be at his aunt's house before midnight. He only hoped he could arrange quickly for the care her neighbor insisted she needed. On occasion his gaze twitched to the forest at the side of the road, to the shadows and dangers there. And chills ran down his spine. Why did he feel as if something dark awaited him?

It was leaving Anya that put him on edge, he reasoned. She was carrying his child. She was liable to do anything without his supervision.

And already he missed her. Against all reason, he missed her voice and her smile and the way she touched him.

How could a small slip of a woman force him to so easily abandon his ideals? Easy. His ideals had been false barriers, an excuse to keep anyone who might break his heart at bay. Anya had battered down those barriers, not with her body but with her own vulnerable heart.

A child. He smiled at the very thought, he who had never even remotely desired a family! The thought of his son or daughter growing inside Anya warmed places in his heart that he did not know existed.

As he approached a bend in the road, his thoughts of Anya faded and he glanced to the rear. Again, the hairs on the back of his neck stood. His instincts warned him that someone watched his every move.

Two men on horseback left the shadows of the forest and approached quickly. One of them grabbed Julian by the back of his jacket and hauled him off the saddle. He hit the ground hard. His breath left him, the world went gray, for a moment. By the time he had the strength to move, the larger of the two ruffians was upon him. Julian's hands were wrenched behind his back, and a dark hood was shoved over his head.

The large man kept Julian's arms immobilized, while the other stepped in noisy circles around them both.

Thieves. Murderers? Julian had no idea what he faced. The world was black, thanks to the hood over his head, but his other senses worked well. He smelled the men; their nauseating scent was a mixture of sour clothing and whiskey and something one of them had stepped in, along the way. There was no other sound but his own pounding heart and the shuffle of the pacing thief. There was no promise of rescue in the far-off sound of horses' hooves on the road.

He was tempted to shake the big man off and go for the knife he had tucked in his boot. He didn't. Not yet. The man at his back had him truly disabled with steadfast, meaty hands.

"If it's money you want," he said calmly, "take it. I don't have much, but you're welcome to it."

"Fine horse," the man who circled around Julian said. "Fine clothes. You even smell like money."

Julian didn't respond by noting aloud how they smelled. "Take it all," Julian said, maintaining his calm. "I—" He got no further, as the pacing man hit him over the head with something heavy.

Anya, he thought as his knees buckled and his world went truly black.

The house seemed empty without Julian. Anya paced in the south parlor, her eyes on the yellow rosebud. He had promised he would be back before the first petal fell. Julian always kept his promises. He was kind, and honest, and would never break his word to her.

"Would you like some tea, Miss Anya?" Peter asked, stepping into the room so silently she did not hear him.

Startled, she spun around. "No," she said sharply. Then she relaxed. "But thank you for asking."

"You didn't eat enough at supper," he admonished gently. "A woman in your condition—"

"I will eat more tomorrow," she interrupted.

Peter accepted her proposal and turned to leave the room.

Anya stopped him with a question. "Peter, why are you not married?"

He stood in the doorway, his stiff back to her, for so long that she thought he might not answer. A few weeks ago she would have commanded a response.

But now . . . if he walked away she would not follow and make any demands. Finally he turned around to face her.

"I was married, a very long time ago," he said softly.

"Where is she?"

"Dead," he said succinctly.

Her heart lurched, breaking a little for him. It must be so terrible to bury a loved one with whom you had planned to spend your life. "Did you have children?"

Peter's eyes clouded. "A daughter. She is also dead," he added before Anya could ask.

"I am sorry," Anya said sincerely. "What happened to them?"

A flash of pain crossed his face.

"You do not have to answer," Anya said quickly. "I had no right to ask. Julian always tells me that I should not be so insolent."

"It is not an insolent question," Peter said, stepping out of the doorway and into the room. "I can tell that you ask because you care, not because you are curious. My wife and daughter died while I was at war. They were lost in a fire, the same fire that consumed the small hotel that had been in my family for three generations."

"I am so sorry," she said again, at a loss for proper consoling words.

"It was long ago."

"I cannot imagine that a thousand years would be enough to erase the pain of such a loss."

He cocked his head. "Erase? Never. But I have learned to live with what happened."

"How did you come to work here?" She remembered more and more about this place where she had lived as a child, as the days went by. Happy memories, most of them. Peter was often there.

"Your father and I fought in the same unit. We were traveling toward home together, the damnable war finally over. He was with me when I arrived home and discovered what had happened."

A picture of a smiling blue-eyed man flashed in her mind, and she dismissed it. "My father was your friend?"

"Friend, fellow soldier. Life saver. He refused to leave me behind, even when I insisted that he do so. He practically dragged me away from the grave markers of my wife and child."

"And he brought you here," Anya said softly.

Peter almost smiled. "That he did. I made him think I didn't mind staying in this house, knowing that at some point he would think me recovered from my loss. At that time I would say my good-byes, leave this place, return to the graves of those I loved"—he set his eyes on her—"and join them."

"You planned to take your own life."

"Yes, I did," he said without emotion. "Until one afternoon a red-haired devil of a little girl who had molasses cookie crumbs all over her mouth and hands came up to me, crawled into my lap, and offered me half of her last cookie because I looked like I was hungry."

"Me?"

237

"You. I refused the less-than-appetizing cookie, but you were so insistent you would not be dissuaded. You shoved a corner of that cookie into my mouth, a wide grin on your face, and wiggled it in until I took a bite and you were satisfied." Peter looked suddenly . . . younger. "You giggled. And I didn't want to die anymore."

"Peter . . ."

He continued, uninterrupted. "Your grandmother needed someone to run the household, and managing the Sedley Mansion was not so much different from running the hotel. I did finally save enough money to leave this place and start again, but I didn't. Valerie and Seymour's father took to the sea and was rarely at home. I felt it was my duty to watch over them. And you . . ." He shook his head. "You did not replace my daughter, but you did remind me that there was much beauty in the world."

"No wonder all my memories of you are so warm," Anya confessed as she crossed the room to stand before Peter. She surprised him with a quick hug.

"Miss Anya," he said, taking a step back when she released him. "If I had known you were alive after the shipwreck, I would have looked for you. I would have searched until I found you."

Anya smiled. "I know."

"We were assured that everyone was lost, that there was no possible way for anyone to have survived."

She laid a comforting hand on his cheek. "You are a good man," she said. "Almost as good as my Julian."

238

Peter smiled. "It does me good to see you and Miss Valerie both happily married. You and your cousins have become very important to me over the years." His smile faded. "If only Seymour would straighten up and become a man. . . ." Peter shook his head. "I have just about given up hope for that boy."

Julian waited until they stopped to care for the horses. He could see nothing since the hood remained in place. His head ached since he'd been knocked out, tied up, and tossed over his horse's saddle like a sack of meal.

But he was still alive, thank God. Why hadn't they taken his money and horse and left him unconscious on the road? For no good reason, he was sure. Did they mean to kill him? Or hold him for ransom?

By the rustle of bushes he imagined they were in the forest, on a narrow path. By the absolute silence, he knew they were far from civilization. The kidnappers might decide to kill him at any moment.

Finally they stopped, and one of the men hauled Julian unceremoniously from his horse and dumped him on the ground.

Julian muttered an indignant *ouch* and sat up gingerly. "Could you untie my hands and remove this hood?" he asked in a calm low voice displaying none of his fear. All he needed was to get to the knife he had tucked in his boot. He didn't want to fight the men who had kidnapped him, but if that's what he had to do . . .

"Why would we do that?" one of the thugs asked hoarsely.

"There are two of you and only one of me. You are both armed and I am not. What difference does it make if I can move or not?"

A moment later the hood was jerked from his head.

Julian surveyed the situation quickly. They had stopped in a small clearing. Complete darkness had fallen, but scant moonlight provided enough illumination for Julian to see. One man, the smaller of the two, was tending to the horses. The larger thief glanced down at Julian with the dark hood dangling from his meaty hand.

"What are you going to do with me?" Julian asked calmly.

"I reckon you'll find out soon enough."

Murder, then. "Never done this before, have you?" he asked softly.

"Lots of times," the man said defensively.

"That's odd. You don't look at all like a cold-blooded criminal."

But what did a criminal look like? The man did not respond, and Julian prepared himself to die. If they killed him here and now, no one would ever find his body. What would Anya think when all the petals fell from the rose and he did not return?

"The least you can do is allow me to write a letter to my wife." The man had obliged and removed the hood, but Julian's wrists were still bound behind his back. His ankles were snugly trussed.

"We ain't got no paper and pen here."

"Perhaps you could take me somewhere where I could obtain paper and pen."

The other man joined them, moving forward suspiciously. "What are you two talking about?"

"Nothing. This fella just wants to write his wife a letter. Don't sound like too much to ask, Milton. Maybe we could—"

"No," the smaller man interrupted, slapping his companion on the back of the head. "And you shouldn't have used my name. What if he escapes? He'll be able to tell everyone that Milton and Jeremiah kidnapped him."

"He's tied up," Jeremiah said. "He's not going to escape. We could let him write a letter to his wife."

"What if he tells her in the letter we kidnapped him off the road? He knows our names now, you moron."

"We can read it before we send it on."

Milton clasped two hands to his head. "Neither of us can read!"

"But I know my name when I see it," Jeremiah argued.

Milton shook a bony finger. "Let's get this over and done with, and then go home. I know you're worried about Nellie."

Jeremiah took a deep breath. "Yeah. I have to get home."

"Who's Nellie?" Julian asked softly.

"None of your business," Milton answered.

Jeremiah shrugged his big shoulders. "I don't mind telling him. He doesn't seem like a bad sort." He dropped down on his haunches. The man was inches away, and still Julian's hands were tied behind his back. "Nellie is my wife and Milton's sister. She's

241

due to deliver our first child in just a week or two, and we're all pretty worried."

"Why are you worried?"

The big man went pale. "In the past two months, every woman in our little town that's had a baby has died. Every single one. The midwife says it's just bad luck, but no one knows when the bad luck will end."

Julian met the man's gaze. "A fever, striking three or four days after delivery?" he asked.

"Yeah."

"Headache? Abdominal pain?" Julian asked quickly.

Jeremiah gave him a suspicious and somewhat muted, "That's right."

"Delirium?" he asked in a softer tone, knowing what the answer would be.

The big, obviously frightened man nodded.

Julian took a deep breath. Whatever these men had planned for him, it wasn't good. He had seen their faces, he knew their names. But he wasn't dead yet. "I can save your Nellie."

"What can you do?"

"I'm a doctor. It isn't bad luck that's been killing the women of your town, it's puerperal fever."

Denial was etched on Jeremiah's face and darkened his eyes. "You're making this up. You're just trying to get me to let you go."

"My wife is going to have a child. Our first," Julian said softly. "After what I've heard, I would ride through hell to keep her from bearing a child in your town. It's almost certain death, and I can stop it. But only if you take me there. Kill me, and I can't save her."

Jeremiah cast a silent, questioning glance to his more steadfast partner.

"Don't listen to him," Milton snapped. "He's just trying to get loose so he can run."

"I give you my word, I won't run," Julian said calmly. "I'll make the preparations, deliver your child, and if your wife lives you let me go."

"If she dies?"

"Then you can continue with your plans for me, whatever they are. Trust me, you have nothing to lose."

Jeremiah paced in the near darkness, never moving far from his prisoner.

"What on earth are you mulling over?" Julian asked loudly, losing what was left of his patience. "Are you unwilling to trade my life for that of your wife?"

All was silent for a moment, as the reverberations of Julian's loud voice echoed in the stillness.

"He's got a point," the big man finally said. "And if he can save Nellie . . ."

"I can."

Milton shrugged in reluctant acceptance.

A rush of relief shimmied through Julian's body. He was not free yet, but he had arranged a reprieve. As long as he could save Nellie, he might even live long enough to see his own child come into this world. "But if she's due to deliver in a week or two, we should hurry."

Jeremiah pulled a knife from the sheath at his

waist, a much larger knife than the one Julian had tucked in his boot. "You promise you won't try to run?"

"You have my word."

The big man hauled Julian to his feet, spun him around, and cut the ropes that bound his wrists. The ropes at his ankles were severed next.

Milton had to have his say in the matter. "Try to run, and I will catch you and make you wish you'd died a quick death."

"Understood," Julian said as he turned about and began to rub his raw wrists.

"And if Nellie dies after you've gone and gotten our hopes up, I'll kill you so slowly you'll beg for death."

Julian swallowed hard. "I'll do everything I can."

The knife was in his boot, accessible and deadly. Yes, it was small, and yes, he had no desire to take a life. He was a doctor, after all, sworn to heal, not to hurt. Still, he wondered if these thieves had any honor in their malodorous souls. He might save Jeremiah's Nellie, and then lose his life, anyway. If he were going to run, this was the time. He had the element of surprise and the darkness of the forest on his side.

But one thing stopped him from attempting escape. In two months not a single mother had survived delivering a child in the small town where these outlaws lived. He could change that. He could stop the horrific cycle of puerperal fever.

"But you will allow me to write my wife a letter, letting her know I have been delayed." He'd have to ask Anya to send someone, Seymour or Peter, perhaps, to check on Aunt Helen.

"Sure," Milton said with another shrug of his bony shoulders. "My wife can read. She'll check it over to make sure you don't say anything that might give us away."

"Do I have your word that you'll let me go if I save Nellie?"

"Sure," Milton said, just as nonchalantly.

The word of a kidnapper and thief, and possibly a murderer, wasn't much, but it was all Julian had.

Chapter Fifteen

The first petal fell. She had known the day was coming, as each morning the rose bloomed fuller, and fuller; as the petals opened wide. The first petal fell, and still Julian was not back.

Anya clenched her fist and fought away the tears. Why was she surprised? Her husband did not like sick people. He did not want children. He had only married her for his ship and the ability to travel where he wished. One could not travel as they wished with a pregnant wife.

She had been so worried when he did not return within days as promised, that she had asked her grandmother to send someone to inquire about Julian's aunt. The woman must be very ill, Anya had thought, to keep Julian away for so long. Just days ago Anya had received word that Julian's aunt had never been ill at all. She was alive and well and had not seen her nephew in months. The letter had been false, Julian's way of sneaking away.

At her request, Seymour checked with the head of operations of Sedley Shipping and learned that Julian had presented himself within two days of his departure from this house and demanded passage to Australia.

Grandmother tried to be cheerful. They had known all along that Julian wished to continue his grandfather's studies. Anya felt silly for having told her grandmother, so confidently, that she would travel with Julian when the baby was old enough. Julian had never promised her such a thing, they had never discussed the future. The matron of the house tried to put a happy face on the situation. Julian was gone, but they had a baby on the way, a child who would fill the house with joy and love.

No one else was up and about yet, though Anya very faintly heard Betsy in the kitchen as she prepared breakfast. Anya stood in the south parlor and suffered this particular heartbreak alone, as was fitting.

Men who promised not to leave always lied. Why had she believed Julian? Why had she let herself love him? He could have told her the truth, instead of lying so well. He could have said good-bye. To make her wait and think he would be back, to promise . . . it was the cruelest thing he could have done.

She picked up the fallen petal and slipped it into the pocket of her gown. Somewhere deep inside herself she thought that maybe everyone was wrong. That maybe she was wrong. There was an explana-

Linda Jones

tion for everything that had happened, and Julian would be back. If not before the first petal fell, then before the last.

In a matter of days she would celebrate her birthday. Uncle Ellis was set to arrive that day or the next, if all went well. Grandmother would be very disappointed if her son did not arrive on time for the party. She was so looking forward to seeing her only living child.

Grandmother still had not forgiven Valerie for eloping with William, but she had invited the newlyweds to the party at Anya's insistence. In time, she would see that the couple had been right in defying her for their love. Anya hoped that time came soon. She missed seeing Valerie every day. Her promised attendance at the party was all that kept Anya on her feet.

Julian had done his job well. When the time for the party came she would know what to say, what not to say, how to dance, how to dress . . . and when that day came she would be a very rich woman. She did not need Julian DeButy, or any other man.

She angrily wiped away a tear. She would not cry, not for *him.* Not for anyone.

She blindly worked the clasp at the back of her neck, and removed the necklace Julian had given her. Without studying it, she dropped the rose and chain into her pocket, where it rested with the soft petal she carried there.

The people of the small town of Miller's Crossroads were cooperative. Milton and Jeremiah took turns keeping watch since they were afraid Julian would run at the first opportunity, but they needn't have feared. There was much work to be done here. Since they had allowed him to pen a letter to Anya telling her that he was well and would return as soon as possible, and to ask that someone from the household check on Aunt Helen, he had quit worrying so much about the time that passed.

The midwife had been furious at his interference, unwilling to listen to his explanations about the infectious disease she carried from woman to woman. She still preferred bad luck as an explanation for the deaths among her clients. But she did join him in cleaning all her supplies, and in gathering what was needed to make sure the epidemic of child-bed fever came to an end.

Chloride of lime was needed most badly, but he also requested turpentine and ordered a thorough scrubbing of Jeremiah's home. He also insisted that the midwife not touch Nellie, or any other pregnant or delivering woman for at least one month.

They were trying to keep his presence a secret— which was only natural since he had been kidnapped. Still, the midwife knew he was there, as did several of Nellie's friends. They had all been sworn to secrecy.

He had been living in a small house with Jeremiah and his wife, sleeping on a pallet on the floor, eating well, making plans to improve the conditions in Miller's Crossroads. What a change from the Sedley mansion! Jeremiah's house consisted of one large room, with a kitchen and table in one corner, a bed in another, and two faded, padded chairs by the fireplace. This home was simple and overly warm, providing only the bare necessities for its inhabitants.

Jeremiah's wife was healthy, young and full of life, and huge with child. She was all belly. When Julian considered slipping past his guard and away in the night, he thought about Nellie. She deserved to live to raise her child.

But he wished she would deliver soon. He wanted to get back to his own pregnant wife.

Jeremiah came home surlier than usual. At least this time he came alone. Julian didn't trust Milton. If anyone saw him out of this predicament alive, it would be Jeremiah.

"What's wrong?" Nellie asked as she laid three plates on the small roughhewn table.

"Nothin'," Jeremiah grumbled.

Nellie gave her gruff husband a smile. "I can always tell when something's wrong."

Jeremiah sat down at the head of the table, more surly than ever. "Milton is going to rob this guy over on the North Road. Seems some merchant fella always comes through with a bunch of money on Monday afternoons. Milton wanted me to tie the doc here up and go with him, since he expects things might get rough, but I told him I didn't trust the doc enough to leave him unguarded."

"That's not the whole truth, though, is it Jeremiah?" Julian asked.

The big man laid his eyes on him and scowled. "You think you know what I'm thinking?"

"Of course not, but I do know you well enough to know that you're not a thief at heart."

Nellie blushed. "I tried to tell him that when he hooked up with Milton. He's just so sure there's big money in being an outlaw, but Milton has been doing this for years, and he doesn't have nothing."

"Worse," Julian said calmly, "you risk your life every time you go to work. And I can't imagine what you tell a child when he or she asks where Father goes when he leaves the house."

Jeremiah scowled, but it was clear to Julian that he had suffered with those same thoughts before.

"You're a big man," Julian said as he reached for the potatoes. "Have you ever given thought to working the land? Raising crops or working with horses, perhaps?"

"Takes money to buy a farm. Takes more than that to buy horses."

Julian smiled. "My wife's family is wealthy. I'm sure I could arrange a loan."

"Really?" Nellie asked brightly.

"I don't want charity," Jeremiah grumbled.

"If you pay back the loan, it's not charity at all," Julian assured him. "And a farm is a fine place to raise a family."

Before they had finished dinner, someone pounded on the door, opening it and walking inside long before Jeremiah could rise and see who was calling.

A harried woman burst into the room and laid her frantic eyes on Julian. "Are you the doctor?"

"Th-there's no doctor here," Jeremiah said ner-

251

vously. "Who said there was a doctor here?"

"Milton, and Miss Hattie, and Nellie," the woman snapped. She laid her eyes on Julian again. "My boy fell. His leg's broken, I know it is. It looks just awful."

"It might not be broken . . ." Julian began optimistically.

"The bone's sticking through his skin."

He had no choice, no matter what he felt or wanted, but to see to the boy. With any luck, it wouldn't be as bad as the woman said.

"I'll need a place to work," Julian said, coming to his feet and rolling up his sleeves.

"Since the inn closed last winter it's been empty."

"It'll do," Julian said, "but I want it cleaned first."

Nellie nodded knowingly. "The doc is a real stickler for cleanliness."

"And Doc," the woman said as together the four of them exited Jeremiah's small house. "My sister has the most awful cough. . . ."

From the safety of her room, Anya heard the chatter of voices below. Her family was here, of course. Valerie and William, Seymour, Grandmother, and the newly arrived Uncle Ellis, who clearly preferred life at sea to spending the week with his family.

But others had begun to arrive. She heard them, laughing and talking in high, bright voices. They were all waiting for her. How many waiting below had been at the Mansfield party? How many had heard Margaret March call Anya a savage?

She told herself it did not matter. If Julian stood beside her she would not be nervous at all, but he was not here. He was at sea, traveling to an exotic destination where he could study life from afar without being sullied by it.

One last time she studied her reflection in the long mirror. Her gown was a becoming shade of sea green, her hair had been flawlessly styled, and the gems at her throat, diamonds and emeralds, were elegant and heavy. She did not look like a savage. She did not look like her heart was broken.

A knock on her door made her heart skip a beat. A moment later it swung open and Valerie stepped inside. "Are you ready?"

Anya nodded.

Valerie could not hide her happiness. "Father likes William," she revealed in a lowered voice. "He didn't exactly say so, but I can tell."

"That is wonderful." Anya tried a small, encouraging smile.

"Come," Valerie said sweetly. "It's time for you to make an appearance at your birthday party."

"I will be right down," Anya said. "I just need to . . ." *Steel my heart. Gather my courage. Cry, one more time.* "To fix my hair."

"Your hair is perfect," Valerie said, crossing the room to take Anya's hand and guide her toward the door.

Downstairs, the bell chimed again as another guest arrived. How many people had Grandmother invited?

Anya allowed Valerie to lead her down the stairs. She had never been afraid before. Why did her heart pound now? Why did she feel that Valerie was her only friend, her only ally? Even together, they could not fight the vultures who circled in the rarely used ballroom.

When Anya and Valerie walked into the ballroom, heads turned in their direction. Some people smiled, others watched as if waiting for the evening's entertainment. Anya did not smile back, and she had no intention of providing entertainment for those vultures who awaited her downfall.

She did not care what they thought of her. They could call her savage and whore; they could laugh at her behind her back and she would not care. But she did care what they said about her child. To her child. Growing up without a father would be difficult enough without being hampered in other ways.

This child would be accepted, where she had never been. This child would never know the pain of being different from everyone else. He or she would be welcomed in any home, in any circumstance. And that meant Anya would be on her best behavior tonight. Tonight and always.

As soon as everyone in attendance assured themselves that Anya was properly dressed and well-behaved, they returned to their activities. They drank and ate, talked and fanned away the September heat. When the music began, they danced. Anya herself drifted through the crowd, never remaining in one place too long. Restlessly, she walked past dancers and those who visited with neighbors they saw too infrequently. When she was asked to dance, she politely declined, citing a sore foot. A lie, but Julian had told her that sometimes a kind lie was better than the ugly truth. Had he thought his own lies kind?

The party was well underway when the door chime sounded in the distance. It was hard to hear over the roar of the party, but Anya heard. And wondered. A part of her heart even hoped.

She was watching the doorway when the newcomer appeared. Her heart lurched in disappointment and an uneasy fear as Julian's *puta,* decked out in garnet, made her entrance. It was more than Anya could bear, to have this woman in her home. She made her way to the door with every intention of throwing Margaret out. Peter would see to it, she thought, though as her eyes scanned the room she saw the butler nowhere.

Seymour, coming from the other side of the room, reached Margaret first. He took the harlot's hands in his, leaned forward, and kissed her on the cheek.

"Why are you here?" Anya asked without preamble as she reached the couple.

Margaret and Seymour held hands and smiled together. "I invited her," her cousin answered in a lowered voice.

"I—" Anya began, intent on uninviting the detested woman.

"Seymour and I are engaged," Margaret interrupted smugly. "Happy birthday, dear. You're the first to hear the happy news. We're going to be one big, happy family."

He had fully expected to be home by now, attending Anya's party, caring for her and their child as no one else could.

Linda Jones

"Push," he said, leaning over to take a look at Nellie's sweating face. "You're almost finished."

The raised bed in the inn lobby that had become his office was well lit, with a number of lanterns scattered around in a semi-circle. The place was clean, at least, and the midwife had not touched Nellie since Julian's arrival. The labor had been long, but Jeremiah's young wife was strong and healthy, and all would be well. It had to be. Milton and Jeremiah awaited the outcome outside the door, armed with loaded pistols and sharpened knives.

Nellie's sister Mary and her sister-in-law Phyllis, Milton's wife, looked on. They had done all they could. Mary held Nellie's hand while the others stood back and waited.

"I'm dying," Nellie said hysterically. "I know I am."

"You are not dying," Julian assured her.

Mary, who had seen too many women die in the past two months, sniffled loudly.

"But it hurts," Nellie moaned.

"I know it does," he said calmly.

There had been a time when the prospect of delivering a child, unassisted, would have made him break out into a sweat of his own. In the hospital where he had worked after his schooling was finished, there had always been other, more well-trained doctors looking on or assisting. He had never delivered a child without someone looking over his shoulder.

But in the last two weeks he had seen and done much more. He had set a nasty broken leg, removed a bullet from Milton's arm, and cleaned and bandaged a child who had fallen off the roof of his home, delivering a lecture on the folly of foolhardy climbing as he worked. He had treated a number of coughs and bellyaches, cleaned a few infected wounds, and lanced more boils than he cared to remember.

And in the process he'd set about cleaning up this town. He'd visited the local general store and café and made suggestions. He lectured those who came to him about cleaning up their homes, and this town in general. Already he could see the change. The town was fresher, sweeter, and Jeremiah and Milton, regularly bathed at their wives' insistence and wearing clean clothes, smelled better.

Miss Hattie, the midwife who had at first rejected Julian's opinion that she had been spreading the puerperal fever from one new mother to another, listened carefully to his lectures on cleanliness and sterilization. She had her own supply of chloride of lime for disinfecting, and when a month had passed without a delivery, she would be able to resume her activities.

Perhaps he had been kidnapped and threatened with death in order to arrive, but when he left this town it would be a much safer place. There was some comfort in that fact.

Nellie's child was born into his hands. A large child, Jeremiah's son came into the world squalling. Julian cleaned the baby quickly and placed him at his mother's breast.

"He's beautiful, isn't he?" Nellie asked softly.

"Yes, he is."

Linda Jones

The other ladies looked him over and agreed that he was a fine, healthy child.

Julian prayed he had done everything correctly. Puerperal fever usually set in within three days of delivery. Jeremiah and Milton had decided that they would release Julian four days after the birth of the child.

In four days, he was going home.

"He cannot marry her," Anya whispered as she and Valerie claimed a quiet corner. "If he marries her, they will live here! I will not live in the same house with Margaret March."

Valerie wrinkled her nose. "Maybe it won't be too bad."

Anya shook her head. "Not too bad? You expect me to live in the same house with Julian's whore?" There was only one thing she could do. She would return to the island where she had passed most of her life.

It would not be a bad life for her child, she mused. And it would definitely be preferable to living at Rose Hill with Margaret and Seymour! This was a big house, but it was not nearly big enough! Even if she thought she could bear to live in the same house with the harlot, she was determined that her child would not grow up under the same roof as that hateful woman.

Anya danced once with her Uncle Ellis. He did not say much, and he always seemed to be looking around the house as if he had lost something and couldn't remember where he had put it. In less than

258

a week he would set sail, and even though he was kind and warm, she got the feeling he would be glad to leave this place and get back to the sea, where he belonged.

Grandmother said her eldest son had never recovered from his wife's death. That he hid from his pain by living at sea, by devoting himself to his work. Anya understood. She had no work to lose her heartache in, but she did have her child. The child she had thought she would never have would be her life.

It occurred to her, as the dance with Uncle Ellis ended, that he could take her with him. He could take her to the island she considered her home. She would not have to say good-bye to anyone, she could simply . . . disappear.

She was twenty-one, a large portion of the Sedley fortune was now hers . . . and she did not want or need it. Without Julian, this place was unbearable.

An excited murmur worked through the crowd like a wave. Voices rose. A woman raised a limp hand to her forehead and fainted into her husband's arms. Anya could not see what they all looked at, so she worked her way through the crowd and toward the wide ballroom entrance.

When she saw the man who stood there, she walked past the last party guest to stand before him, dropped quickly to her knees, and placed her forehead on the floor.

"Your majesty," she whispered.

"Anya, stand up," he said lowly, his voice only slightly more accented than her own. "This is America."

259

Linda Jones

She lifted her head and saw the large offered hand before her. Laying her own hand on his palm, she stood slowly.

As always, Sebastian was decked out in a loincloth, a feathered necklace, and the crown that marked him as the King of Puerta Sirena. His dark blond hair fell straight and long down his back. His dark blue eyes danced with humor. His bare, muscled chest was bronzed by the sun, and the royal rose oil that was applied regularly by his servants made that chest and his muscular arms glisten.

"Why are you here?" she whispered.

He smiled, flashing straight white teeth on his handsome sun-darkened face. Everyone was listening. You could not even hear the rustle of skirts or the sounds of the guests breathing.

"I have come to take you home."

Chapter Sixteen

Anya led the way across the house to the south parlor. Sebastian trailed behind her. His mother, Queen Carola, had traveled to America with him, along with half a dozen servants. The procession was regal and colorful and decadent.

King Sebastian was dressed as always, but the others had made some small concessions to the culture into which they had traveled. Queen Carola and the two female servants wore simple shifts made of silk. Their arms were bare, and as the shifts ended just beneath the knee their limbs and feet were uncovered, but they were not naked. The four male servants were bare chested, but they wore knee-length skirts more substantial than their normal island loincloths. The skirts were made of the same colorful silk, in red, blue, green, and yellow.

Seymour and Peter and William held back the

party guests who wanted to follow the half-naked king and see what transpired. They had their work cut out for them.

Anya had just decided to return to Puerta Sirena, so why did Sebastian's appearance and his insistence that he was there to take her home shake her so? Her heart pounded too hard, her mouth went dry.

In the south parlor, Sebastian took the largest, most luxuriously padded chair available. Queen Carola stood behind the chair as if protecting her son, a severe expression on her beautiful face. Her dark brown hair fell straight and silky to her waist, the green eyes she had inherited from a French pirate father were bright and intelligent. Like the other females, she wore a red silk shift, but she had added a crown and a necklace of coral to her ensemble.

Anya insisted that the servants wait outside the parlor, and she closed the door and instructed them to wait there.

When she turned back around, leaning against the door for support, she found Sebastian smiling at her again. His feet were planted flat on the floor, his knees spread wide. He had found his throne and was as at home here in the Sedley mansion as he was in his own island kingdom.

"I never should have given permission for you to leave the island. The giving of that permission was a mistake and is hereby rescinded."

Anya's heart lurched. "I would like very much to go home."

His smile widened.

DeButy & the Beast

"But some things have changed," she added quickly. "I have taken a husband."

Sebastian's smile faded quickly. "A husband. Without asking my permission?"

"He has put me aside," Anya explained succinctly, "but in my heart he is still my husband. In my heart, he will always be my husband." No matter where he was, no matter what he did . . . "If I do go home, it will not be as one of your concubines. Even if he does not want me," she admitted softly, "I will remain loyal to my husband."

Sebastian raised his eyebrows in a rakish and very royal way. "Do you expect me to believe that you, Anya, a goddess of love, will live the rest of your life without a man?"

"If I must."

Sebastian was not overly perturbed. "You will change your mind," he said. "When your heart is healed."

"There is more," she said quickly.

"More?"

Anya glanced at the queen. "I am going to have his child."

The room was eerily silent for a long moment.

"But you are barren," Sebastian said.

Anya licked her lips. "Apparently I am not."

Sebastian and Queen Carola knew the significance of this news, and they quickly came to the same conclusion Julian had. If Anya was able to bear a child, then it was very possible that Sebastian was infertile.

"A miracle," the queen said with a tight smile.

"The child you carry is a miracle, and a blessing for your devotion to King Sebastian."

"Yes," Anya agreed quickly. She laid her eyes on Sebastian. "Perhaps I can return to Puerta Sirena in another role. As a teacher, perhaps. Have you ever heard of Shakespeare?"

"No. Should I meet him?"

"He is dead, Sebastian," Anya said, slipping into their easier mode of friendship, now that the difficult news had been shared. "He has been dead a very long time. But he wrote the most fabulous plays. Oh, we could have plays of our own!"

"Perhaps." He looked her up and down. "Why do you wear so many clothes?"

"It is the way things are done here," she explained simply.

"The fabric is very pretty."

"It itches," she revealed in a confidential voice.

Sebastian smiled, and in that instant Anya realized that she had missed him. Not as a lover, but as a friend.

"I have an idea," the queen said softly. "Anya, you wish to come home."

"Yes."

"You could come home as queen."

"But . . ."

"No one but the three of us need know that the child you carry is not Sebastian's."

Anya shook her head vigorously. "I cannot tell that lie. I will not—"

"Your child will one day be queen or king. You would deny your son or daughter such a gift?"

Sebastian was Queen Carola's only child. If he did not have an heir, Carola's line would die with him. Who would rule, then? There might be war, among those who thought they had a claim to the throne, or who wished to take it by force.

"But it is not true," Anya whispered.

"If I say it is true, it is true," Queen Carola said regally. "If I say this child is Sebastian's, it is Sebastian's. I hereby declare your marriage undone." She waved her hand. "You will marry Sebastian, and the throne of Puerta Sirena will have an heir."

Sebastian was king, but on Puerta Sirena the power had always passed through the women of the family that had ruled for more than a hundred years. Terrence Whetherly had become king because he married Queen Carola. If they had had a daughter, it would be she who ruled. Queen Carola was mother of the king, her word was law. And she had just declared Anya and Julian's marriage dissolved.

In a matter of hours, Sebastian had turned the Sedley household upside down, even more completely than Anya had when she arrived. He chose his bedroom, and Queen Carola chose hers. A large chamber was chosen for the servants to share, where they would be close by.

They decided to stay for a few days, in order to give Anya time to think over their offer. Besides, Sebastian had taken quite a liking to the comforts of the Sedley mansion.

Grandmother magnanimously and hopefully offered the services of her tailor, but Sebastian refused to wear anything other than his loincloth and crown and one or two of his favorite necklaces.

Anya, who had still not given an answer to the queen's proposal, was more distressed by the fact that Margaret had moved in than she was by the presence of a primitive royal court in her grandmother's home. Whenever she turned around, Margaret was there. Watching. Smirking. Planning something, of that Anya was certain.

Peter was quite put out by the new demanding guests. He seemed particularly annoyed with the queen, who was always tracking him down with one request or another. Sometimes he saw her coming and turned quickly, heading in the opposite direction. Sometimes she followed.

Nothing disturbed Sebastian. He seemed not to care that Anya could not decide if she wanted to be his queen or even that it looked as if he would never father a child of his own. He seemed content, as long as he was well fed and his personal servants saw to his needs. Every morning they rubbed his body down, using the special oil they had carried with them for that purpose. For the past two days this had happened late in the morning, in the garden where his bare skin could catch the rays of the sun.

Yesterday Anya had caught Margaret skulking in the north parlor, watching the procedures in the garden. When the harlot had turned about and found that she was not alone, she had said that Anya's king was an animal, and should be kept in a zoo. The look she cast at Anya said what Margaret did not say aloud. That no matter how finely she dressed or how well she behaved, Anya was an animal, too.

Anya would never like Margaret, but she was beginning to understand the woman. Margaret wanted desperately to be loved. She craved affection from men, and became whatever the object of her interest wanted or needed. For Julian, she had pretended to be his ideal—sweetly seductive. With Seymour, she let her more manipulative personality traits run free. She flirted subtly with Peter, who ignored her, and if there was a man in her range of vision he had her attentions. Apparently no one man was enough; Margaret always wanted more. If there was anything at all likable about Margaret, Anya might even feel sorry for her. For some reason, the unpleasant widow was starving for love. And Anya suspected no amount of adoration would be enough.

Mealtimes were especially stressful. The food was strange, there was never enough of it to suit Sebastian, and Grandmother was fidgety. Having two scantily clad savages at her table, with six more standing close by to see to their needs, was almost more than she could take.

Uncle Ellis, who had surely seen many things, was not at all perturbed by the presence of their visitors. Seymour seemed more amused than disturbed, and spent most of his time fawning over Margaret.

Anya was lost. Where was home? Not at the Sedley mansion. Not as queen of Puerta Sirena. She had come to the conclusion that her home was wherever Julian happened to be, and he did not want her.

If she stayed here, she would forever listen for Julian's return. She would forever wonder if he would

267

Linda Jones

come home to her. And as long as there were people like Margaret around, no one would ever forget that she had once been a king's concubine.

Queen or pariah? It was not much of a choice.

Sebastian insisted on sitting next to Anya as they shared lunch with the family. Huge bowls of chicken and dumplings were carried to the table. The aroma was heavenly; at last Sebastian seemed satisfied.

"People here are very strange," he said conversationally, stirring his food and glancing down at Anya. "You have been here for a long time. Do you understand them?"

"No," she said succinctly.

"They seem to know nothing of love," he said as he began to eat.

"I have often had the same thought," she said.

If those around them listened, they showed no sign. Anya no longer cared.

"I think the women here have no instruction on the art of making love," he said.

Anya glanced at Sebastian. "This is true. How did you discover this sad fact?"

He waggled a spoon at Margaret without lifting his eyes from his bowl. "This one does not seem to know the simplest things. Not even the *Torcere de Flavia!*"

Margaret choked on her wine, and Seymour went white.

"This is quite good," Sebastian remarked, lifting another spoonful of chicken and dumplings to his mouth.

"Margaret," Seymour whispered hoarsely. "What is he talking about?"

"I . . . I . . . I have no idea," she finally said.

Sebastian looked up and smiled. "Do not be ashamed. With the proper instruction, I am sure you could become an adequate lover."

"Margaret!" Seymour whined loudly.

"I . . . I went into his room by mistake, thinking it was yours," she hissed. "And he . . . he attacked me. He grabbed me, and . . . and threw me on the bed . . . and—"

Sebastian continued to eat, unperturbed. "I have never attacked a woman. She came into my room and begged me to make love to her, so I did." He glanced at Seymour. "I thought you had sent her as a gift, and so in keeping with your traditions I accepted her offer."

Grandmother stood. "I'm going to my room," she said softly. "Wake me when my home is safe once again for an old woman." She left the room with a regal air of her own.

Sebastian glanced down at Anya and smiled. "I am sure she meant well, but she lay there like a fish on the beach, with the occasional flop as she died." He demonstrated with his hand. And smiled.

"I never!" Margaret said, jumping to her feet. "How dare you?"

Sebastian ignored her. "If I did not think it would have been thought inhospitable, I would have kicked her out of the bed after the third time."

"The third time?" Seymour groaned.

"She . . ." Sebastian knit his brow and stared at Margaret. "What is your name again? I cannot remember."

Linda Jones

"You're a vile savage," Margaret seethed.

Sebastian grinned. "That is what she said last night, too. Many times. She seemed to like vile savages, then."

"Seymour," Margaret said tightly. "Defend me. Kick this this—"

"Vile savage," Sebastian supplied as he began to eat again.

Margaret bristled. "Throw him out of our house. He is a coarse, uncivilized, liar."

Seymour leaned back in his chair, pale and tight-lipped. "No, my dear. I think it's you who should be packing." He glanced up at her. "You betrayed me. You offered your body to a savage."

"A king," Sebastian said with a wag of his spoon. "A savage *king*."

"And don't think everyone we know won't hear about this," Seymour finished. He did not look at all hurt. He looked angry, and vindictive.

Margaret swayed on her feet. "You wouldn't."

"Of course I would. Good God, the servants are all listening from the kitchen, you know. I'd be surprised if word hadn't already begun to spread."

Margaret took a step back.

"Run far and fast," Seymour said softly. "And maybe the tales of your behavior in this house won't catch up with you."

Anya expected Margaret to do just that. Run. But she turned to Sebastian with a girlish trembling lip. "You could take me with you," she said.

Sebastian seemed to consider the offer, for a moment. Then he shook his head. "You are too un-skilled to be my concubine."

Margaret went red in the face.

"But I can always use another servant," he contin-ued. "Someone who will wash my clothes. Clean my hut."

"Do these servants rub that oil onto your body?" Margaret asked, wide-eyed.

"Only those who are specially chosen."

"Could I be chosen?"

"Perhaps one day—what is your name again?"

Anya stifled a smile. "Margaret," she supplied softly.

"Ah," he said with a smile. "If you serve me well for many years, Margaret, then you might be allowed to undertake that task on occasion."

Margaret looked almost smug. Like it or not, Anya knew the way the woman's mind worked. She actu-ally thought that she could seduce Sebastian if she had the time and opportunity. Apparently she had set her sights on Sebastian now, and would become the woman she thought *he* wanted her to be. A wan-ton. A passionate woman. A love goddess. No doubt Margaret had her sights set on the throne at his side, as well as his affection.

"If she goes to Puerta Sirena, I will not," Anya said simply. "I do not like her."

"Then she will not go." Sebastian dismissed Mar-garet with a wave of his hand. "I did not want to take her, but did not want to be rude."

"He doesn't even want you to clean out his royal

271

chamberpot," Seymour said loudly as Margaret left the room.

When the woman was finally gone, Seymour laid his eyes on Anya. "What's this about you going to Puerta Sirena?"

Anya lifted her eyes and straightened her spine. "Sebastian has asked me to be his queen." She took a deep breath. "I have decided to accept his offer."

"It's been four days," Julian argued, his eyes on the barrel of Milton's revolver. "Nellie and the baby are doing fine. You gave me your word . . ."

"I changed my mind," Milton snapped. "My wife says we need a doctor here in Miller's Crossroads, and you seem to be a good one. You can just stay right here."

The three of them met in the inn, where Julian now lived as well as practiced. The room upstairs was comfortable, but it was also temporary. Anya was waiting for him, and he thought of nothing more than getting home.

He clenched his fists. "You can't force me to stay here."

Milton aimed his six-shooter at Julian's foot. "I think I can."

"Now, Milton," Jeremiah began.

"Shut up!"

"My wife will be expecting me," Julian said calmly. "I told her in the letter that as soon as I delivered the baby . . ."

"This letter?" Milton asked, taking the note Julian had written from an inside pocket of his leather vest.

Dirty, folded in a smallish oblong shape, it looked very little like the note he had so carefully penned weeks ago. "Did you really think I'd deliver it to her personally?"

"You said you'd leave it at her house," Jeremiah said.

"Well, I decided it wasn't such a good idea."

"Let the doc go," Jeremiah insisted.

"If we let him go," Milton said testily, "the man who hired us will ask for his money back. I don't know about you, but I already spent that money."

"The man who hired you?" Julian repeated softly. "I thought you two were working on your own. You were going to rob and kill me, right?"

Jeremiah shrugged. "Well, no. We usually just do the robbing part. And we weren't supposed to kill you, we were supposed to get you on a ship headed to the opposite side of the world." He looked sheepish. "Sorry."

"You were trying to shanghai me? Who hired you?" Julian asked, his worst fears riding to the surface.

"I'm not tellin'," Milton said with a smirk.

The knife Anya had given him before he'd left the Sedley mansion sat on a table six feet away. He had not been tempted to use that weapon on a human being in the weeks he'd been here, but at the moment he wished it was in his hand.

The people of Miller's Crossroads had given him a gift. He could heal. He could cure. He had a power in his hands that was more potent than he'd ever imagined. And he was no longer afraid. With that power, how could he possibly wish to injure a man as he now wished to injure Milton?

Easy. He had no personal enemies. He'd never done anything important or fearless enough to make an enemy. The only reason for anyone to try to get rid of him would be to get him away from Anya. So she'd be unprotected. And he would do anything to protect Anya.

Julian reached out and grabbed the six-shooter before Milton knew what was happening. He twirled it in his hand, gripped it easily, cocked the hammer, and pressed the muzzle against Milton's chest, there above his very tiny heart. "Oh, yes you are. You're going to tell me everything."

Chapter Seventeen

Anya stared down at the day dress that had been spread neatly across the bed. The blue, frilly gown suddenly looked like a monster. A monster that threatened to swallow her alive.

Without another thought she went to her chest of drawers, opening the one that contained her scarves. She simply picked two from the top, a green and a red silk that Grandmother would insist did not match.

Once the scarves were in place, she opened the jewelry box Grandmother had given her. She donned it all, pendants and bracelets and rings encrusted with many jewels. If she were to be Queen of Puerta Sirena, she must dress like a queen. If she were to leave the woman she had become for Julian behind, it was just as well that she start now.

Scarves in place and jewelry dangling, she shook

out her hair. There was no need for combs and brushes and pins this morning. The red strands curled and waved around her face and down her back, and when she ran down the stairs it danced around her head.

Peter waited in the dining room. He looked her up and down and sighed tiredly. "What would you like for breakfast this morning?" he asked without commenting on her attire.

Anya lifted her chin and prepared to do battle. "A plate of fresh fruit and a slice of roasted boar." The rumbling in her stomach protested. Her nose twitched, her mouth pursed. Still, Peter waited silently. "I suppose a couple of biscuits and a slice of ham will suffice," she said grudgingly, thinking fondly of Betsy's tender biscuits. "And coffee," she added. "With lots of cream and sugar."

"Anything else, Miss Anya?"

"Is King Sebastian up yet?"

Peter's face went stony. "He is in the garden. I suggest you wait here."

Anya ignored his suggestion and turned. "I will return in a few minutes for my breakfast."

"But Miss Anya . . ." Peter began.

"Do not be a prude, Peter. I know very well what is going on. What difference does it make? Sebastian will soon be my husband." Her heart lurched and her stomach, which had been behaving well of late, turned over. Julian was her husband. In her heart he always would be her husband. It did not matter that he did not want her, or that Queen Carola had declared their marriage void.

No one would ever know that she was such a sentimental fool.

Completely bare, Sebastian rested face down on the ground, a pile of soft blankets beneath him, his back soaking up the sun as two of the servants, one male and one female, applied the royal rose oil and rubbed it into his back and shoulders and legs.

He lifted his head when he heard her footsteps, and smiled widely when he saw her.

Sebastian dismissed the servants with a wave of his hand, and indicated that Anya should sit beside him. She did so, sitting cautiously so as to maintain the annoying modesty she had acquired as Julian's wife.

"Soon we will go home," he said, grabbing his loincloth and putting it on while he sat on his pile of blankets.

"Yes," she whispered.

If she seemed less than enthusiastic, he did not notice. His smile did not dim as he tossed his dark blond hair back so his oiled chest was presented to the sun. "I am glad you are the one, Anya. You will make a good queen." He laid his deep blue eyes on her. "I missed you more than I expected I would."

"You have . . . other women," she protested. "You can have any woman you desire."

"Yes, but you are the only one who speaks to me as if I were a person as well as a king," he said, his smile dimming. "The others, they agree with everything I say. If I say the sea is red, they nod and agree that it is so. You were the only one who dared to tell me when I was behaving badly, or when I was wrong. You were the only one who made me laugh."

He reached out and placed his big hands on her face, one on each cheek. "And now you will give me a child. Maman wishes for a girl child to carry on the traditions, but I hope it is a son. I have always wanted a son."

"This is not your child," she whispered. "You know that."

"It will become my child because I claim it as mine." His smile dimmed. "But I fear we will never have another. I should have many sons by now, but . . . I cannot."

"Perhaps you should see a doctor before we go back. Maybe . . ."

"No. This child is all we need." His face came nearer to hers. He tilted his head as if he were going to kiss her. Impossible.

"I do not love you," she said when his lips were almost on hers. "I want to go home, Sebastian. I *need* to go home. But I do not love you."

A spark of sadness flashed in his eyes. It was quickly gone. "You still love this husband who abandoned you?"

"Yes," she whispered.

He moved his head back slightly, so the threat of a kiss was gone. His thumbs rocked over her cheeks. "I forgive you," he said magnanimously, "Because I know that in time you will come to love me. You will love me because I am king, and because I am your husband, and because I make myself father to your child." He pinned his eyes on her. "And because I will never abandon you."

Her heart lurched. It should be so simple, but she suspected it was not.

"What the bloody hell is this?"

Anya's head snapped around at the sound of that angry voice. "Julian?"

Julian drew the knife from his boot and stalked toward his wife and the near-naked man on the ground. He had ridden like the hounds of hell were at his heels to protect his wife. He had ridden through the night, sending Jeremiah to Wilmington to find the thug who had been hired by someone in this house to arrange for the abduction, so Julian could rush to his wife's side and assure her safety. And here she sat, in her scarves and jewels, allowing a huge, greasy, *naked* man to touch her.

He grabbed her hand and pulled her to her feet. The large, almost naked man rose slowly, as if he didn't have a care in the world.

Julian forced Anya behind him and raised the knife so it pointed at the man's slick chest. White-hot fury bolted through his blood. "If you ever lay a hand on my wife again, I'll cut out your goddamn heart and feed it to you."

"Julian!" Anya whispered urgently, tugging on his shirt.

He did not take his eyes from the long-haired savage who stood a couple of inches taller and surely weighed fifty pounds more. "Do we understand each other?"

The big man looked down at the weapon. "Anya,

279

I gave you this knife as a gift. How did this man come to have it?"

"I gave it to him."

Julian shook his head. "This knife was a gift from some would-be island royalty who's . . ." *far, far away, right*? He would never have to meet King Sebastian face-to-face. It would be too much. He didn't want to know—

"I am King Sebastian," the man said calmly, not at all concerned about the knife at his chest. "And if you draw so much as a drop of blood, my men will kill you."

Julian glanced over his shoulder. Two other men, only slightly more clothed than the king, stood close by, extremely large knives clasped in their able hands. Somehow, Anya held them off.

"I tried to tell you," she whispered. "Where have you been?"

Julian looked the king over. Anya had said he was young, and strong, and handsome, and virile. He had not expected that the king would be no older than Anya herself, and possessed of blond hair and blue eyes and the ability to smile while a knife was pointed at his heart.

"I don't care who you are," he said softly. "If you ever touch my wife again, I will kill you."

"She is your wife no longer," the king said calmly. "Soon she will be my queen."

Julian dropped the knife to a non-threatening position and turned to look down at Anya. Her eyes were wide, her soft cheeks pale.

"You need a shave," she said softly.

"Anya, what is he talking about?"

Her eyes and her mouth hardened. "You said you would come back, and you did not. You promised—"

"I was kidnapped," he interrupted.

She wasn't so sure she believed him. He saw, too easily, the skepticism on her face. "It matters little. Queen Carola has declared our marriage void."

"Queen Carola, whoever the hell she is, has no jurisdiction in North Carolina," he said testily.

"But on Puerta Sirena she rules second only to me," Sebastian said lowly. "In a few days, we will leave for that island, and there Anya will become my queen."

Julian turned to the annoying man. "Anya is my wife, and she's carrying my child. If you think—"

"The child is mine, now," Sebastian declared. "I have claimed it."

"You can't just—"

"I can."

Julian turned and pulled Anya toward the house. "We need to discuss this in private." The guards blocked their path, and when he tried to skirt them they stepped to the side to remain between him and the house. Anya's little knife didn't seem much of a threat, since the blades they carried were four times longer and twice as broad.

"Anya is to be queen," Sebastian said with an almost intolerable serenity. "She goes nowhere without my permission and the guard of my most trusted men."

Julian tugged on Anya's hand and pulled her close. She was well, which assured him that the per-

Linda Jones

son who had arranged his foiled shanghai meant her
no harm. For that he was grateful. But this new development . . .

"I have been so worried about you," he whispered.

"There was no need," she said crisply. "I have been
fine without you. I did not miss you at all. You deserted me without a care, and . . ."

"I did not desert you."

"You did." He saw the sharp hurt in her eyes, the
indecision. "Perhaps you are telling the truth and
the leaving was not of your choosing, but the result
was the same. You broke your promise."

The expression in her eyes was enough to do any
man in, there was such deep longing and pain there.
Julian moved his mouth close to hers. One kiss, to
tell her he loved her. One kiss, to make things a little
bit better, until they had the time and opportunity
to work this out. His mouth moved toward hers, but
at the last moment she turned her face and presented her cheek.

Julian looked different, Anya thought as he stormed
into the house. His hair was longer, his beard a few
days old, his clothes unkempt. But the change she
saw was much more than skin deep. His eyes . . . a
new passion flickered there, something deep and
true that she had not seen in him before.

"He threatened to kill me," Sebastian said with humor and horror.

"He did not mean it," she said as the king came
up behind her.

"I believe he did."

Why had he come back? And with that ridiculous story about being kidnapped. Maybe he had forgotten something. Maybe the captain of his ship had tossed him off the way the pirates of Puerta Sirena had been tossed off their own ships, and he had nowhere else to go.

Maybe he had realized that he truly did love her.

Too late. She would not allow herself to be hurt again. Even if Julian did love her, that love would not last. Eventually he would leave again. He would break her heart again.

Sebastian could never hurt her, for one simple reason. She did not love him.

Peter appeared in the north parlor doorway. "Miss Anya, your breakfast is getting cold."

At Sebastian's orders, the servants who had defended him from Julian's knife fell into step behind her. She now had her own personal guard, it seemed. Could they keep Julian away?

She hoped so. She could not stand another broken heart so soon.

Her eyes cut to the side as she made her way to the dining room, waiting for Julian to appear. He did not, but Grandmother joined her at the table.

"Anya, why are you wearing that . . . that outfit?"

"I wished to do so."

"You have so many beautiful dresses—"

"Julian is home," Anya interrupted.

Grandmother's eyes went wide, her cheeks lost their color. "He is? I thought . . . Seymour said he had taken a ship to Australia. What happened?"

Anya shrugged and played with one of the biscuits

283

on her plate. "I do not know." Why share his ridiculous story about being kidnapped? It was an excuse for his behavior, and she chose not to believe him. "I told him I was going to return to Puerta Sirena with Sebastian, and he left."

"Anya," Grandmother said crisply, "you are not returning to Puerta Sirena." She nodded sharply in that way she had, leaving no room for argument.

"I belong there," Anya said quietly.

"You belong *here*."

Anya shook her head.

In truth, she did not belong anywhere. Not here, not on Puerta Sirena. Oh, she was going to make a terrible queen!

"Well, where is Julian now?" Grandmother asked tersely.

"I do not know. Maybe he left. Maybe he is here in the house, still." Yes, he was here in this house. She felt him. After weeks of missing her husband, she actually felt his presence in this house.

Grandmother gave her a small smile. "Perhaps he came back because he missed you, and he now realizes that the two of you should remain here. Together. He'll do away with that ridiculous pagan king, and everything will be the way it should be." Again, she nodded.

Anya picked at her biscuit. She had a sinking feeling nothing would ever be as it should be, not ever again.

Julian had not slept for more than twenty-four hours, and it was beginning to show. After leaving Anya and her damned king, he'd stormed through the house looking for Seymour. Jeremiah would come with the truth, when he found it. He would get the information from the man who had hired him and Milton, he would learn who was behind the plot.

But Julian knew what had happened. Who else but Seymour would hire thugs to see that Julian left this house and didn't return? Seymour, who had been so distressed by the news that Anya wanted a dozen children. Seymour, who had been so happy that his sister would turn her back on her share of the Sedley fortune for love. Seymour, who apparently wanted it all for himself.

It had been Peter who'd finally told him that Seymour had gone out the night before with friends and had not returned. The butler was not concerned. This was normal behavior for Seymour.

Julian had washed his face in cool water and now laid back on his own bed. His heart pounded erratically, his vision was cloudy. He could not think straight! In truth, the shock he'd received on his homecoming probably had more to do with his state of mind than something so simple as lack of sleep.

He closed his eyes. So that was King Sebastian. A new fury rushed through his blood. He had painted a picture in his mind, a picture he could live with. In spite of Anya's insistence that the king was young and handsome and virile, in his mind he'd given Sebastian an ugly face, a spindly body, and a grating voice no woman would care to hear. He had made the king old and ugly and . . . less than ordinary.

How else could he live with the fact that Anya had once been his concubine?

But Sebastian was none of those things. Most women would probably find the heathen attractive. And the bastard had asked Anya to be his queen, and wanted to make Julian's child his heir.

Never. He would follow them to Puerta Sirena, if he had to. He would fight to the death for his wife and child.

At least she was safe, he thought, the rage he was unaccustomed to fading slowly. And well. Pregnancy agreed with her. How could she be more beautiful than he remembered? Her hair redder, her lips more perfect, her eyes brighter. He had dreamed of her, while imprisoned in Miller's Crossroads, and even in his dreams she had not been so beautiful.

As soon as his head cleared and Anya was calm enough to be reasonable, he would explain again what had happened on the road. She would understand, and forgive him.

A few hours of sleep, that was all he needed. Julian took a deep breath. He could hear people moving throughout the house and voices muffled by the thick walls. A man, a woman. A voice he knew, another he did not.

Below stairs, something fragile hit a wall or the floor and shattered with a resounding crash. Julian smiled and drifted into an uneasy sleep.

Chapter Eighteen

Anya was surprised to see Julian come down to dinner. What had she hoped? That he would leave? That he would follow her around and beg her forgiveness? She had not seen him all day, though Peter had said he was resting in his room. She had been tempted to open the door and peek in, but she had not. Angelo and Hector, the guards Sebastian had assigned to her, never left her side, even though she had tossed more than one vase their way and had ordered them several times to leave her be.

For the evening meal, Julian had bathed, shaved, and put on clean clothes. He wore a very nice black suit Grandmother had insisted he have, a conservative contrast to the scarves Anya continued to wear. He looked very gentlemanly, but for the gleam in his dark, hooded eyes.

Anya took a seat at the table. Sebastian sat in the

chair at her right. Julian took the chair to her left. Her heart almost thudded through her chest when the two men bracketed her.

There was quite a crowd at the table tonight. Grandmother at the head, as usual, Queen Carola at the foot, the place she had chosen for herself. Julian, Anya, and Sebastian were on one side of the table, a yawning Seymour and the Mathias newlyweds on the other, along with a disinterested Uncle Ellis. While Grandmother had not forgiven Valerie for defying her, she did concede whenever Anya asked to see her cousin, and of course Valerie wanted to spend as much time as possible with her father before he sailed away for parts unknown again.

The islanders from Puerta Sirena, four men and two women, stood close by, silent and ready to defend their king and the queen mother. And Anya herself, she supposed.

Sebastian leaned down and placed his mouth close to Anya's ear. "I do not think the man who was your husband likes me much," he said, a hint of teasing in his deep whisper.

"I doubt he cares enough to dislike you," she answered in a voice as low as his own.

"I disagree."

Julian laid a hand on her knee, and Anya jumped. He leaned close, and nudged her hair aside as he whispered, "When did you take to wearing scarves and jewels again, my dear?"

"They are more comfortable," she answered turning the back of her head to Sebastian and glancing up at her husband, who remained so close, so very close. No. As Sebastian said, Julian was the man who used to be her husband. She waited for a lecture on proper clothing for a lady. Instead, Julian's fingers slipped higher on her bare leg.

"I like it," he whispered in her ear as his hand traveled higher.

"You do?"

His fingers stopped short of their intended target, swaying on the tender skin at her inner thigh and going no higher. "Of course I do."

Grandmother cleared her throat loudly, and again Anya jumped. Good heavens! She had almost forgotten that she and Julian were not alone.

"Julian, where on earth have you been?" Grandmother asked sharply.

Julian's eyes raked over everyone at the table. "While on the road to my aunt's house, just a few hours after leaving here, I was set upon by robbers and kidnapped."

Grandmother raised a hand to her chest. "How terrible."

Valerie and William expressed their horror, as well, and even Seymour showed his surprise.

Betsy had made a fine roast, and it was passed around the table, along with the vegetables she had prepared.

"What bad luck," Seymour said as he piled potatoes onto his plate.

Julian stared at Anya's cousin. "It wasn't bad luck at all," he said darkly. "The note summoning me to my aunt's house was false, a ruse to get me on the road alone."

Linda Jones

"They meant to kill you?" Valerie asked, horrified.

Julian's fingers tightened at Anya's thigh. "No, they meant to shanghai me."

This last statement got Uncle Ellis's attention. "Shanghai?"

"Yes. Someone wanted, very much, to get me as far away from this house as possible."

Anya lifted her eyes cautiously. When Grandmother passed Julian the large bowl of potatoes, he had no choice but to remove his hand from Anya's leg and take the food. "So it is true?" she whispered. "You were abducted?"

"Yes," he said. "Did you really think I'd simply leave you without a word?"

Anya nodded. That feeling she did not like welled up inside her. Fear. Trapped tears.

"Well, how did you escape?" Seymour asked brightly. "It sounds like a grand adventure. I'm sure it makes for an exciting story."

Julian laid his eyes on Seymour. "Not tonight," he said calmly. "I have more important things on my mind."

Grandmother cleared her throat again. "Well, Anya, now that Julian has returned, I'm sure you've reconsidered your plans to return to Puerta Sirena. Goodness, Julian, we thought you'd taken off for Australia. That's what we were told. I imagine the same ruffians who kidnapped you also arranged for us to hear that story."

Julian scoffed. "The ruffians who kidnapped me are incapable of planning anything so devious. No, someone hired them to shanghai me. That's the person who made sure you all thought I had taken off for . . . where did you say? Australia?"

"Who did it?" Valerie asked, her cheeks flushing pink. "Who hired them?"

"I don't know," Julian said. "But I will find out." He turned his attention to Anya. "You didn't answer your grandmother's question, my love. Do you still plan to return to Puerta Sirena?"

"Yes," she said quickly.

"Why?" he whispered.

Her heart thundered. Her hands shook. "I belong there," she whispered. "I do not belong here."

All of a sudden her stomach roiled. She pushed her chair back and stood quickly. "I do not feel well. I am going to bed."

Sebastian and Julian rose in a synchronized motion. They both looked as if they intended to accompany her. She lifted her hands, one palm presented to each man. "No. Leave me alone, both of you."

When Angelo and Hector stepped up as if they intended to follow her, she lost her temper. "And you two! I am sick of turning around and running into you! Stay away from me!"

They looked to Sebastian, and with a wave of his hand he gave them permission to do as she asked. When they stepped back Anya turned and ran from the room, heading for the stairs and blessed solitude.

The royal guests had been put in another wing, thank goodness. The queen was in Valerie's old room, and the damned king was in a room near Sey-

Linda Jones

mour's. Guards had been posted at Anya's door, but they likely didn't know that the three rooms along this corridor were connected by inner doors. Julian slipped through the door from the shared sitting room into Anya's bedchamber.

A lamp burned low on a bedside table, illuminating the lump beneath the covers. Anya immediately sat up and twisted to face him.

"I see you're still wearing my nightshirt," he said softly.

She nodded and grasped the bodice with one hand. "What are you doing here?" Like him, she kept her voice low, so the guards in the hallway wouldn't hear.

He held the plate in his hand high, and offered the glass of milk. "You didn't eat. I thought you might be hungry."

"I am starving," she whispered.

Julian sat on the edge of the bed and offered her the plate and glass. He had put together a roast beef sandwich and cut it into four pieces, and he'd sliced an apple. Anya took one of the small sandwiches and began to eat.

"You must think about the baby," he admonished. "Skipping a meal is not a good idea."

"I know," she said between bites. "But I could not eat. Not with—"

"We're not going to talk until you've cleaned this plate and drunk all the milk," he interrupted. And then he wasn't leaving this room until he and his wife settled this . . . this thing between them.

Anya didn't look at him, not directly, as she ate

292

and drank. Even when she was finished and he took the plate and glass and set them aside, she only looked at him out of the corner of her eye. He couldn't stand it. He took her face in his hands and forced her to look at him. Immediately, her eyes filled with tears.

"Don't," he whispered.

"I cannot help it."

He wiped away a tear with his thumb. "I don't understand," he confessed. "Do you really prefer a life with that . . . that Neanderthal king to a life with me?"

"Yes," she breathed.

"Why?"

Anya only shook her head in inadequate answer.

"I hate him," Julian said, refusing to release his hold on her. "Never in my life have I really wanted to kill, but when I look at him . . ."

"Stay away from Sebastian," Anya said, showing fiery emotion for the first time.

Julian dropped his hands. Had he been so wrong about her? He'd been so certain that Anya loved him, but the way she defended her bloody king made him wonder.

Anya was keeping a secret, and he couldn't figure out what it was. Did she love her king so much? Did she want to be queen so badly that she'd do anything to have that title? Had everything between them, everything that had come before, been false?

No, he didn't believe it. Couldn't. When he leaned forward to kiss Anya, she turned her head and presented her cheek. He wasn't deterred, but planted his lips there, kissed her, raked his mouth down to her throat.

"While I was gone," he whispered, "I thought of you every day. Every moment of every day. I dreamed of you at night. In the worst moments, I remembered the way you felt, the way you laughed, the way you smiled. When I lost hope, I thought of you and knew I had to do whatever was necessary to get home. To get home to you. And now that I am here, it seems that you don't want me."

She shuddered, long and deep. "Julian . . ."

"Marido," he corrected. "You used to call me *marido.*"

"But you are my husband no longer," she said, almost desperately. "Queen Carola has declared—"

"Queen Carola can kiss my ass."

"Julian!" Anya said, drawing slightly away from him.

"She can't undo what we've done." He raked his hand down Anya's side.

"It is best," Anya whispered.

"Best for whom?" Julian asked impatiently. "You? Me? King Sebastian? You can't tell me that taking my child to an island in the Caribbean to be raised as a savage is best."

"It is best for everyone," she said, not very convincingly.

Julian raised his eyes and met her watery gaze. "Do you love him? Is that what this is all about?"

"Sebastian? She shook her head. "No, I do not love him."

"Then why—"

"I will never fit in here," she snapped. "Never."

"You are my wife. You will fit in wherever we are."

She shook her head in denial. "Did they hurt you?"

"What?" he asked, confused by the abrupt change of subject.

"The kidnappers," she explained. "Did they hurt you?"

"No, not really."

"Good." She reached out and brushed a strand of hair off his shoulder.

She had, at least, accepted the fact that he had not purposely deserted her. That was a step in the right direction, he supposed.

"I missed you so much," he confessed.

"And I missed you."

Julian smiled. Everything was going to be all right. He reached out and placed his palm over Anya's belly. "You've grown a little, I think."

"I know."

He placed his other hand on her breast. "Here, too."

Anya nodded.

With a gentle shove he laid her back on the bed and hovered above her, one hand on her belly, the other on a soft, yielding breast. "I want you," he whispered.

Anya shook her head, but she didn't move away or shove his hands aside.

"You're my wife, and I need you."

Again, she shook her head.

"Don't you want me?" She didn't answer, not even

with a shake of her head. He kissed her throat again, laid his body against hers so she could feel for herself how he needed her. She answered, with a long, deep shudder.

His hand slid down from her belly. He grasped the tail end of the nightshirt Anya wore and lifted it slowly to bare her thighs. Enough talking. She would show him how she felt, as she always did. They would handle the king tomorrow. They would handle everything tomorrow. Tonight . . . tonight was for this.

He ran his palm up her bare thigh, cupped her hip, and drew her closer. He kissed the tender spot beneath her ear, trailed his lips down to her shoulder. She moaned and brushed an easy hand down his side, then slipped that hand between their bodies to caress the length beneath his trousers. A few buttons, a moment more, and he would be inside her.

"Show me you love me, Anya," he whispered.

It was, evidently, the wrong thing to say. Her entire body stiffened. "We cannot do this," she said, drawing away from him.

"What do you mean we can't?"

She scooted away from him. "It is too late."

"How can it be too late?" he asked, exasperated.

Anya drew her legs up and hid her body beneath the quilt. "Sebastian will kill you."

It was more than he could stand. "Sebastian again, son of a bitch." He left the bed and raked his hair back with the fingers of both hands. "So you really want to be queen, is that it?"

She shook her head. "No, but I am promised to

Sebastian, now. Even if I did . . . want you, it would not be right."

"Anya, you're my wife—"

"No," she interrupted. "My grandmother bought you for me. You did your job well, and now our time is done. Go, Julian," she said softly. "Travel around the world, write your books . . . live the life you wanted before you met me."

"Our marriage might have started that way, but things have changed."

"Have they?"

"I love you." Let her argue with that!

"I know," she whispered. "Now, please go."

Julian threw his hands in the air and did as she asked.

Sebastian left his guards behind and crept down the stairs and into the kitchen. He was still hungry. They never fed him quite enough in this house.

A light still burned there. Good. If someone was about he might not have to fend for himself.

He saw her long before she saw him. Her back was to him as she bent over some menial task at a work table. Betsy, he remembered. Her name was Betsy, and she was a servant in this household.

As a servant, she would surely give him whatever he asked for, and at the moment his rumbling stomach was the least of his problems.

She was attractive, in an ordinary sort of way. Brown hair, green eyes, upturned nose. But her body . . . beneath those plain clothes she wore she had a magnificent body. She had breasts just the right size, a waist so small he could span it with his hands, he was certain, hips that swelled in invitation.

Betsy turned and jumped when she found him standing there. "I didn't hear you," she said softly. "Are you hungry?"

He nodded once and gave her a smile to still her nervousness. The smile did not work on her, as it usually did on females of all ages. It seemed to frighten her. "Why do you work so late?"

Betsy turned and resumed her task. "I have no choice. We're shorthanded, and have more guests than usual, and I can't get Hilary to do a thing in the kitchen. The part-time girl who was supposed to help me tonight was scared away by one of . . ." She stopped abruptly.

"One of what?" Sebastian prompted as he walked up behind her.

"One of your men," she finished crisply. "Alice had never seen a bare-chested man before, and she was quite frightened."

"Silly Alice," he said, coming upon Betsy and laying his hands on her hips.

She squealed, spun around, and pushed her small, ineffectual hands against his own bare chest. "How dare you?" she said, blushing a pretty pink.

"I want you," he said with a smile. "Come to my bed."

In answer, she lifted her small hand and slapped him soundly across the cheek. He was so surprised his head snapped back.

"I'll have you know I'm not that kind of girl," she said indignantly.

"What kind of girl are you?"

"I'm a . . . I don't . . . You shouldn't . . ."

"Ah," he said, suddenly enlightened and forgiving Betsy for her inappropriate striking of his face. "You are a virgin."

She huffed and turned away from him, but he trapped her against the table. His body touched hers, his hands reached around her and grasped the edge of her worktable. Yes, Betsy was trapped, and she trembled. "Do not be afraid. I like virgins, truly."

"Please go away," she said softly.

He had thought her trembling was caused by desire, but when he realized it was fear that made her tremble, he dropped his hands and stepped back. "You are very beautiful," he said. "Why are you a virgin?"

With some distance between them, she felt safe enough to turn and face him. Good. He liked watching her face as she spoke. It was more than ordinary, he decided. That face was quite beautiful. "I've spent enough time with Miss Anya to know that on your island things are different, but here nice girls don't sleep with men until they're married."

"So you are waiting for marriage?"

She scoffed and crossed her arms across her chest. "I'm never getting married."

"Why not?" Was she afraid? In love with someone she could not have? He found he wanted to know why such a woman would choose a life of loneliness.

"I have eleven brothers and sisters," she said. "Most of my life I've been more mother than sister to all of them. Why do you think I work here? I spent

299

Linda Jones

half my life wishing to get away from home. Why would I trade it for a bunch of kids of my own?"

"You do not want children?"

"No," she said emphatically. "Therefore, I want no husband. Besides," the ever intriguing Betsy added, "I don't like you."

Sebastian was taken aback. Everyone liked him! "Why not? Have I offended you in some way?"

"You're going to take Miss Anya away, when everyone knows she loves Dr. DeButy. It just isn't right."

"She wishes to go," he contradicted in a dangerous tone.

"No, she doesn't, you dolt," Betsy argued.

He paused. In a way, Betsy was right. Anya did love Julian. She had admitted it freely. So why was she leaving this place? So she could be queen? So her child would be heir to the throne? No, he suspected her reasons were more personal. To be honest, if she changed her mind he would not berate her, or force her to return to Puerta Sirena. He liked Anya. He wanted her to be happy.

Besides, there were other interesting women in the world, he decided. Other women who would argue with him. As for the bloodline that ruled on his island, perhaps it was time for a change.

"If you will not come to my bed, will you at least feed me?" he asked, taking a step toward Betsy.

"Of course," she said. "That's my job."

He was aching for a woman, and almost wished that that woman Anya did not like—what was her name?—was still around. Perhaps even she would be better than no woman at all.

300

Mother's servants, Maida in particular, would not be averse to a night in his bed. She had accommodated him on occasion during the long voyage from Puerta Sirena to America.

But Sebastian found he did not want Maida, or even that woman whose name he could not recall. He did not even want Anya, who slept above his head.

He wanted this woman, the one who had refused him, the one who had called him a dolt.

But for now, he would settle for the plate of food she prepared and placed on the kitchen table. He could charm her, if not tonight then certainly tomorrow. No woman could resist his charms.

"Sit with me?" he asked as she poured him a glass of cider.

"I have work to do," she protested.

"Please."

When a king said *please,* you obeyed. Betsy sat beside him. "Tell me," he said as he picked up a piece of sweet bread and brought it to his mouth, "all about your brothers and sisters."

It was well after midnight when Peter found his way to the pantry. The kitchen was dark, so he assumed Betsy had finished and gone to her bed. Like him, she had a room in a wing off the kitchen. All three of the live-in servants had chambers there. There were two other rooms along that corridor, but as Anya had turned the household upside down, they never kept help very long, these days.

He carried his single candle to the end of the

long, narrow pantry, and sat on the stool there. Placing his candle on an empty space on the shelf, he reached behind a few canned goods and found the bottle he had stashed there. Some days he needed a good stiff drink more than others.

His time here was almost done. He didn't know where he'd go next, but he knew it was time to move on. He'd stayed all this time for the children who were not his own. Valerie had William Mathias, now, a good man to take care of her. Anya had Julian DeButy, if she'd come to her senses; a king to care for her if she did not. Seymour . . . Seymour was beyond hope.

He tilted his head and took a long swallow.

When the door opened, he tried to hide the bottle, but it was too late. Beside, it wasn't the lady of the house checking on her butler or her brandy, it was that damned queen who had been following him everywhere! Every time he turned around, she was there. Demanding something, asking questions, watching him with those haunting eyes.

His patience was gone. "What do you want?"

She closed the door behind her and walked toward him. Dark hair swinging, hips swaying. She lifted her hand and pointed at the bottle in his hand. "Some of that would be nice."

He offered her the bottle, and she lifted it to her lips to take a long swig. Her slender throat worked as she swallowed.

Her arms and legs were bare, that red silk chemise she wore was not much better than nothing at all. The woman was demanding, annoying, a nuisance!

And Peter was reminded of how long it had been since he'd had a woman he hadn't paid for.

He started to stand. "Please, have a . . ."

She laid her hands on his shoulder and forced him back down, then perched on his knee. "I will sit here."

"You really . . . shouldn't." She handed him the bottle, and he took another drink.

"You are a practical man," she said, resting her hands easily on his shoulders while she sat on his knee. "I cannot sleep for all the questions in my mind. Perhaps you can answer them for me?"

"If I can."

"Sebastian cannot father children, and he is my only child. My husband Terrence and I wanted more, but he became ill not long after Sebastian was born. He had a fever that kept him in bed for more than the cycle of the moon, and after that . . . after that he could no longer be a true husband to me. As queen, I should have taken a lover. It was my responsibility to provide an heir. But we had Sebastian, and I did love my husband. Very much. Too much to take another man into my bed while he lived."

"How long has your husband been gone?"

"Two years," she said softly. "He stepped down from the throne and made Sebastian king, when he knew he had such a little time left."

Peter nodded. "I'm sorry."

"Do you have a wife?"

He shook his head. "I was married once, but she's gone, now."

303

"Dead?"

Peter nodded, and was surprised to feel a soft hand in his hair. "I am sorry, too."

"You want Miss Anya for the baby, don't you?" he asked, more kindly than he had intended.

"Yes. She is my only hope." The queen shifted, leaned closer to him. "Well, until a while ago I thought Anya was my only hope. Now . . . I wonder."

"You wonder what?" he asked, taking another long drink.

"If I had another child," she said, tracing a finger over his face. "The line would continue. I am not yet forty years old. It is not too late for me to have a child. Or two." She laid her hand over the hardening length in his trousers.

Peter jumped. He would have stood, but the queen's position prevented him. "Your, uh, majesty. Queen—"

"Carola," she said softly. "You will call me Carola."

"No, I should—"

She laid her mouth on her ear. "Carola," she whispered.

"Carola," he said, giving in too easily.

"You are the man I have chosen to be the father of my child."

"Why me?" he asked, settling his hands at her waist and trying to decide if he should argue or simply comply. His brain said argue. His body said comply.

"You are handsome and strong, and I like you."

"Why on earth do you like me?"

"I like the lines of your face." She traced his jaw with her finger. "I like the strength of your body."

Her other hand raked down his chest. "I like the way you care for the people in this house. And most of all I like the way you look at me."

"I . . . I don't look at you at all," he protested. And when he did, he had been very careful to make sure no one was watching him.

"Yes, you do." She turned to straddle him, her legs parting and wrapping around him. "And I have dreamed about you, every night since I came here."

"You have?"

"My dreams are highly regarded among my people. They often come true." She flicked her tongue across her bottom lip and moved the hand in his lap. "Sometimes you have to make dreams come true."

Peter wrapped his arms around her and pulled her close. "Why not?" He didn't tell her that as she began to remove his clothing she was making quite a few of his recent dreams come true.

Chapter Nineteen

After a restless night, Julian woke with the sun. He combed his hair with his fingers, and threw on a shirt and a pair of dark trousers. If Anya was in the garden with that blasted half-naked king, she needed a chaperon.

But no one was in the garden. In fact, it seemed the rest of the house slept—all but a cheerfully humming Betsy who was already at work in the kitchen.

Julian stood in the garden alone, for a while, and watched the day come alive. What next? He would not allow Anya to simply sail off. Letting her go that way would be impossible. He loved her, she loved him. And he couldn't quite figure out what was getting in the way. She didn't love Sebastian, and he didn't believe that she wanted to be queen of Puerta Sirena so badly that she'd sacrifice their marriage for the throne.

Dammit, if he had to he'd follow her. If Anya could learn to be civilized, he could learn to be a barbarian.

Something had happened while he'd been gone. Something to make Anya question her feelings for him. He could plead with her to tell him, he could follow her and her contingent of guards around and beg for an explanation he could understand . . . or he could show her why she was wrong. He could remind her, in a way she was sure to understand, that she was his wife and always would be.

He returned to the house and made his way to the kitchen. Above stairs, people were beginning to stir. He heard their muted movements. Soon the house would be alive. What would the day bring? It was impossible to guess.

Coffee. He desperately needed a cup of Betsy's coffee.

"Good morning, doctor," the servant said brightly as he entered the kitchen. She even cast a bright smile over her shoulder.

"Good morning," he responded, suspiciously narrowing one eye.

"It's a beautiful day, don't you think?" she continued. Betsy was usually so reserved. So quiet. Not this morning.

"Beautiful," he muttered.

"The heat of summer is gone, the morning is autumn mild. Why, we couldn't ask for a more beautiful day."

"Is the coffee ready?" Julian asked. He was really in no mood to hear how lovely the new day was.

Linda Jones

"Of course, sir," Betsy said sweetly. "You have a seat in the dining room and I'll bring it right out, along with a nice, big breakfast. You look like you could use a bit of fattening up. Didn't those nasty kidnappers feed you?"

Julian shook his head. "They fed me as well as they could."

Betsy shooed him out of her kitchen, that wide smile on her face. Julian took a chair at the dining room table and settled back, stretching his legs.

Jeremiah might arrive at any time. With any luck, he'd have the name of the person who had arranged the kidnapping. It had to be Seymour, though Julian refused to move forward and accuse Anya's cousin until he had proof. Once he did have proof, he was going to kick Seymour's scrawny ass from here to Wilmington.

The violent thought surprised him, but he didn't deny it was exactly what he intended to do.

Betsy flew into the room, a cup of coffee in her hand. "Here you go, doctor," she said cheerfully, setting the cup before him. "You drink this while I make you a breakfast fit for a king." She leaned forward, so she could look at his face. "And doctor, don't worry," she added in a lowered voice, "everything's going to be all right."

Then she patted him on the head as if he were still a lad in short pants. Julian sipped at his hot coffee and watched Betsy return to the kitchen with a spring in her step. The woman had lost her mind.

*   *   *

Anya stayed in bed as long as she dared, not ready to face Julian or Sebastian or anyone else in this household. But eventually she had to rise and dress. She was hungry, she was tired of lying in bed with the covers over her head, and besides . . . she wanted to see Julian. She could not love him, she could not stay with him; but at the moment she had a deep and undeniable desire to see him.

She dressed in a comfortable linen blouse and a pale blue skirt. Perhaps it would be best if she wore something more suited to this civilized country, for the remainder of her time here. She even twisted her hair up and pinned it atop her head. A few tendrils escaped, but for the most part her red tresses were contained.

For now, she would deny the wild aspect of her personality. Her husband—the man who had once been her husband—had tried to seduce her last night. A prim woman would be more steadfast in resisting a man like Julian, she supposed. For now, she would be the proper wife he had taught her to be.

No, she reminded herself as she left the room. She was not his wife any longer. Queen Carola had declared the marriage undone. While that might not be of any importance in North Carolina, as Julian said, Anya had spent too many years on Puerta Sirena to dismiss the queen's decree.

Hector and Angelo leaned against the wall on either side of the door. As Anya stepped into the hallway, they jerked away from the wall and stood up straight.

Linda Jones

"Were you here all night?" she asked.

"Yes," Hector answered, his eyes on the floor. "We are to be your guardians."

Anya sighed in disgust. "Go to bed," she commanded.

"But, my queen," Angelo began.

"I am not queen yet," Anya snapped. "But I soon will be. And I order you to get some sleep!"

They obediently left to do as she commanded. Thank goodness! She did not want them underfoot all day long.

And she had other, more important problems, she noted as she walked down the stairs, her eyes on the man at the foot of the stairway.

This was Julian as she had never seen him. The beast she had always known lurked within him had been released. His hooded eyes were dark and dangerous, his long, wild hair fell about tensely squared shoulders. He had not shaved this morning, and a coarse beard darkened the lower half of his face. His hands balled into fists as he pinned his eyes on her.

"Good morning," he growled.

"Good morning," she said, her own voice sweet and tame.

"I had begun to think you would sleep the day away." He smiled at her, a joyless grin that made her heart lurch.

"I have been very tired lately."

As she reached the bottom of the stairs, the harsh iciness of his face thawed, a little. His eyes went dreamy, for a moment. "It's the baby," he said softly. "You need lots of rest when you're carrying a child."

"I know," she whispered.

"Come," he said, reaching out and taking the hand she had not offered. "Sit in the south parlor and I'll bring your breakfast in on a tray. Everyone else has already eaten."

"I will eat in the kitchen," Anya protested.

Julian's grip on her hand was firm. Warm. Unyielding. "Betsy has started preparing lunch," he explained. "You'd just be underfoot."

"I . . . do not want to be underfoot," she agreed softly.

Julian, his hand gripping hers, led her into the south parlor. He guided her to the couch, stood before her as she dutifully sat. Then, instead of releasing her hand, he remained before her, legs spread wide so she had no hope of escape.

He lifted her hand to his mouth. "You look beautiful today," he said, laying his lips on her knuckles, the back of her hand, and then twisting it to kiss her wrist. His tongue flickered there, and Anya's heart almost came through her chest. "Of course, you have always been beautiful to me." He reached out and touched a freckle on her nose, trailing that finger down over her lips and her chin to rake across her neck. His progress was stopped only by the high neckline of her blouse. Thank goodness she had not worn those scarves today! If he touched her more intimately than he already had, she would capitulate without so much as a word of dissent!

"We made love here, once," he reminded her.

"I know, but we were married then," she said primly. Her voice was calm, but her body responded to Julian's words, as he no doubt knew it would. Her temperature rose, her heart pounded hard. And deep inside she quivered as she remembered that night when they had come together, here where she sat.

"We are married now," Julian said huskily. "We will always be married." He knelt before her, forcing her legs apart so he could fit between her knees. A shiver worked through her body, she throbbed. His hands settled over her outer thighs, but went no further. "We will always be married," he repeated in a soft voice. "Anya DeButy. Anya the Beauty." He smiled crookedly. "A few months ago I was so certain I could sail away from you without a second thought. How stupid I was."

Anya shook her head.

"You're my wife, and you carry my child. You can't run away from that, no matter how much you want to."

Right now she did not want to run. She wanted to reach out and pull Julian to her. She wanted to hang on to him and laugh and cry. Most of all she wanted to love him, one more time. She could not.

Just as she was about to leap from the couch and push Julian away, he stood and stepped back. "Let me see about that breakfast."

Since Betsy was busy in the kitchen preparing lunch, Peter knew he wouldn't be likely to find any rest in the pantry. So he made his way to the Captain's Walk and sat there, looking toward the sea and thinking about sneaking a quick nap. He hadn't gotten three hours of sleep last night, thanks to that . . . that . . . that magnificent woman.

He hadn't thought he could want a woman that intensely, not ever again. He hadn't been a celibate since his wife died, but there hadn't been any real passion in his life, either. Only necessary physical release, and even then, he always walked away disappointed. It had been, what, more than two years since he'd had a woman?

Last night had definitely made up for his recent lack of female companionship.

He started to stand when the door to the Captain's Walk opened, but when he saw it was Carola who joined him he settled back down and smiled, patting the weathered floorboards beside him. She sat, without saying a word.

"I followed you," she said softly.

"I've been here for a few minutes."

She stared at him with fascinating deep green eyes. "I waited on the stairs a moment, uncertain if I should join you."

There was a look of indecision on her beautiful face. If she regretted what had happened the night before, he didn't want to know it. Not now, not ever. "I'm glad you did."

She turned her face from him and gazed out as he had, toward the sea. "I joined Sebastian on his journey to reclaim Anya in order to keep him from doing anything foolish. If I had not come, I would not have met you."

"That would be a shame," he said sincerely.

"Yes." She looked at him, brave and yet more vulnerable than he had ever seen her. "Last night we made a child. I know it. I felt it, when you first shuddered inside me and gave me your seed."

His heart lurched. "How can you be sure . . . so soon?"

"I knew," she whispered. "The first time we came together, we made a daughter."

A daughter. For a moment he could not breathe. He'd buried one daughter. To go through that again . . .

"You are not pleased," Carola whispered.

"It's not that," he said. "This has happened so fast." No time to think, no time to worry . . . "The first time." He frowned. "You came to me hoping for a child. If you knew you'd conceived the first time we . . ." No matter how he tried, he could not say the words. "Then why was there a second time? And a third? And a *fourth?*"

"Those times were for us," she said softly. She reached out and touched his face, placing a soft hand on each cheek. "Just for us."

"It was very nice." The words were inadequate, he knew. But what do you say to a woman who changes your life in a single night? "I'm glad we had that time, just for us."

"It was very nice," she whispered. "But it was not enough. Come home with me, Peter. Be my king. Make more babies." She brought her mouth toward his. "Love me."

The night before she had loved him four times, their bodies had joined and found pleasure in ways he had never imagined. But Carola had never kissed his mouth. He hungered for that lush mouth on his as much, more, than he hungered to feel her body around his again.

She kissed him, long and slow. Carola made love without restraint, without boundaries. But she kissed like a woman who had never kissed before. Her lips trembled. The hands on his face shivered.

"Why?" he asked as he took his mouth from hers. "Why me? You barely know me."

"I have been watching you since the night we arrived. At first you fascinated me, and I did not understand why. I still do not understand why, but . . . the fascination has only grown." She sighed. "I have dreamed about you. I have awakened in the morning wanting only to see your face."

He kissed her again, taking the initiative this time, parting her lips with his tongue. "I've dreamed about you, too," he confessed. "Good Lord, Carola, you are the most beautiful woman I have ever seen."

She smiled. "Truly?"

"Without doubt. And I . . ." How far did he care to go? How much could he say? For all he knew this was a game to the queen, a game she played everywhere she went. He had not taken a chance in so long. Did he dare take a chance now?

"I love you," he whispered against her mouth. "Will you marry me?"

She smiled and threw her arms around his neck. "Yes!"

He held her close. Tight. He would never let her go. "And Carola, my dear," he added as he clasped her against him. "Our daughter, queen or not, will wear clothes."

"Yes, *querido*," she whispered. "Whatever you say."

She settled nicely in his arms. "We should not tell anyone, not right away. I need to tell Sebastian before we share the news with everyone else."

"Will he be disappointed? Upset?"

Carola considered the question. "I do not think so, but he did love his father very much. I am not sure how he will respond to his mother taking another husband."

Some things were the same, world round, he imagined.

"Tonight," she promised. "I will tell him tonight." She lifted her face and smiled. "And then I will come to you."

Anya still loved him, he now had no doubt. So why was she so anxious to run?

She *was* running. He'd always thought her so strong, but she had a bit of a coward in her. She did not want to face him. She did not want to be alone with him, not even for a few minutes.

For the third time on this trying day, Julian cornered Anya. This time she was in the garden. Her guards had awakened and watched her, from a distance, but he didn't care. He would fight them for this time with Anya, if he had to.

She sat at the small wrought-iron table she and Valerie had shared, on occasion, her arms folded on the top, her eyes pinned on something in the garden. A flower. A bird. Whatever it was, it held her full attention. She didn't know he was coming until he sat beside her. She actually jumped, as if he'd startled her.

"You again!" she said, pinning her sea-green eyes on his face.

"If you don't want me to sit with you, I'm sure all you have to do is raise your hand and snap your fingers, and your bodyguards will arrive to carry me away."

Anya glanced over her shoulder, and her guards stepped forward. She shooed them away, and they moved back, almost to the house. Ah, they were a little bit afraid of her. What had she thrown at them lately?

Beneath the table, he laid his hand on her knee. She jumped, but did not push his hand off her leg or jump up to run away. He took that as a good sign, and moved his hand higher on her leg. Her face flushed pink, she trembled deep. "I missed you," he whispered. "Didn't you miss me at all?"

"Yes," she confessed without looking at him.

"Are you still determined to leave here with that pea-brained king?"

She hesitated, but finally breathed, "Yes."

A flash of anger flared within him, but he pushed it deep. Rage wouldn't win Anya; it wouldn't make her change her mind. "Ah," he said, "you have a spot of something on your cheek." He reached out and brushed his fingers over the non-existent smudge. That done, he trailed his hand down to her chin and then to her neck. This time, he didn't stop at the flimsy barrier her blouse afforded. His hand continued, moving lower to cup one breast, teasing the nipple that hardened at his touch.

Her back was to the guards, who stood a good distance away. Unless she moved or protested, they would never know how he touched her. He brushed his fingers over one nipple and then another, and Anya didn't move. She didn't protest.

"You said that on your island a man and woman could—what did you call it? Make love without love. Lie together for pleasure."

"Fardini," she whispered.

"Fardini," he repeated, just as softly. "You want me, I want you. So why can't we . . ."

"I am to be queen," she said. "It is not as if I am not promised. I am not free."

"No," Julian said sharply. "You are not free. You're mine."

"No more."

"Always."

His hand left her breasts and trailed down to her stomach. "If marriage had not made you mine, if love had not made you mine . . . even if none of that bound us together, this child makes you mine."

She turned her head and laid her eyes on him. Strong, fiery, pained eyes. She wanted him. Dammit, she still loved him. Why did she deny him so staunchly? The answer hit him with a force that had the power to knock him to his knees.

"Has he touched you?" he whispered.

Anya remained silent.

"Since coming here," Julian asked, his voice rising slightly, "has that damned king touched you?"

Anya shook her head quickly. "No. You taught me too well, Julian. I do not think I would care to ever again lie with a man without love. And I do not love Sebastian," she added softly. "I will never love Sebastian."

"Then why are you leaving? Do you want to be queen so badly?"

She shook her head.

"Then why?"

She laid her hand over his, and together they cradled the child they'd made. "You have always been jealous of Sebastian," she whispered. "You never said so, but I knew. I saw it in your eyes when you asked about my life on the island. You should not have been jealous, because Sebastian never touched me *here.*" She took his hand and carried it to her heart, where she pressed it firmly. "And because he never touched me here, he cannot hurt me here."

"Are you afraid I'm going to hurt you?"

"You did hurt me. I know you did not mean to, but . . . the hurt is there all the same. How can I live that way? How could I survive if you left me again?"

Julian raised his free hand to her cheek. "I'm not leaving you, and you're not leaving me. Not like this."

Anya reached out and raked her fingers through his hair. "I am afraid, and I do not like to be afraid. It hurts, and . . . it is like when the storms come, and inside I . . . I . . ." She jumped out of her chair but did not release his hand. She ran toward the house, grasping his hand tightly, pushing past the scantily clad guards who tried to protest.

Julian followed, his hand in hers and his eyes on the back of her head. She ran into the foyer and stopped before the portrait of her father.

"I remember," she said, grasping his hand tightly. "He left me floating on the sea, and he promised he would return. He promised!" Her eyes filled with tears. "But he lied, and it still hurts."

"Oh, honey," Julian said, slipping his arm around her waist and holding on tight. "You know he would have come back to you if he could've."

"He left me to save my mother, and they both died." She sniffled, and big tears ran down her face. "How could I forget?"

"You were a child, Anya. It's only natural that you would forget a traumatic experience like the shipwreck and the death of your parents."

She turned her head and looked up at him. "It would be easier not to love at all. If you do not love, you cannot be hurt."

"Perhaps," he said, reaching out to wipe away the tears on her cheeks. "But think of everything you'd miss. Think of everything we'll miss if you run away from our love because you're afraid of being hurt."

She swayed into him and laid her head on his shoulder. "I do love you," she whispered. "I do not want to leave. I do not want to be queen."

"Good. What would you think about moving to a little town called Miller's Crossroads?"

She lifted her head and smiled wanly. "It is a nice little town?"

"No," he said honestly. "It is a horrid, dirty little town. But it has potential," he said optimistically.

"And they need me. They need a doctor."

"A doctor with patients?"

"A doctor with infinite patience."

She rested her body against his, soft and yielding. The island guards who had followed them inside took a threatening step forward.

"Back off," Julian ordered brusquely. Amazingly, they did. "My wife doesn't need any bodyguard but me."

The two men looked at each other and said nothing.

"Go now," Anya commanded with a haughty wave of her hand. The guards obeyed, though they seemed reluctant.

"It is true," Anya said when her bodyguards were gone. "I will not be queen. I am staying here with my husband. No, we are not staying here, we are going to a horrid little town. Together." She looked up at him and smiled. "I do love you, *marido*. I never stopped."

"Then kiss me, Anya."

She came up on her toes and kissed him, long and deep.

Julian lifted her off her feet. Relief washed through him, relief and the need to lie Anya down in the bed upstairs and make love to her all afternoon. And all night. And all day tomorrow. So much for his earlier fears of excess.

Footsteps headed their way, and Anya kissed him quickly and stepped back to straighten her hair.

"What are you doing?" He didn't want to hide the fact that they were back together from anyone. In

321

fact, he wanted to stand at the top of the stairs and shout the news for everyone to hear.

"We cannot let everyone know that I am going to stay, not until I have a chance to tell Sebastian. I owe him that much."

"You owe him nothing," Julian seethed.

"I will tell him tonight," she whispered as she walked by. "I am going upstairs to take a nap, *cher*," she added. "Perhaps you would care to join me?" With that she walked on, exiting the foyer just before Seymour stepped into view.

Chapter Twenty

He had planned to give Anya a five-minute head-start, no more, before joining her, but after she ran up the stairs and Seymour left by way of the front door, there was another interruption. Mrs. Sedley appeared almost on Seymour's heels.

"Julian," she said, her voice too lively. "Just the man I wanted to see."

"What can I do for you, Mrs. Sedley?" he asked. *And make it snappy.*

Her smile faded. "There's no one else I can turn to," she said in a lowered voice, taking Julian's arm and leading him into the south parlor. "What are we going to do?" she whispered. "How are we going to keep Anya here where she belongs?"

He opened his mouth to tell her that Anya had already decided not to return to Puerta Sirena, but something stopped him. "I'm doing my best," he said simply.

"She can't go back there," the old woman said desperately. "All the wasted years! I need her here, Julian. She cannot leave. All my children are gone. First Ellis left me, and then Robert, and now Valerie. I can't lose Anya again. I would do anything to keep her here."

"Anything?" *Including having me shanghaied?* His heart hitched. "What do you suggest?"

"She loves you. You can convince her to stay."

He considered telling her that he and Anya would not be staying here in this house. Good heavens, suddenly it was all so clear. Elizabeth Sedley had bought him as Anya's husband knowing he would leave, knowing he and Anya would never suit. The prudish doctor and the love goddess. Who would've thought they would fall in love?

"And once that's done," the woman continued, "you'll have to convince Anya that she can't travel, not in her delicate condition."

"Travel?"

"She told me that the two of you would . . . sail around the world, or some such nonsense," Mrs. Sedley said, her temper short, red spots flaring up on her cheeks.

So that's what had triggered the kidnapping. How far would the old woman go? What lengths would she take to keep Anya here? "Perhaps I could kill him," Julian suggested in a lowered voice.

"What?" she snapped.

"Anya's king. I don't like him, much, and neither

do you. Don't tell me murder never crossed your mind."

"Well," she said, her face turning deep pink. "I might've thought of it, but I dismissed the idea of killing as extreme. If you think that's best, though . . ."

She was quite willing to be a party to murder. Elizabeth Sedley truly would do anything to get her way.

"I'll think it over," he said, shaking his head. Sick inside not only that this woman he had once admired had turned out to be so devious, but that he would have to tell Anya. The news would break her heart, and he didn't want to hurt her again.

Julian burst into the room without warning, but Anya was ready. Her prim clothes had been discarded, her hair had been loosened and brushed out, and she sat on the side of the bed waiting for her husband to come to her, as he had said he would.

To think, she had almost left him! The power of her love for him was so strong that it scared her, but she would not turn her back on that love again. She would not pretend that she did not need him.

He should be as happy as she was, but he did not look at all pleased, as he closed and locked the door behind him.

Whatever was wrong, she would make it better. She lifted her hand and invited him to her. She smiled, to let him know without words that she loved him.

"Oh, Anya," he said as he walked to her. "I did so want everything here to be perfect for you."

"Nothing is perfect," she said as he sat beside her. The bed dipped under his weight and she rolled into him, her body searching out his warmth and support. "But if I have you, everything will be fine. Perfect or not."

He lost his hands in her hair, held her body against his as if he searched for the same comfort she did. "I've never in all my life wanted to protect anyone or anything the way I want to protect you. I want to keep everything ugly and hurtful away from you. You've been hurt enough."

"Something is wrong."

"Yes." He nodded slightly. "I'm afraid so."

"And you must tell me what it is that bothers you so?"

"Yes."

"Can it wait until after you make love to me?" She raised her head, brushed aside a length of dark hair, and kissed the side of Julian's neck. He smelled so good, he tasted of love and warmth. Her fingers raked over his beard-roughened cheek.

"I don't want to do this, but I really should get it over with," he muttered.

She laid on her back and drew him down with her. "No. Things are not always going to be as perfect as we want them to be. When that happens, we should learn to stop time for a while."

"Stop time?"

"Time should stop for love, do you not think?"

"It's a nice idea, but . . ."

She began to unfasten the buttons of his shirt.

"Until I came here, I did not even know what love was."

"But you were a love goddess," he said, muttering the words that so obviously hurt him, still.

"A love goddess who knew nothing of love," she said, wrapping her arms around his neck. "You were a most excellent teacher, *marido*," she whispered.

He smiled when she called him husband. "And you have always been an excellent student, my love."

She pressed her body snugly against his, arching her back, winding her legs around his. "We must stop expecting perfection, I suppose. Storms will come, and they might bring pain and confusion and fear, but it should all stop for love. If we can make time stop for love, then nothing can ever tear us apart again." She reached between their bodies and touched him. "See? You want me. No matter that things are not perfect, no matter that a storm may be coming."

"All right," he said huskily, lowering his head to kiss her neck. "You've convinced me. It can wait. Everything can wait."

She had forgotten how much she loved this, the feel of the length of his body along hers, the heat and tenderness of his mouth, the urgency that began to grow, so slowly, from the first moment he touched her.

How could she tell him that none of her teachings on the island had ever prepared her for the perfect melding of sex and love? That with him she experienced something she had never expected, a powerful joining that went beyond the physical. She did not have to tell him, she suspected. He knew.

She helped him shed his clothes, never hurrying and yet with that underlying urgency coloring each and every movement. Julian was hers. Her husband, her lover, her friend.

"I was so afraid I would never see you again," she whispered as he aligned his body to hers.

"Don't be afraid," he said, taking her face in his hands and kissing her deep. "Not ever again. You have to know I would never leave you. Life would be too hard without you. It wouldn't be life at all."

"I love you," she whispered, and he surged forward to fill her waiting body.

They came together like lovers who had been apart too long. Fast and furious, they reached for each other. They danced and swayed in their own time, their joining primitive and still delicately lovely. Intense pleasure built to a fever's pitch and then broke over them at once. Anya cried out, and Julian caught her cry through parted lips. She caught his growl on her tongue, tasted his pleasure and his sharp surrender.

For a long while his body rested over hers, protective and loving. Anya lay there with her hands threaded through long strands of dark hair. Time truly had stopped. Nothing else mattered but this.

Finally, he raised up and looked down at her. The unhappy indecision had come back. He brushed the hair away from her face and made a poor attempt at a smile. "I think I know who tried to have me shanghaied."

"Who?" she whispered.

He kissed her forehead, with tenderness and an offering of comfort that only he could give. "Your grandmother," he whispered. "I'm sorry, Anya. I'm so sorry."

"Did she tell you this?"

"No. But . . ." He shook his head. "She's willing to do anything to keep you here. You told her you and I would travel together?"

"Yes. I would not ask you to give up your dream for me."

"You are my dream," he whispered.

"Grandmother?" Anya asked, more confused than ever. "She is the one who tried to take you from me?"

Julian nodded. "I can't prove it, not yet . . . but I think she's the one. As soon as I hear from Jeremiah, I'll have the proof I need."

Sebastian stepped into the silent, empty kitchen. Where was she?

He had never met a woman like Betsy. Last night, after he had eaten and they had talked for a while, she had finally allowed him to touch her. Gently, quickly, and not at all in the manner he desired. She had refused to take off her clothes. She hadn't even removed her apron!

Such prudish behavior should have angered him, it should have sent him running to Maida. But it had not. Instead he had settled down to a night of dreams the like of which he had never known.

"Betsy," he whispered, walking toward the back door. He noticed the narrow doorway at the back of

329

the room. It opened onto a slender hallway and more rooms. He had not known a house could be so large! His entire village could likely live here in comfort.

"Betsy?" he whispered again. From not so far away, he heard a bed squeak. Sebastian stepped gingerly, on bare feet, down the narrow hallway. He peeked through first one doorway and then another. Finally, he peeked into a small room and saw Betsy laying on the bed. She was fully dressed, all the way down to her apron, and she lay on her side with her cheek resting against her hands. Like a child, and then not at all like a child.

He would let her sleep, he decided. She worked too hard and likely needed her rest. Sebastian leaned against the doorjamb and stared at Betsy. How he would love to take her home with him. She would never again have to cook, unless she wished to do so. She would never again be forced to rise at dawn to prepare breakfast for a house full of people, or to slave over a hot stove all day, until she was so tired she slept . . . like this.

She stirred on the bed, opened her eyes, and when she saw him standing there she sat up quickly, bringing her hands to her chest. "What are you doing here?"

"I came to see you," he said.

Her eyes were pinned to his bare chest, then they snapped up to his face. "You shouldn't be here," she whispered. "I might get fired."

He stepped into the room and closed the door behind him. Betsy's face flushed pink, but she didn't tell him to get out. "No one will dismiss you," he promised. "I would not allow it."

She shook her head. "Well, you won't be here forever, and once you're gone Mrs. Sedley will do exactly as she pleases. She always does."

"Do you like working here?" he took another step toward the bed.

"Most of the time," she said softly.

"Do you ever wish for . . . more?"

"Of course I do," she snapped.

"Do you ever wish for a man?"

"Never," she said sternly, but again her face flushed pink, and her lower lip trembled.

"Do you wish to remain a virgin forever?"

"Yes."

"Why?"

Betsy threw her legs over the side of the bed. "I told you last night, I don't want children. What other reason is there for . . . you know?" This time she turned a bright red. "Oh, I can't believe I said that." She pointed at the door. "Get out."

"Why?"

"Because you shouldn't be here. It isn't right and you . . . you . . . you disturb me."

Sebastian smiled. "What if I could show you a very good reason not to remain a virgin, and yet you would still be a virgin when I was finished with you?"

"There's nothing you can say . . ."

"You liked it when I touched you last night," he said, taking another step closer. "When I laid my hands on your breasts, when I kissed your neck. You did like it. Did you not?"

Linda Jones

"A little."

Sebastian grinned. She lied so badly! "No one has ever touched you that way before."

"No."

He sat on the bed beside her. "Let me touch you again. I promise, you will be left with your precious virginity."

"Then I suppose it would be all right," she conceded. "As long as no one knows! Mrs. Sedley would fire me just for having you in my room."

"No one will know," he promised. "Lie down."

"But . . ."

He laid his finger over her lips to silence her. "Lie down," he repeated in a lowered voice.

She did, twisting her body around, falling slowly back until her head hit the pillow. She lay there stiffly, waiting.

"Close your eyes," he commanded, and she obeyed. He lay down beside her, stretching the length of his body alongside hers. The bed was too short for him, but he paid that inconvenience no mind. "We are on Puerta Sirena," he said lowly. "On the beach. There is no one else on the beach but you and me. No one for miles and miles. The sun shines warm on your face, the water laps just a few feet away."

Betsy sighed and relaxed. "It sounds so beautiful."

"It is."

"Are there flowers?" she asked breathlessly.

"Hundreds. No, *thousands*," he whispered. "Flowers in every color you can imagine, and some you cannot. Would you like your bed to be made of the petals of these flowers?"

"Yes," she whispered.

"It is done." Finally, he reached out and touched her, tracing the lines of her face with his finger, trailing that single finger down to her neck. "When the sun becomes too warm, the shade of a nearby tree travels our way to cool us. Do you feel it?" he asked. "The shadow that covers us?"

"Yes," she whispered.

"Do you feel the soft petals beneath your back?"

"Yes." The word was so low it was less than a whisper.

He unfastened the buttons of her bodice and slipped his hand inside the opening in her blouse to touch her sweet, bare skin. Her eyes remained closed. Her breasts rose and fell with each deep breath she took. "The breeze that washes over us smells of the ocean. Can you smell it?"

"I do," she said, her voice touched with wonder.

He caressed her breasts with one hand, while with the other he unfastened every blasted button and tape he found. There were many, on her unnecessary layers of clothing. When her breasts were bared, he leaned over and took one nipple into his mouth, suckling deep, tasting without hesitation. Betsy breathed deep and arched her back, but she did not open her eyes.

"Oh, my," she whispered as he moved his mouth to her other breast. Her hands reached out to find and grasp his head. Her fingers threaded through his long hair and she held him tight.

Linda Jones

"Day turns into night," he whispered when he took his mouth from her and rolled her onto her side to push some of her clothing down and aside. "Do you see the stars? They shine so bright, just for us."

"I do," she said with wonder. "I do see them."

"They are beautiful," he said as he slipped her already unfastened skirt down. "And so are you."

She shook her head. "I'm not—"

"You are," he interrupted. "By the light of a full moon, you are the most beautiful sight I have ever seen." One by one, he discarded the unnecessary pieces of clothing she wore. Her skin had never seen the sun, it was pale and soft, silky and inviting. He touched her, always gently, always with a wonder he had never felt before.

"And while the moon and the stars shine down on us, I make love to you." He rolled her onto her back again, and his hand raked down her chest to her flat belly, and then lower to cup her where no man had ever touched her before.

"Yes," she whispered.

"The pleasure is so great we scream at the night."

"Yes."

He moved to tower above her, parted her thighs with his hands, and then laid his mouth against her, tasting her innocence and her passion. His tongue flickered, his fingers aroused. He toyed with her, bringing her close to completion and then backing away to whisper against her. "The pleasure is so great, it is an ecstasy you cannot live without. A pleasure like no other."

She moaned, and he took her hips in his hands

and laid his mouth on her again, flicking and fluttering his tongue against her. She shattered, with a
moan and an arching of her body. With her hands
grasping the sheets and a scream caught in her
throat, she found fulfillment.

When Betsy came to her senses she opened her
eyes, and found herself not on Puerta Sirena but in
her own bed. Sebastian moved so that he again laid
beside her, stretched on his side, staring at her with
a wide smile on his face.

"Oh, my," Betsy said, and then she glanced down
and squealed. "I'm naked! How did I get naked?"

Sebastian gave her his most innocent look, as she
tried to cover herself with hands on her breasts and
her legs clasped together. "I made you naked," he
said. "It was not necessary, but . . . preferable."

She was different from the women he knew, and
he wondered how she would react to what she had
just experienced. Would she cry? Be angry? Would
she thank him?

She surprised him. Her hands reached out to
touch his face. "More," she said. "I want more."

He smiled, caressed her bare hip, and left the bed.
"Not today, *querida*."

"Why not?" she asked, sitting up in her bed.
"Don't you want me?" There was real hurt in her
eyes.

Sebastian turned about and faced her. "All you
have to do is look at me to know that I want you."
His loincloth did little to hide his condition. "But
when I came to your bed I promised that when I left

the room you would still be a virgin. I am a king and a man of my word."

"Oh."

The disappointment in her voice was almost enough to make him break his promise. "Tonight, if you still want me, come to my room."

"I can't—"

"If you come to me, you needn't worry about finding yourself with child," he said, telling his secret at last. "It appears that I cannot father a child."

Another man's child would be his heir. A woman who loved that man would be his wife. A couple of days ago he had not minded that prospect, but now . . . it seemed he was being cheated out of something. Something intangible.

"If you come to me tonight, I will give you more," he promised. "I will give you everything."

Betsy's answer was a nod.

Chapter Twenty-one

Dinner had been strained, at best. Queen Carola had been oddly quiet. She normally voiced her opinions on everything, so Julian had to wonder if she was ill. Sebastian had seemed distracted as well. He'd barely eaten two plates full of chicken and potatoes. Seymour had whined loudly because he'd lost a bundle at cards the night before, and his grandmother had finally told him to shut up. Ellis was obviously anxious to return to sea.

Even Betsy, who was always reserved and rarely spoke, seemed different tonight. She tripped over her own feet while carrying a tray of chicken to the table, and barely saved their dinner from being thrown about the room. Once she'd recovered and placed the tray on the table, she'd blushed and stammered an apology. Her eyes only left the floor once, to sneak a peek at the king who was usually so hun-

337

Linda Jones

gry he demanded more and more and more. Julian imagined poor Betsy was tired of trying to feed the great ogre.

Anya, who had dressed in a very nice blue gown for dinner, was quiet throughout the meal. Julian wondered if Mrs. Sedley noticed that her grand-daughter barely glanced her way during the long, torturous meal. Julian had wished, more than once, that Valerie and William had made the trip over for dinner again. They had not, and their absence left a noticeable chasm at the table.

Miller's Crossroads was several hours away, by horse, but it was a bit closer to the Mathias farm than the Sedley house. Once they were settled there, he'd make sure Anya and Valerie had time to visit with each other, to maintain the kinship they had recently rediscovered.

When the strained meal was blessedly over, everyone gratefully went their separate ways. Mrs. Sedley pleaded a headache and retired to her room. Seymour declared he was off to win some of the money he'd lost the night before, and Ellis simply wandered off. The queen started to follow her son to the south parlor, his favorite room and the one he had all but taken over, but at the last minute she sighed and pleaded a headache herself. The queen, flanked on either side by the two island girls, walked up the stairs without looking back.

Julian followed Anya toward the south parlor, where she was headed to break the news to the king that she would not be returning to Puerta Sirena, when Peter waylaid Julian.

"Sir, there's a gentleman here to see you."

Julian reached out and touched Anya's arm. He didn't want her to deliver this news alone. To be truthful, he didn't want her alone in the same room with Sebastian, not ever again. She stopped and waited while an exhausted looking Peter delivered the message.

"I use the term *gentleman* loosely," the butler said in a lowered voice. "I suggested that he wait in the garden, as I feel quite sure the silver would not be safe if I invited him indoors. And," Peter added with an upturned nose, "the creature smells."

Jeremiah. Julian shook a finger at Anya. "Wait for me. I'll be right back."

"But . . ."

He grabbed her by the shoulders and faced her head on. "Wait for me." With that, he lowered his head to give her a quick kiss. Peter did not seem at all surprised, and Anya promised. As he left, she perched on a delicate chair that had been placed in the foyer.

By the dying light of day, Jeremiah paced on the garden path. He lifted his head when Julian appeared, and stalked with long, swaggering steps in the direction of the house. Julian met him halfway.

"Sorry I took so long, doc," the big man said in a lowered voice. "Turns out the man who hired me and Milton was hired by someone else, and I had to track him down before I knew for sure who was behind it all."

Julian nodded his head. "Go on. What did you find out?" He knew what the answer would be, but he needed proof. He had to be certain before he confronted Mrs. Sedley.

"You're not going to like it, doc," Jeremiah said, leaning slightly forward. "I was kinda surprised myself."

Julian didn't think he would be at all surprised.

"I mean, the man lives right here in this very house!"

Julian began to nod, then stopped. "Man?"

"Seymour Sedley," Jeremiah whispered. "Your wife's own cousin!"

"Seymour." He shouldn't be surprised, not knowing Seymour as he did. But he had been so sure Anya's grandmother was behind it all. After all, she was willing to kill Sebastian to keep Anya here! No, she was willing to allow Julian to kill Sebastian. It had, after all, been his idea.

"Thank you."

Jeremiah shuffled his big feet. "I decided you were right," he said.

"About what?"

"About . . . farming. I've had enough of this. I just don't make a very good criminal!"

"I think you'll make an excellent farmer," Julian said with a small smile.

"When are you coming back?" Jeremiah's half-smile faded. "I told Nellie you'd come back, and if you don't she'll have my hide."

"It won't be long," he said. "How is everyone?"

"Old Mrs. Blythe has the croup, and Jim Mc-Connell has a frightful rash."

Julian gave Jeremiah instructions for both patients, then promised to be in Miller's Crossroads in no more than a few days. As Jeremiah ambled toward his horse, Julian headed for the big house. It was grand, it was beautiful. And he couldn't wait to get Anya out of it.

Anya waited, as Julian asked, but she was anxious to tell Sebastian that she would not be returning to Puerta Sirena with him. He might be angry at first, but she would make him see the right in her decision. But before Julian returned, Queen Carola waltzed down the stairs and toward the south parlor, alone. She had left her companions above stairs.

Sebastian and his mother were very close. He often sought her counsel on island matters, and she did truly seem to have his best interests at heart, always. Anya laid her hand over her own flat belly. She understood that, now. She only wanted what was best for her child. Julian was best, for her and for the baby.

But she wanted to tell Sebastian of her decision in private, and Carola went into the south parlor and closed the door behind her. The queen would be angry when she found out that Anya's child would not be Sebastian's heir. They would have to find another solution to their dilemma.

Julian came up behind her, assisted her to her feet, and practically dragged her out of the foyer and toward the stairs. He glanced around, checking to see if anyone else was about. They were, of course, all alone. "It wasn't your grandmother," he said lowly. "It was Seymour."

She sighed in relief. "Thank goodness. Of course it was Seymour," she said. "He is such a terrible person. But why?"

"I suspect it was your comment about having a dozen children," Julian snapped.

"Why should he care how many children we have?" Anya shook her head. "It makes no sense."

"Money," Julian said. "He didn't want to have to divvy up the Sedley fortune into such small pieces."

"Money? Money means nothing." She didn't like Seymour, and she knew darn well he had never liked her. But to have Julian taken from her for money . . . The news raised her ire to new levels.

Julian took her hand. "Let's go tell that blasted king now that you're not going back with him. Then we'll kick him out of the house."

"I have a better idea," she said. "Let's just leave. We can pack our bags, sneak out of the house, and go to this horrid little town you told me about."

Amazingly, Julian smiled. "Feeling cowardly?"

"A little." She rose up on her toes and kissed his cheek. "We cannot tell him now. He is with his mother."

She laid her head against Julian's chest. Queen Carola had declared her marriage undone. Julian said the island queen did not have the authority to declare their marriage void, but still . . . She did not like that declaration hanging between them. She had lived too long on the island to completely disregard the dictate of the queen.

"Later, then," Julian said gently. He took her hand and together they headed for the stairway. A noise

342

at the top of the staircase startled them, and Julian dragged her aside and toward the entrance to the library. They entered the dark room and Julian took her in his arms.

"As soon as Queen Carola leaves the south parlor," Anya said. "We will tell Sebastian the news."

"Until then?" he whispered.

Anya rose up on her toes. "Kiss me."

Sebastian remained in his seat, but his face grew hot and his hands balled into fists. "Who is he?" he asked. "I will kill him with my bare hands." The man who had touched his mother did not deserve to live. He thought of all the men of Puerta Sirena who had shown her attentions. Jean Pierre, that blasted pirate. Leonardo, with his wide smile. That devil Manuel.

"You are not going to kill anyone," she said gently. "This is for the best. The line will live on through me, and you will be free. You never wanted to be king, Sebastian. With the birth of this child, you will be free."

"What of Anya?" he asked through clenched teeth. "Her heart will be broken that she will not be queen, that her child will not be heir."

His mother waved a slender hand. "Nonsense. She still has feelings for that man who was once her husband. The only time she is happy is when he is with her. Do you not see it?"

"Of course, I see it. But I came all this way for her, and to simply—"

"No," she interrupted. "We did not know it at the

time, but we came here so I could meet the man who is father to my baby."

Sebastian narrowed his eyes. "You met him here? And you already carry his child?" He rose slowly to his feet. "It is that sea captain, is it not? Ellis Sedley. I will have his—"

"No," she cried, sounding horrified.

"Then who?" he thundered.

"Peter," she said gently.

"The *servant*?"

"He is a fine man," she said defensively. "A former soldier, a strong, caring . . ."

Sebastian clapped his hands over his ears. He did not want to hear any more.

"My son," a soft voice intruded, in spite of the hands over his ears. "Do you want to be king?"

He shook his head. "No. I hate it when people expect me to make their decisions, to settle their disputes. I do not like that they expect so much from me." He never had. His mother had been the one to make most of the decisions. He just sat on the throne and smiled and said what his mother told him to say. "But that does not mean I like the idea of you taking a . . . a . . ." *Lover.* He could not say the word.

"Husband," she supplied.

"You are going to marry him?" Somehow that seemed worse.

"Yes. You can stay on as king for a while, teach him about the people and the island, and then when you are ready to step down, Peter and I will rule until our daughter is old enough to sit on the throne."

"You know it is a female?"

"I know," she whispered.

Sebastian took his seat. "He is a coward for allowing you to tell me this alone. Why is he not here?"

"He wanted to be. I told him I preferred to tell you myself, and I also told him that I would share the news later tonight. Otherwise I imagine he would be here, despite my wishes."

In truth, he had not seen his mother looking so happy in a long time. Not since before his father had died. "Do you care for him?"

"Very much."

"So I suppose I should not kill him."

She heard the surrender in his voice, and smiled. "I very much wish you would not."

A soft knock on the door interrupted, and a moment later it opened. Betsy peeked in. When she saw the queen standing there, she paled, mumbled an apology, and started to back away.

"No," Sebastian said, lifting his hand. "Come in."

She did as he asked, stepping in with her hands clasped before her and her face flushing pink. "I just thought I'd see if you'd like some tea."

One would not think, to look at her, that Betsy hid a great passion behind that meek expression and under those plain clothes. But she did. He wanted to uncover every element of that passion, one layer at a time.

"I would love some tea, later," he said. She curtseyed once, and left the room, all but running.

"Fine," he said, feeling a bit better after seeing

Betsy's pretty, not-quite-as-innocent-as-it-was-this-morning face. "You have my blessing."

"Thank you."

He did not think his mother had ever thanked him before, not for anything. "This Peter, he is important to you."

"He is," she said, sounding more than a little surprised herself.

Julian and Anya waited in the library for what seemed like hours, but they didn't mind. They kissed, they whispered of future plans, they talked about names for the baby.

"Surely Queen Carola has gone to bed by now," Anya whispered.

"Let's go find out."

Decisions made, plans finalized, they wanted this confrontation over. The one with Seymour would come next, he imagined, but since the rogue rarely came in before dawn that would have to wait.

The door to the south parlor was closed. Anya knocked briefly before opening the door and stepping inside. The king, looking oddly flushed, sat on the chair he had made his throne. A rumpled blanket was thrown over his lap on this cool night. The queen was nowhere to be seen.

"Anya," he said, a bit too brightly. "It is always good to see you."

Julian stepped into the room behind her, and the king's smile faded.

Anya clasped her hands, acting almost nervous. "Sebastian," she said gently. "I have to tell you some-

346

thing very important." She started talking gibberish. The same kind of gibberish she had sometimes reverted to in her early days here. Spanish, French, Italian, a little bit of English, and some island words no one else would ever understand.

Sebastian responded in kind. Julian didn't know what he said, but since he didn't seem at all upset, he was afraid the king just didn't get it.

Julian stepped around Anya and took her hand. "Would you two stop this? I can't understand a word. Sebastian," he said, steely eyes on the king. "Anya is my wife. She carries my child. She is not going back to Puerta Sirena with you."

"So she tells me," he said calmly. "Though her words were much more eloquent than yours." The man actually smiled. "I wish her only the best."

Julian, who was more than prepared to fight for Anya, blinked. "You do?"

"Of course. Anya is my dearest friend. If she wishes to remarry you and stay here in America, I will not object."

"What do you mean, remarry," Julian said. "We were never *un*married."

"Actually," Anya said, squeezing his hand. "We were."

Sebastian raised one hand high. "I will perform the ceremony myself," he said with a magnanimous air of authority.

Julian rolled his eyes and was about to tell the king that there was no way in hell there would be any heathen ceremony performed by a half-naked king, when he looked into Anya's face. She was so happy, so openly delighted.

And she had never been completely satisfied with the first ceremony. How many times had she told him that something was missing?

"Fine," Julian muttered. "As long as the ceremony happens soon, I'll be—"

A soft sneeze interrupted him, and Julian snapped his mouth shut. It hadn't been the king or Anya or himself who sneezed, but someone who was hiding behind the king's wide chair. Anya stepped to the side and began to circle the chair, and a disheveled Betsy rose from behind the makeshift throne. Her hair was mussed, her cheeks were pink, and her lips looked well-kissed.

"Betsy!" Anya raised a horrified hand to her chest.

The maid tried a smile that didn't quite work until Sebastian offered her his hand. When she took it and rounded the chair, he yanked her down onto his knee. "You heard," the king said.

"Yes," Betsy muttered.

"I told you she would stay here with the doctor."

"No," Betsy said, turning her head to smile at the king. "*I* told *you* she would stay here with the doctor."

"Come to Puerta Sirena with me," Sebastian said.

"Sebastian!" Anya snapped. "What have you done?"

It was Betsy who answered, glancing up at Anya with a smile on her face. "I'm going to be a . . . a . . ." She lowered her voice. "A love goddess. Sebastian's going to teach me everything."

"Oh, he is?" After a moment, Anya smiled. "You

will love Puerta Sirena," she said gently.

Betsy sighed. "I know."

Once again, the Sedley mansion was in an uproar. Seymour, who had confessed that he had paid a man in Wilmington to have Julian kidnapped but pled that it was Margaret March's idea, would be going to sea with his father—against his wishes and at the older man's insistence. Two of Sebastian's men were guarding Seymour, in case he should try to escape. Life at sea would not be easy for Seymour, Anya suspected.

Grandmother was livid. She was losing her son once again, as well as her granddaughter, her grandson, her butler, and her cook. All in one day. She was not happy. She had tried to bribe everyone into staying, and had even tried to offer William Mathias money to send Valerie home, but no one accepted her offers. Seymour would have gladly stayed, Anya knew, if his father had allowed it.

Valerie and William came for the wedding, at Anya's insistence. When the ceremony was over and the others left for the ship that would take them all to Puerta Sirena and would then take Uncle Ellis and Seymour to points unknown, Anya and her husband would leave this place for Miller's Crossroads. She very much looked forward to living in the horrid little town where Julian would be doctor. The night before they had made great plans for a new home. One of the sections of the house they planned would be an office where Julian could see his patients.

Until then, they would live in what had once been

Linda Jones

an inn. Anya did not care where they lived, as long as they were together.

For the momentous occasion, Sebastian wore a brightly colored skirt, his crown, and a coral necklace. Nothing else. At Julian's insistence, Anya wore her white scarves and the jewelry she had worn to their first wedding. This time, a delicate gold rose rested atop the other, more extravagant necklaces. Julian wore his trousers and a shirt, but had left the jacket off. This was, after all, a casual affair.

They stood in the north parlor, where they had been married before. The preacher, Anya remembered, had stared at the floor and frowned. In contrast, Sebastian grinned and looked her and then Julian in the eye.

"Marriage is a wonderful thing," Sebastian said in a rich, accented voice. "I did not always think so, but I have changed my mind. It is a gift to find the one person in the world who is yours in heart and soul and body. The one person in the world who completes you. Apart, you are fine, but together . . . together you are better." He glanced at Betsy as he said this, and Anya saw a spark of life in his eyes, something she had never seen before.

"Anya, is this Julian DeButy the man you wish to spend your life with? The man you put above all others?"

"Yes," she said breathlessly.

"Do you wish to take him as your mate for life?"

"I do."

Sebastian turned a gaze that was not quite so tender to Julian. "Julian DeButy, is Anya the woman

350

you wish to spend your life with? The woman you put above all others?"

"Yes."

"Do you wish to make her your mate for life?"

"I do," he said, his voice deep and clear.

Sebastian lifted both arms, somehow encompassing the newlywed couple and everyone else in the room in the sweeping motion. "By the power granted to me by the people of Puerta Sirena and God in his heaven, I now pronounce you husband and wife."

Anya faced her husband and lifted her lips to his for a kiss to seal their vows. The kiss he gave her was sweet, tender, and all too brief. His mouth came back toward hers, perhaps for another kiss, but he stopped when his lips were an inch away from hers. Julian glanced to the doors behind her, the double doors that opened onto the garden, and he smiled as he whispered, "Run."

Into The Woods
LINDA JONES

When those village kids, Hanson and Gretchen, mention the old witch, Declan Harper knows he needs her help. Only the Candy woman can brew a love potion. But his hopes are dashed when he finds her cottage in the woods; the old lady is dead and her granddaughter claims to know nothing of concocting love tonics, though her face seems aphrodisiac enough for Declan.

Matilda Candy has been content to remain unwed, but when the handsome Mr. Harper appears at the door, she wants him. But the man is seeking aid in seducing the most beautiful girl in Mississippi. Still, Matilda has hope; she knows Declan has a good soul, and with a little magic of the heart, his otherwise crummy plan will lead to a happy home for all.

The Indigo Blade
Linda Jones

Penelope Seton has heard the stories of the Indigo Blade, so when an ex-suitor asks her to help betray and capture the infamous rogue, she has to admit that she is intrigued. Her new husband, Maximillian Broderick, is handsome and rich, but the man who once made her blood race has become an apathetic popinjay after the wedding. Still, something lurks behind Max's languid smile, and she swears she sees glimpses of the passionate husband he seemed to be. Soon Penelope is involved in a game that threatens to claim her husband, her head, and her heart. But she finds herself wondering, if her love is to be the prize, who will win it—her husband or the Indigo Blade.

___52303-5 $5.99 US/$6.99 CAN

Dorchester Publishing Co., Inc.
P.O. Box 6640
Wayne, PA 19087-8640

Please add $1.75 for shipping and handling for the first book and $.50 for each book thereafter. NY, NYC, and PA residents, please add appropriate sales tax. No cash, stamps, or C.O.D.s. All orders shipped within 6 weeks via postal service book rate. Canadian orders require $2.00 extra postage and must be paid in U.S. dollars through a U.S. banking facility.

Name_____
Address_____
City_____State_____Zip_____
I have enclosed $_____ in payment for the checked book(s).
Payment <u>must</u> accompany all orders. ❑ Please send a free catalog.
CHECK OUT OUR WEBSITE! www.dorchesterpub.com

One Day, My Prince
LINDA JONES

Joe White is the most dangerous and best-looking gun-fighter in town, which makes him powerful enemies who bushwhack him and leave him for dead.

But Joe is saved. And though his woes dwarf those of his rescuers, the answer to their problems mirror the solution to his own. The seven newly orphaned Shorter sisters are in danger of being separated, and only a prissy schoolmarm named Sarah Prince can save them. And while the Shorters know that the bewitching Sarah is just what the wounded marshal is looking for, *he* doesn't know it yet. Miss Prince's kiss will open Joe's eyes to love—and one taste of forbidden fruit will keep them open forever.

___52388-4 $5.99 US/$6.99 CAN

The Seduction of Roxanne
Linda Jones

Roxanne Robinette has decided to marry, and Calvin Newberry—the sheriff's new deputy —has a face to die for. True, he isn't the sheriff: It was Cyrus Bergeron whose nose for justice and lightning-fast draw earned the tin star after he returned from the War Between the States, a conflict that scarred more than just the country. Still, with his quick wit and his smoldering eyes, Cyrus seems an unfair comparison. And it is Calvin who writes the letters she receives, isn't it? Those passion-filled missives leave her aching with desire long into the torrid Texas nights. Whoever penned those notes seduces her as thoroughly as with a kiss, and it is to that man she'll give her heart.

___52357-4 $5.99 US/$6.99 CAN

Dorchester Publishing Co., Inc.
P.O. Box 6640
Wayne, PA 19087-8640

Someone's Been Sleeping In My Bed

A Faerie Tale Romance

LINDA JONES

**WHO'S BEEN EATING FROM MY BOWL?
IS SHE A BEAUTY IN BOTH HEART AND
   SOUL?
WHO'S BEEN SITTING IN MY CHAIR?
IS SHE PRETTY OF FACE AND FAIR OF
   HAIR?
WHO'S BEEN SLEEPING IN MY BED?
IS SHE THE DAMSEL I WILL WED?**

The golden-haired woman barely escapes from a stagecoach robbery before she gets lost in the Wyoming mountains. Hungry, harried, and out of hope, she stumbles on a rude cabin, the home of three brothers, great bears of men who nearly frighten her out of her wits. But Maddalyn Kelly is no Goldilocks; she is a feisty beauty who can fend for herself. Still, how can she ever guess that the Barrett boys will bare their souls to her—or that one of them will share with her an ecstasy so exquisite it is almost unbearable?
_52094-X $5.99 US/$6.99 CAN

BLUE CHRISTMAS

Sandra Hill, Linda Jones, Sharon Pisacreta, Amy Elizabeth Saunders

The ghost of Elvis returns in all of his rhinestone splendor to make sure that this Christmas is anything but blue for four Memphis couples. Put on your blue suede shoes for these holiday stories by four of romance's hottest writers.

___4447-1 $5.50 US/$6.50 CAN

EMMA CRAIG

Cooking Up Trouble

Heather Mahaffey is a beauty, true, and clever, but her father has a tendency to run off at the mouth. And that can be a problem—especially when he is praising her to the wealthiest rancher around, telling him that she can out-cook anyone in the New Mexico Territory. The whole situation is mortifying, especially when Heather knows she has difficulty boiling water. Worse, the wealthiest man in the territory is also the best looking. Philippe St. Pierre has a face women would die for . . . and a body to match. And then there's the devilishly handsome man who offers to assist her—one Mr. D.A. Bologh. Is he on the up and up, or does he have a purpose far more sinister? Either way, with one kiss from Philippe, Heather is in the kitchen and cooking up trouble.

__52398-1 $5.99 US/$6.99 CAN

Dorchester Publishing Co., Inc.
P.O. Box 6640
Wayne, PA 19087-8640

Please add $2.50 for shipping and handling for the first book and $.75 for each book thereafter. NY, and PA residents, please add appropriate sales tax. No cash, stamps, or C.O.D.s. All orders shipped within 6 weeks via postal service book rate.
Canadian orders require $2.00 extra postage and must be paid in U.S. dollars through a U.S. banking facility.

Name _____
Address _____
City _____ State _____ Zip _____
I have enclosed $_____ in payment for the checked book(s).
Payment <u>must</u> accompany all orders. ❏ Please send a free catalog.
          CHECK OUT OUR WEBSITE! www.dorchesterpub.com

The Wild Swans
Kate Holmes

King Richard has had it with frivolous females filling his ears with their foolishness. Yet for all his castles and dragon-slaying, he still needs a wife. Preferably one who won't plague him with womanly whining. One who knows when to shut up. So why not lay claim to the sweetly saucy—and utterly silent—wench he encounters in an enchanted forest?

Princess Arianne has had it with meddling males making her life miserable. When her twelve brothers anger an ogre, *she* is the one stuck spinning nettles into shirts to save them from eternal servitude as swans. And she has to complete the task in total silence! To make matters worse, along comes chatty King Richard, wanting to bed her, wanting to wed her. Rugged Richard makes her virginal knees weak. But could even a king know a woman's mind—without her speaking it?